The Goblin Wood

Also by Hilari Bell

A MATTER OF PROFIT

HILARI BELL

The Goblin Wood

An Imprint of HarperCollinsPublishers

Library of Congress Cataloging-in-Publication Data
Bell, Hilari.
The Goblin Wood / Hilari Bell.— 1st ed.
    p.   cm.
Summary: A young Hedgewitch, an idealistic knight, and an army of
clever goblins fight against the ruling hierarchy that is trying to rid the
land of all magical creatures.
    ISBN 0-06-051371-3 — ISBN 0-06-051372-1 (lib. bdg.)
    [1. Witches—Fiction. 2. Knights and knighthood—Fiction.
3. Goblins—Fiction. 4. Magic—Fiction.] I. Title.
PZ7.B38894 Go 2003   2002015281
[Fic]—dc21   CIP
                                                                    AC

Typography by Hilary Zarycky

1 2 3 4 5 6 7 8 9 10

First Edition

This book is dedicated to my father,
who loved Makenna because he despised "wimpy" heroines.
Thanks, Dad, for everything.

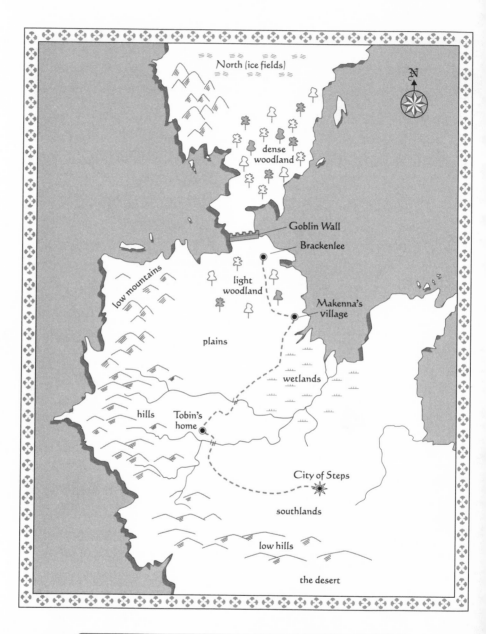

North (ice fields)

dense
woodland

Goblin Wall

Brackenlee

low mountains

light
woodland

Makenna's
village

plains

wetlands

hills

Tobin's
home

City of Steps

southlands

low hills

the desert

REALM OF THE BRIGHT GODS

CHAPTER 1

The Hedgewitch

MAKENNA HAD TO STRETCH onto her toes to reach the small stone lamp, for the shelf that held it was higher than a grown woman's head, and she was only eleven. She'd drawn the fire rune in the sweet-smelling sawdust that littered the floor of Goodman Branno's workshop. Now she set the lamp in its center and murmured the word, the essential name of fire.

Nothing. She clenched her hands to still their trembling and lifted the lamp. Carefully she smoothed the sawdust and drew the rune again. It was hard to get the lines right, in dark. Replacing the lamp, she repeated the word, a call this time, almost a prayer. A tiny orange spark glowed before her. She leaned forward and blew on the wick, and the flame flickered to life.

The light bloomed slowly, filling the toolshed, spilling out the cracks in its walls and under the door. It was dangerous—if anyone saw it they might guess she was there, for Goodman Branno, the carpenter, was sound asleep at this hour. But Makenna's hatred flared stronger than the light. Let them come. Likely she could kill a few before she was taken.

She stared around the shed at the tools that covered the walls—she wasn't sure what she'd need. Finally she chose a saw, a hammer and chisel, and a hatchet. Surely one of them would be sufficient to cut through the thick screw.

The tools were awkward, too large for her hands as she packed them into the big grain sack that already held her mother's spell books. She snuffed the light and hauled the heavy sack out of the shed; it clanked when she bumped against the door frame and Grulf, the carpenter's dog, gave a tentative bark.

Her heart thumping, Makenna called to him softly— if he raised an alarm it would draw people more quickly than the light!

Grulf whined, and Makenna hurried over to reassure him that she was a known, good person. No spells of calming needed here; she knew every dog in this village, where she'd grown up.

Hate rolled and boiled in her stomach, making her feel sick and fearless and strong. There wasn't a man or woman in that mob that her mother hadn't healed or helped—either them, or someone in their families. Branno himself—she'd cured his infected thumb just last year, and she'd charmed the weevils out of the meal bin when his youngest daughter left the lid off. But that was before Mistress Manoc came.

Branno had started suckling up to the new priest immediately, but Makenna's mother had seen through Mistress Manoc, right from the start.

"She speaks against the goblins," Ardis said thoughtfully, the whisper of the spinning wheel making music under her words. "By St. Spiratu, they're pesty enough! But if we stop putting out the goblin bowls, they'll only get more pesty. Besides, goblinkind and ours have been living together since the beginning. It's dangerous to meddle with things like that, Makennie love. Upsets balances you can't even see, turns nature against you. And besides . . ."

Makenna blotted out the rest of the memory, angrily wiping away tears. She needed to be strong, not weak and weeping.

She gave Grulf a final pat and made her way to the back of the work yard. The light of the near-full moon sifted through the newly leafed branches, making it easy to avoid the stacks of cut timber. But hauling the big sack over the wall was awkward, and her skirt tore resoundingly. She froze, knowing her dark brown hair and faded clothes would blend with the shadows. No dogs barked. No neighbor stuck his head out the window to see what was going on.

She wasn't dressed for this kind of scrambling thievery, but when she'd put on her clothes this morning she'd expected nothing more from the day than her ordinary chores and the fascinating struggle of a magic lesson.

Tears crept down her face again, and she wiped them

away, sniffing. She'd have thought there'd be no tears left in her, but they kept coming. Well, let them come. They didn't matter. Nothing mattered anymore except to lift the gate and cut the screw.

She couldn't go back to her own home. They were watching it. But Krick's house was only a few doors down. He was almost her size, and his mother was lazy about taking in the wash. Makenna's mother had cured their baby's croup a few months ago.

She stole a pair of Krick's britches off the drying rack and put them on. A dark shirt that belonged to his brother was only a little too big. There was a heavy cape on the hook by the door—almost a cloak for her—and she took it, too.

She was almost out of the village when she realized that she ought to steal some food as well—once she had cut the screw, she would leave. And after that? Her mind boggled over the question—she was too tired to think. After she cut the screw, she would eat and rest and plan for the future.

She chose the house of Goodwife Marra, whose apple trees her mother had cured of a blight. The back door was latched, but the shutters on the kitchen window were open. She left her sack outside and wiggled through easily in her stolen britches.

Inside the kitchen she paused a moment to let her eyes adjust. After the bright moonlight outside, the small square of silver that came from the window and the glow of the banked fire seemed very dim.

Bread, hard yellow cheese, and the last of the dried apples went out the window to join the spell books and tools. She was fumbling at the back of a high shelf for the tight-sewn bags that held strips of dried meat when her elbow tapped a bowl. It fell to the floor and shattered.

Makenna froze, staring at the fragments of pottery. Her mother had dropped the scrying bowl that morning.

It had begun with the chiming of the tiny copper bell on the mantle, warning them someone was passing the ward stone her mother had placed on the path to their house. They lived almost a quarter mile from the village. Hedgewitches needed more privacy than most, because folk didn't always want their neighbors—or the priest—to know they'd gone to a hedgewitch for aid. Ardis liked to have a bit of warning when someone was coming, but her lined face held only cheerful curiosity as she wiped the dough off her hands and poured water into the big clay bowl she used for scrying.

Makenna watched as her mother drew the runes and murmured the words that turned sight through water into Sight through water. Makenna couldn't make runes in water, though she'd often tried.

Light flickered from the bowl, casting faint upward shadows on her mother's face. Then her expression had changed, stiffened, and she leapt to her feet. The bowl fell and shattered, spilling the water in a widening pool on the floor.

The faint creak of a door hinge brought Makenna back to the present with a rush. She heard steps on the boards over her head. Someone had been wakened by the crash and was coming to investigate. Makenna spun toward the window, but the window could be seen from the stairs! No time.

She raced silently to hide in the dark corner by the hearth—not good enough, especially if someone lit a lamp.

With shaking hands she raked a handful of cold ashes from the corner of the hearth, flinching as a live ember singed her fingers. Plain dust was the best essential object for this spell, but any powdery substance would do.

The footsteps had almost reached the bottom of the stairs. She flung the ashes on the floor in front of her and blew to create an even layer—no time to do this spell over and over until she got it right.

She traced the rune, an eye outside a circle, and whispered the last of the words as Goodwife Marra stepped into the kitchen.

Several pieces of broken bowl lay in the square of moonlight, and the goodwife went to them, hopping and muttering a curse as she stepped on a piece in her bare feet.

Then she came over to the hearth. Makenna held her breath. The look-away spell worked better if you didn't move or make any noise.

Goodwife Marra lit a candle and stood gazing around the kitchen. Aside from the broken bowl, Makenna saw nothing out of place—and evidently Marra didn't, either. She muttered something about accursed cats and went to latch the shutters.

When she returned the candle to the hearth, her eyes passed right over Makenna, and she didn't even blink.

Makenna listened to her footsteps going up the stairs and waited until Marra had had time to go back to sleep before unfolding her fear-stiffened legs. She took two bags of dried meat and let herself out the kitchen door, leaving it wide with a quiet wish that every cat in the village would invade the place.

On her way out the back gate she kicked over the goblin bowl. She flinched reflexively as it tipped, but of course there had been no milk or table scraps in the goblin bowls for months now—no bad luck, likely, from tipping over an empty bowl.

But the fragment of memory she had suppressed earlier swirled through her mind. *"It's dangerous to meddle with things like that . . . upsets balances . . . turns nature against you. And besides . . . if she's getting rid of the goblins, likely we hedgewitches will be next."*

Makenna clung to the side of the road where the scruffy bushes promised some cover. It was hard going, hauling the now-stuffed grain sack through the brush. The village was in the center of a vast area of reclaimed marshland. The soil was rich, the lake behind the dike provided sufficient water even in the driest years, and the land was almost completely flat. You could see several miles down the road from the village. Makenna was taking no chances, not now, with her goal so close.

7

She'd come almost far enough to walk on the road without being seen when a stick, concealed in last year's dead grass, caught her foot and she fell. She lit soft, but she had fallen earlier and skinned her knees—it was the memory as much as the pain that made her breath catch on a sob.

Her arms overflowing with the large, untidy collection of her mother's spell books, she hadn't even seen the rock that turned under her foot. She was running, so she fell hard, the books exploding out of her arms, sending loose sheets of parchment flying among the willows that ringed the house.

"Hide the spell books," her mother had whispered fiercely, piling them into her hands. "They're my life's work, love. Hide them and keep them safe. Use them."

Scrambling on bleeding knees after the notes and fragments of spells, herbals, scraps of granny lore, and even ordinary recipes that her mother not only inherited from her mother, but had gathered from every passing tinker and vagabond hedge-witch, Makenna was still near enough to peer through the screen of branches when the mob reached the house.

They had milled uneasily outside the door, some looking down as if to conceal their faces, but she knew them all, oh, yes, she knew them. Including their most recent resident. Mistress Manoc looked sober, except when she forgot to control her expression. Then a smug look twitched over her face and lingered until she banished it.

Makenna heard Goodman Branno's voice raised to shrillness. "Come out, Ardis. You're accused of sorcery. Your power comes from demons, and you know their names."

That had stunned Makenna, for her mother knew no more of demons' names than anyone else in the village. In fact, she'd sometimes wondered if her mother believed in demons—or even the Dark One.

She could barely hear her mother's quiet voice replying, soothing, delaying them while Makenna got the books away. She'd been told to save the books, so she'd gathered them and hidden them, wasting time she might have spent thinking ahead, finding tools to cut a chain, finding a weapon. . . .

Makenna's stomach was twisting again. Her eyes stung, but she refused to weep anymore. Weeping wouldn't get it done.

She stood and hauled the sack onto the road. She hated these books now, but her mother had told her to save them and she would. They were her mother's life's work—the fragments of knowledge she had snatched up and preserved, despite the church's decree that only priests could possess any knowledge of magic. It had not occurred to Makenna until much later that in sending her to save the books, her mother had been saving her as well.

It was easier walking on the road, and she made good time. Better time than she had made that morning, crawling through the bushes on the far side of the dike, striving desperately to get to the long dock that hung over the lake in time.

Now as she drew near the dike, she missed the rhythmic thudding of the pump that started every dawn when old Haren hitched the oxen to the wheel. The noise of the pump, pulling the night's seepage back up to the lake, was as much a part of the dike as the scent of mud—its absence made her feel like a stranger in an unfamiliar place. She'd thought she and her mother had a place in the village. Friends. It was dangerous to disobey a priest, for the teachings of the Hierarch's church were backed by the swords of the Hierarch's guards. But the villagers could have warned them! Not one had. So much for friendship.

With the hatchet, it took only a few minutes to reduce the pump's cog pins to splinters. They would never get it working in time.

She turned off the road before reaching the dock, for she knew she couldn't face the sight of it, and cut across a field of new corn, carelessly trampling the tender shoots. It was a hard scramble up the dike, for the sluice gate was set where the land was lowest. At the top, the fresh wind that blew off the lake struck her like a slap. The sound of the waves lapping the shore brought everything hurtling back.

She had watched them from behind a screen of brush and grass as they dragged her mother, struggling now, over the dock's rough boards. It took two men to carry the heavy chains and shackles. They always drowned a sorceress, so she couldn't use the power of her dying breath to summon demons or to curse.

As soon as the last man had moved onto the dock,

Makenna scrambled underneath it and ran forward. By now the men who held her mother had reached the end. She heard the thudding of their feet as her mother fought.

The water met Makenna halfway. She was in it up to her knees before the thought struck her—what was she going to do? She couldn't fight. Then the scream rose, a terrible, wavering shriek, and her mother's body flashed down, wreathed with chains, her face mindless with terror, like an animal caught in a trap.

A tremendous splash and a swirl of bubbles cut off the sound.

Makenna was swimming then, hearing the feet tramping overhead, not caring anymore if they heard her.

When she reached the end of the dock the water was still, and she stared helplessly at its softly heaving surface.

What could she do? She could dive for her mother, but the water was deep here. Even if she reached her, she had no way to break or unfasten the chain. And no swimmer could haul up that weight.

The desire to scream rose in her, to scream and scream and go on screaming until the world was blotted out by the sound. It took all her will to suppress it.

Screaming was useless. Her mother was dead.

She moaned, clinging to the rough wood pillar that supported the dock. Then some instinct for survival stirred and, though she clung there, drifting in the light wash of the waves for a long time, she made no further sound.

Makenna shuddered, pulling herself out of the past,

and went to the wheel, that twisted the screw, that lifted the sluice gate. It took all her strength, but once she got it turning, it spun easily.

The dike shivered under her feet with the violence of the current surging beneath it. Only when the screw reached the top of its length and jammed did she look down at the water shooting out, rushing through the ditches, already swamping the low end of the fields and covering the base of the pump. The sight gave her intense satisfaction, and she realized that, for the first time that day, she felt no desire to cry.

Looking carefully at the thick wooden screw, she decided the saw would be quickest. She set the blade as low as she could, where the screw vanished into the gate mechanism. At first, the saw jerked and buckled, but she struggled on, and soon each thrust bit deeper into the wood. When the saw broke through, she twisted the top part of the screw free and threw it into the pond, which was deepening rapidly at the base of the dike. It already stretched over several fields. Makenna could no longer see the water spurting in, but the surface beneath her feet roiled furiously. Good, the gate was underwater. With the screw cut, they wouldn't be able to get it closed for days . . . maybe never.

Makenna looked back at the sleeping village. When the lake reclaimed its own, most of those houses would be under water, destroying the food stored in their cellars. The rooftops would be the only dry places.

The water would rise gradually. Only a few might drown. But fields under water would grow no crops, and much of the livestock that made it to shore would escape. They would all be left with nothing. All would suffer. All would grieve. The thought warmed the chilled place inside her, and Makenna smiled.

"May the Dark One devour the lot of you," she whispered. It was the worst curse she knew. She wished she knew the Dark One's name, so she could call on him with real effect.

Makenna turned and dragged her sack of spell books along the dike toward the highland. She wanted to be a long way off by sunrise.

CHAPTER 2

The Hedgewitch

MAKENNA DRIFTED NORTH. She wasn't sure why she chose that direction, but she wanted to leave her old life behind, and the deep woods and soft, rolling hills were completely different from the flat, open land she'd known. Her mother had traveled in her youth. She'd told Makenna that staying in one place, in a village where you knew folks, and they knew you, was safer.

At first Makenna's grief for her mother felt like tearing claws, and she cried herself to sleep each night. But after the first few days, the difficulties of survival occupied more and more of her attention.

She stole food from the villages she passed. Soon she grew bolder and acquired better clothes, a knife, a bedroll, and a big oilcloth sheet she could hang when it rained.

She felt no guilt—the empty goblin bowls told her that the villagers she robbed had fallen in with the priests' demands. Makenna wondered what the goblins did, with no more table scraps set out for them. Thinking of the mischief they could make, she almost felt sorry for the villagers. Almost.

Makenna took care never to be seen, and she moved on quickly, never robbing any village twice. And one of the first things she did was to twist some stolen bronze wire into a hiding charm so no one could find her with magic. It took her more than a dozen attempts to set the magic into the bronze, and she wept again for her mother, who had so easily made these charms for poachers.

In the beginning Makenna had intended to live by trapping small game. Krick and Rolan, near her own age, had taught her how to set snares in the days when they'd run wild together. When they'd been . . . when they had pretended to be her friends. But the first time her wire captured a squirrel, the sight of its frantic struggles made something twist inside her. She couldn't kill it. She soon discovered that she couldn't kill anything in a trap, although she had no qualms about eating the meat she stole.

As the weeks passed into months, Makenna began to look for snares in the forest around the villages. If they were empty, she sprung them. If there were animals in them, she set them free. Sometimes her spell of calming failed and she was clawed or bitten, but freeing trapped creatures became something that she had to do.

As the first gold touched the leaves, she realized it was nearly harvest month and that she had had a birthday a few months back. She was twelve now. It didn't seem to matter. Birthdays were a part of humanity, and she hardly considered herself human anymore.

But harvest would soon be followed by winter. She'd need better gear, perhaps even a permanent shelter. She began to look for an area where she might stay. It had to be within raiding distance of at least three villages, but not so close to any of them that she was likely to be discovered.

She traveled almost another week. The sun was sinking behind the hills when she came across a barn that looked promising. The blackened ruins of a farmhouse nearby explained why it had been abandoned, but the barn looked strong and in good repair. The people who owned the well-tended orchards that surrounded it probably stored things there, but the harvest was past; they might not go near it till spring.

Makenna couldn't see anyone among the trees now, but she knew better than to take chances. She found a clump of bushes from which she could watch, and waited for moonrise.

It was several hours after darkness had fallen, and the moon was high above the trees before she moved, slowly and carefully, toward the darkened barn. The trails she'd found in the grass seemed to indicate that the farmhouse had been moved downstream a bit and behind a hill—out of sight, but not necessarily out of hearing. Makenna had seen no sign of a dog, either, but that didn't mean there wasn't one, so she had the well-chewed bone she used as an essential object for her calming charm ready to hand.

There was no lock on the door, just a big latch, which probably meant they stored nothing of value here. Good. But the door's great iron hinges moved with the silence of grease and use, which meant they opened this door a lot. Bad. Or at least, a puzzle. The barn was dark, only a few small windows catching the moonlight. The old straw on the floor would substitute for sawdust. Makenna knelt and charmed fire into the wick of one of her stolen candles. The spell was coming easier, now that she worked it every night for campfires.

The light revealed the barn's plain plank walls. No animals moved restlessly in the stalls at the coming of light; only their scents lingered in the cool air. They must have moved the livestock to be nearer to the new house. The stalls held the tools of farm and harvest: baskets for gathering, which were cheap enough, but also steel tools, saws for cutting dead wood, hoes, and shovels. And at the far end was a cider press, and in the stalls near it, dozens of new barrels, their strapping gleaming in the candlelight. Makenna scowled. Either folk around here were more honest than any she'd ever known, or she was missing something. Could she have tripped some magical alarm without sensing it? But magical wards were usually harder to come by, and more expensive, than a dog—more expensive than a cider press and the new barrels warranted.

She was reaching out with her other senses, letting her eyes stray, when she saw it—just a glimpse of a long-nosed brown face, about the size of a small melon, peering down from one of the eaves. It was gone in an instant, but Makenna jumped back, tripped over a bump in the straw covered floor, and fell.

This barn was far from unguarded. Her heart started to pound. "I didn't take anything," she said rapidly. "I didn't hurt anything. I'm leaving now, and I've done you and yours no harm. All right?"

The silence stretched. The back of Makenna's neck prickled. The goblin doubtless knew every move she'd made, but she still held out her hands to show they were empty as she fled from the barn.

She was free of the farmyard and deep into the orchard before she began to relax. Wild goblins were pesty, but her mother had told her that nothing guarded a farm better than a loyal one. She was lucky she'd seen him before she'd taken something. Besides, if these folk still had their goblins, likely they'd let their hedgewitches live as well.

The tension in her neck and shoulders eased slowly. She was almost to the edge of the orchard, and no alarm had sounded. It was all right. With the unthinking gesture of someone who had been raised around apple trees, she reached up, picked an apple, and bit into it.

A flurry of movement in the leaves proclaimed her mistake.

"I'm sorry!" she cried. But goblins didn't care about sorry.

A shrill whistle sounded in the tree above her. A clatter of metal, loud enough to carry to any number of farms, sounded from the barn. Followed by the distant baying of dogs.

Makenna dropped the apple and ran.

Drying her soaked boots by the fire, Makenna cursed her carelessness. "But you think no more about picking an apple in harvest than about scratching an itch!"

She'd begun talking to herself more and more often lately. Not that she wanted anyone to talk to. She wondered if it was just her imagination, that feeling that the rustling canopy above her was listening. It had taken most of the night, climbing trees and wading for miles up shallow creeks, to lose the dogs. Makenna banked her fire and went to bed.

It was just after noon when she finally wakened, stretched, and pulled on her boots. The exertions of the previous night had made her hungry, and she walked quickly to the tree where she'd hung her gear. She was reaching for the lowest branch when she noticed both her sacks lying on the ground.

After being robbed by several animals, Makenna had learned to climb a tree and lower her food sack on a rope so it dangled in the air, safe from the clever paws of raccoons and other creatures.

"Dung!" She reached the sacks in two long strides.

The spell books were there, the food was gone. But how? Had something chewed through the rope?

She pulled the rope through the fallen leaves and one glance at the end told her everything. Not chewed—cut. Goblin work. She should probably be grateful they hadn't taken the spell books and hidden them out of pure mischief—but she wasn't grateful.

Anger burning through her veins, Makenna packed her gear and set off. There was no point in staying. Once the goblins got a grudge against you, it lasted till you appeased them. She had no milk to offer and they'd stolen all her food, so she had no choice but to flee.

They chose to follow her.

By the third day of the goblins' pursuit, Makenna was near weeping with weariness and frustration.

She could keep from starving by eating what she stole on the spot, but she couldn't store any food unless she kept it in her pockets. She'd tried clutching her food sack in her arms as she slept—and wakened to the sight of a scrawny, long-nosed lady, about two feet high, dragging her spell books away. She'd raced to recover them and returned to find her food sack gone. The empty bag fell over her head later that day, and by the time she tore it off, there was nothing to be seen. The woods echoed with shrieks of goblin laughter.

She combed the spell books for a charm to keep the goblins off, but aside from dozens of bits of useless lore and rumor, all she found was a note in a strange hand that said only the priests' magic was strong enough to affect goblins, whose magic was innate.

Since the priests tried to keep magic out of the hands of any who weren't priests, Makenna's mother and grandmother had collected their lore from many different sources, but Makenna had never heard of innate magic before. Did that mean they didn't have to study to bend the natural world to their wishes? Some humans had magic, some did not, and those chosen for priests were chosen, Makenna's mother had claimed, solely because they had more magic than others. But even the priests, who needed no essential objects, no complex rituals, had to spend years learning to wield their magic.

Makenna was beginning to believe that her mother was right that magic was part of the nature of the world itself, not something handed out by gods. It was heresy, of course. But Makenna had no more dealings with gods now than she'd ever had, and the spells that hid her tracks or settled the mud in ditches where she dipped her water jug were coming easier to her. But there were still days when she couldn't bring a spell to life, no matter how hard she tried.

Makenna knew her magic was weak, even for a hedgewitch. She barely remembered the day the priests' chooser had come to the village, to test the latest generation of children for magical ability. But she remembered the old man's nasal voice, passing his judgment. "Her holiness is not sufficient."

"It's all right, Makennie," her mother had soothed her. "The priests do priestly things, but we hedgewitches, we do well enough without their help. We do fine."

Still Makenna had heard her weeping in the night and known she had wanted her daughter to be chosen, to have possessed magic that was strong enough for real teaching, real knowledge. Ardis had never again, by word, look or deed, let Makenna see her disappointment.

The goblins' persecution continued. If they couldn't get Makenna's food, they stole bits and pieces of her other gear. Which they left, teasingly, in place of her food when they stole it later. The first time they did this, she swore and stamped her foot. It lit on a sharp stone, and as she hopped about, clutching her sore foot and cursing, she could hear them snickering.

The only way she could keep everything was to stay awake all the time—and in the past few days she had fallen asleep more and more often. She was almost certain they were casting spells on her—if she realized it in time, she could fight the wave of drowsiness. But more often she simply woke, lying across the trail with a crick in her back and another piece of gear missing.

Makenna fought back a tired sob. This couldn't go on. Much as she hated the idea, she had to set a trap.

That night she crept into a blacksmith's shop to steal what she needed. The moon wasn't up yet, but the glowing coals in the forge gave her enough light to search. Goblins, with their clever fingers and sharp copper knives, were almost impossible to trap, but they couldn't abide the touch of iron or steel. One of the scraps of lore in her books speculated that that was because iron and steel were man-made things, not found in nature, but no one seemed to know for certain.

It took awhile to find the things she needed, and she stole a net as well. Walking back to camp, she was smiling for the first time in days.

It was a good thing she slept lightly. The thrashing snap of the bent branch that primed her hidden snare wasn't loud, and only someone dozing in all her clothes could have reached the moon-shadowed grove in time, for the small creature bent over his bound ankles had his fingers in the wire, pulling it loose. In a moment he'd be gone! Makenna raced toward him and tripped over the bent sapling of the trap she'd left in plain sight.

The young tree whipped upright in a storm of thrashing leaves, taking the net and food sack with it. Makenna fell, rolled, got her feet beneath her, and sprang into a flying dive. Her outstretched hands fell on the goblin just as he slipped free of the wire. "Got you!"

She tightened her grip against his wiggling and dragged him forward till she could sit up and look at him.

He was thin as a scarecrow, about two and a half feet tall, and the lines and bones of his face were long and sharp. The elbows of his rough jacket and the knees of his britches were neatly patched, but his hair straggled into his eyes. Dark, angry eyes.

Even though Makenna had set the deceptive double trap—one snare in plain sight, the other hidden as well as she could hide it—she hadn't really believed it would work. Now that she had her hands on one of her tormentors, she had no idea what to do with him.

"How could you undo the wire on your ankle?" she asked. "I thought goblinkind couldn't touch steel or iron."

"Well, I can. Not that it's any of your business." He gritted his small sharp teeth and a gleam came into his eyes. He glanced down at Makenna's unprotected wrist.

She shook him slightly, in warning. "Don't even think it, little man."

He sniffed. "As if I'd soil my teeth on a great dirty creature like you."

"You're not that clean yourself!" Makenna retorted, stung. He spoke true; living wild, her bath days had become few and far between. "What's your name, little man?"

"What's yours, great wench?"

Makenna scowled. For a prisoner, he was awfully rude. But it was pure bravado, for she held him tightly enough to feel his heartbeat. The rapid heartbeat of a trapped creature. What had she thought to accomplish with this? Even if she could kill him, there would always be more goblins. Why bother? She pushed him away and stood stiffly, brushing the wet leaves off her clothes.

The goblin stared at her suspiciously. "What's this about, wench?"

"My name is Makenna. And you're free. Go away."

"What for?"

"Because I don't want to spend the rest of the night talking to rude goblins. Go on, get!"

"No, great stupid one, I meant what do you want for freeing me?"

Not pure bravado after all, Makenna decided. At least half his rudeness sprang from plain bad temper. She turned to the sapling to pull her food sack down.

"Well, are you going to make me stand about all night? What do you want?"

Makenna shrugged. "Nothing. I just can't stand to hurt anything in a trap. Not even surly goblins. Not that it's any of your business."

She skinned a knuckle untying the knot and swore as she lowered the net that held the food sack. She'd have to eat all she could before going back to sleep, for the rest would likely be gone before she woke. When she turned back, the goblin was still standing there.

"You must want something." His voice was anxious, almost pleading. "You must."

"Well, it would be nice if the lot of you would leave me alone, but I'm sure that's too much to ask." She sighed wearily. "Just go."

"Ahhh!" His anguished shriek rent the silence.

Makenna sprang back, tripped and sat down abruptly, blinking in astonishment. "What the—"

"You've done it! Curse you, wench, may your children be devoured by ducks, you've gone and done it! Ahhh!" He stamped his foot. Makenna wished there'd been a sharp rock beneath it. Her lips twitched.

"Done what?" she asked, clambering to her feet.

"You don't even know, you great stupid creature. What have I done to deserve this, what?" He clutched his hair, elbows akimbo, eyes wild.

Makenna couldn't help but laugh. It sounded a bit rusty. Was this the first time she'd laughed since her mother's death? "Look, all I want is for you to go away. I'll give you some food, all right?"

"Ahhh!"

Makenna clapped her hands over her ears.

"You've done it again!" the goblin cried.

"Done what?"

"You've gone and indebted me! Now I owe you! Guarding, serving, gold—who knows where it'll end? Why do I have to meet up with the one human who won't strike an honest bargain—even a greedy one! What an accursed night this has been. I'll be about!"

He turned and stomped toward the bushes.

Makenna tried to stifle her giggles. "Look, I don't want—"

The goblin spun. "Don't you go indebting me again, wench, or I swear I'll get violent, indebted or not!" He stalked away, radiating fury. At the edge of the clearing he paused and looked back to snarl, "My name's Cogswhallop," before he vanished.

When Makenna woke the next morning all of her food was still there, and a pile of fresh-picked blueberries had joined it.

Cogswhallop was seldom seen after that, but he made his presence felt. Food still vanished, but more appeared. Gear was mended and fires stayed alive all night.

Sometimes when she was traveling, he turned up to warn her of trouble ahead or guide her to an easier path. He was never polite, much less friendly, but she finally got him talking enough to learn what she'd done to upset him so.

"Humans! Do you never give folks any balance?" he complained.

Makenna frowned over the cold pigeon pie that had probably come from some villager's windowsill. She had just thanked him for it. "What do you mean?"

Cogswhallop snorted. "If you go doing more for someone than they pay back, then they're indebted to you—surely even a human can understand that. And if you're indebted, you can't be in balance with them. Or with yourself, for that matter. You're . . . unequal. Like with me, owing you a life debt. It'll take a cursed mountain of pigeon pie to pay that off."

Makenna took a moment to think this over. The folk

of her village had surely taken more from her mother than they'd paid back, even before— She swallowed and put down the pie. They hadn't been equals, that was certain. "So if you owe someone a favor, you always pay it back, so that you won't be indebted. Not for them, but for you."

"Good wench. I knew you could understand, if I said it in wee, simple words."

Makenna grinned. Prickly as he was, it was nice to have someone to talk to. Almost a friend. "But what about friendship? Surely you don't keep track of every little thing friends do for one another? Or families?"

"You think friends don't need to be equal? And families need balance more than any, I'd think. Though with friends, we don't keep such close track of the amount of the debt. You can pay back favors with just a token, a rock, a pinecone, whatever's to hand. With friends, or with family, it's just a symbol. The real debt gets paid out in time."

It made sense to Makenna, in an odd sort of way. Once she understood the rules of the goblin's game, she came to enjoy it. When the other goblins, who still followed her, stole things, she put out food to ransom her possessions back. When she had plenty, she put out food as an offering, and they always did her some favor in return.

It was good to know that someone listened when she spoke her thoughts aloud, even if she couldn't always see them. So Makenna felt nothing but pleasure when Cogswhallop appeared before her as she hiked along at dusk.

"Drop those bags and follow me," he commanded.

Makenna did, rubbing the sore spot the rope always left on her shoulder. He led her toward the road that meandered east through the woods.

The leaves had all fallen now, and they were far enough north that an occasional pine gleamed green through the barren branches.

As they approached the road, Cogswhallop dropped to his stomach and began to crawl, and Makenna followed his lead, trying to be as silent as possible wiggling through the dried bracken. Cogswhallop made no more sound than a soft breeze. Of course he was smaller. He stopped under a bush at the top of a hill, and Makenna crawled up to join him.

A campfire blazed beside the road below and something bubbled in the iron pot above it. A tinker, a small man with more gray than brown in his hair, was cooking his evening meal.

But it was his pack that drew her eyes, a huge leather pack, with wide shoulder straps designed to be carried comfortably day after day. It looked enormous, stuffed with his gear and the tools of his trade. It would probably be too big for her, but likely the goblins could adjust it—

"I thought you'd like it," Cogswhallop murmured.

CHAPTER 3

The Hedgewitch

MAKENNA CREPT INTO THE tinker's camp, inch by silent inch, alert for the slightest variation in the rhythm of his snoring. She spared an irritated thought for Cogswhallop who'd vanished shortly after leading her to her prize—he could have done this much more quietly. But evidently the goblins' strange rules put this beyond the bounds of his "indebtedness."

The pack lay next to the tinker's bedroll. The worst part, Makenna thought as she eased forward, would come when she reached the pack. Tinker's tools had a tendency to clank. It might be better to try to unload the pack right there beside him, if she could be quiet enough. If he continued to snore like that, likely he'd not hear if she rattled the pans in his ears.

Heart thumping, she crept forward as silently as she could. The rhythm of his snoring never changed. She reached down, touched the pack buckle—and a hard hand closed around her ankle.

Makenna dove away. The force of her movement pulled the tinker half out of his blankets, but he didn't let go, and she fell, already twisting to face him, kicking as he seized her other leg. The dirt beneath her was dry and loose. Quick as thought, she grabbed a handful and cast it at his eyes, but he closed them before it hit.

He kept his face turned away and swarmed up her body like a man climbing a tree. It wasn't until he was sitting on her stomach, pinning both her wrists to the earth, that he finally looked down at her face. "Why, you're only a lass!"

Struggling was useless, so Makenna stopped.

"I'm not 'only a lass,'" she replied with as much arrogance as she could muster. "I'm a hedgewitch, and a powerful one. If you hurt me, I'll curse you in the names of all the demons I know, so you'd better let me go, now!"

"Ah, you know the demons' names, do you?" He didn't look frightened. In fact he looked like he was trying not to smile.

Makenna's fear vanished in a wave of outrage. "I do know them. Lots of them! And . . . and I've got hordes of goblin slaves who'd avenge me, too!" She only hoped they weren't listening, because she had no idea how they might react to that.

The tinker chuckled. "Hold back your hordes, lass, for Todder Yon means you no harm. If I let you go, will you promise not to claw my eyes out?"

"Aye," said Makenna slowly. What was he up to?

He released her and stood, and she scrambled to her feet, glaring up at him. Now she understood how Cogswhallop had felt.

"Why'd you let me go?"

"Why not?" Todder Yon shrugged. "If you'll stay awhile, and behave yourself, I'll even heat up some stew for you."

"But why?"

"Because you're a powerful hedgewitch, of course." The corners of his eyes crinkled as he bent over the fire to stir it up. "We lesser minions ought to stick together."

"Lesser what?"

"Minions." The amusement left his face—he looked older. "Haven't you heard it? The Hierarch decided that any power that doesn't come from the Seven Bright Ones, like the priests' power does, must be coming from the Dark One. He declared that all hedgewitches, seers, even the light healers, are lesser minions of the Dark One. Bad as demons, he said, just not so strong."

"But that's nonsense," Makenna burst out. "Mother never had anything to do with the Dark One. And neither have I. We don't even know any—" She stopped abruptly, but he wasn't slow.

"Demons' names? That's fine with me, lass, for I'd hate to be cursed. Did something happen to your mother?"

Makenna said nothing, but he read the answer in her face.

"I'm sorry," he said softly. "You don't have to talk about it. No father, either?"

"No," said Makenna shortly. Ardis had always claimed Makenna's father had loved her, loved both of them. But not enough to stay with a hedgewitch. Ardis had never blamed him for it, but Makenna had.

"On your own, then? Well, you'd best have a care for yourself, since you've no one to care for you. The Hierarch decreed that all the Dark One's minions are to be slain or turned over to the church. The Decree of Bright Magic, they're calling it. And you'd best watch out for your goblin horde as well—they've been declared lesser minions, just like the rest of us."

"But why?" Makenna demanded. "I know they never approved of hedgewitches, but that's no reason to kill us!"

"I don't know the real reason." Todder sighed. "They say it's because the barbarian attacks in the south are growing worse. They had to recruit more men into the army last winter, and they'll need even more this year. Soon there'll be all-out war on the southern border."

"So?" demanded Makenna. A border war was the Hierarch's business, and perhaps the lords'. The barbarians had been raiding the southern border for as long as anyone could remember. "What does that have to do with hedgewitches? It's knights and priests that fight a war."

"Ah, but the knights and priests are commanded by the Hierarch, so you can hardly expect them to take the blame, now can you? The logic is that the Bright Ones have stopped favoring the Hierarch's army, because he's been tolerating the presence of the Dark One's servants in his own land. If he casts out the 'evil ones,' then the army will start winning again. It's pigdung, but that's what they say." He shook his head ruefully and stirred the bubbling pot. "By St. Spiratu's truth, I'd give a lot to know what they're really up to. Of course, those with power blaming those without isn't exactly a new thing in the world."

"But that's absurd. Hedgewitches have nothing to do with whether the army wins or loses. And seers and light healers can't do anything but predict or heal—and not even as well as a hedgewitch can! To blame us for what happens to some distant army is . . . is . . ." She could think of no word strong enough.

"Despicable? Aye, so it is. But unless the Decree is revoked, it'll go hard with all of us."

Hatred was rising in Makenna, a cold, solid hate, not at all like the blazing fury that had led her to flood her village. "Why do you keep saying 'us,' tinker? Do you have power?"

"Not a scrap." He ladled stew into a bowl and gave it to her. "You might as well sit down." He sat himself, leaning comfortably against his pack.

"The Hierarch says the way we rove about—tinkers, and the gypsies, too—serving no lord is a sign of lawlessness. And lawlessness comes from the Dark One. Myself, I think the Hierarch is more concerned about the news we spread."

As Makenna ate, he proceeded to spread news. He told her about failed harvests, which were also being blamed on the Dark One's minions. One village had even been completely swallowed by flood when its sluice gate was mysteriously damaged, though no one there was killed.

Makenna tried to hide her riveted attention and evidently succeeded, for the tinker went on to talk about scandals, dishonest lords, and rumors of corrupt priests. At first, satisfaction at the success of her revenge distracted her, but eventually she began to listen. She was most interested in his talk of the priests' intention to push the goblins into the north woods, where they could be imprisoned behind the great wall.

"But that'll never succeed," Todder remarked. "It didn't work three hundred years ago, and it won't work now. Especially with all the holes that have grown in the wall over the centuries."

"Why's the Hierarch killing hedgewitches and not goblins?" Makenna asked. It felt strange, talking to a human, but good, too—pleasure and discomfort mixed, like stretching out stiff muscles.

"Have you ever tried to kill goblins, lass? It's not impossible, but killing them all would take far more men and magic than the church can spare. Driving them out's hard enough."

He still hadn't run out of gossip when he caught her yawning and tossed her a couple of blankets.

"By the by, lass, what was it you wanted here?"

"Your pack." Makenna was too tired to lie. "I need something stronger to carry my things in."

"Hmm," said the tinker. "Well, I can't give you that one, for I've need of it myself, but I've an old one here you might make use of." He dug into his pack as he spoke, and pulled out a heap of crumpled leather. "It's pretty well in tatters; I've been using bits of it for leather scrap. But perhaps that goblin horde of yours could mend it for you." He winked as he handed it over. "There you go, and St. Veschia's charity with it."

Makenna snorted. "You have the most blasphemous opinions I've ever heard, but you offer a saint's blessing? A saint's nothing but a priest who went and did something memorable enough to get himself talked about."

"And so? Veschia was a good woman, by all accounts, priest or no. Why shouldn't the poor folk she cared about invoke her name?" His face was sober, but his eyes danced. He knew she had no answer.

"Humph." Makenna turned away. She didn't like feeling indebted, any more than Cogswhallop did. Especially to someone who laughed at her.

She took the battered pack with her, when she crept out of camp just before dawn, listening to Todder Yon's deceptive snores.

Speaking with another human had roused the aching loneliness the goblin's company had almost cured. And he'd been kind, she supposed. But the villagers had seemed kind before they turned on her mother. She didn't trust him. She preferred the goblin's system of favor for favor, even though it took two weeks to set out enough food to get the pack mended.

She hadn't seen Cogswhallop in all that time and was beginning to think she never would again. She was surprised how much she missed him, but she'd become accustomed to loneliness once—she'd come to accept it again.

So when Cogswhallop shook her awake one morning, she sat up gasping in astonishment. He had never touched her before. Her delight at seeing him was washed away by the tension in his thin face.

"I thought I'd paid it," he fretted. "I thought with finding you a pack I'd cleared my debt, for good and all."

"You have," said Makenna promptly. "You owe me nothing, Cogswhallop. Paid in full."

"Aye," he said glumly. "But that's about to change. It may be too late already, wench, and I'm not even sure if there's anything you can do, but I've some friends who need help. Badly."

Makenna stared at the wood piled under the towering oak and groped desperately for a plan. The thought of what she might have to witness sickened her.

"It's that great chain they've laid in a circle around the tree that's the problem," Cogswhallop told her grimly.

Makenna squinted through the crack between the

boards of the old barn where they were hiding. She could only catch glimpses of the chain, between the bodies of the milling mob. "I thought you could touch iron."

"Oh, it's not that it's iron. It's spelled against goblins, like the doorsills of the churches. Not one of us can get within six feet of it. Keeps us out and the Greeners in. Real effective, that priest, may foxes chew off his buttocks! I was hoping you could get past it."

"If the chain's only spelled against goblins, then I can," said Makenna. "The problem isn't the chain, it's that great crowd of people."

A wave of despair swept over her. Trapped, the lot of them. She hadn't been able to save her own mother. What made Cogswhallop think she could save his friends? Even with unexpected help.

She could feel the hopeful gazes of her goblin allies. When they'd arrived at the farm, four strange goblins had materialized and followed Cogswhallop out of the bushes. Cogswhallop had seen her staring.

"You didn't think I'd ask you to do it all on your own, did you? These are Oddi and Beekin, the lass is Narri, and the little one's Pimo. They're the ones who've been following you all these weeks."

It felt strange to see the faces of her pursuers.

"Good enough, if all we needed was tricks with a food bag," Makenna had said grimly. She had no great faith in the goblins' abilities, for all the bedevilment they'd given her, but it had been nice to have allies. Until she saw what she was up against. Now they were just four more people she might fail.

Returning her thoughts to the present, Makenna stared into the bare branches. The tree was an ancient giant. Almost all its leaves had fallen, but she still couldn't see anything in it.

"Are you sure they're trapped up there?"

"Aye, a whole family of Greeners. Five of 'em. They're keeping still, hoping the humans will think they're gone and the farm folk'll be able to talk the mob out of it. Those farmers are the only reason they didn't set it alight at dawn."

Makenna had guessed that without being told. A farmer was speaking furiously with the priest, who wore the seven-rayed sun symbol of his calling upon his breast. The farmer had the look of a man who'd been arguing for a long time. His wife stood off a bit, weeping into her apron. A little boy, also sobbing, clung to her skirts. An older boy stood beside her, but he wasn't crying. He looked grim and angry, and his hands flexed as if he wanted a weapon in them. The priest looked sober, even sympathetic, but there was a smugness about him that reminded Makenna of Mistress Manoc from her village. He'd already won, and he knew it.

Anger surged through her, burning away her helplessness. These were her mother's enemies, in spirit, if not in person. "The farmers won't be able to talk them out of it," she said quietly, turning to face her small troop.

Cogswhallop's sharp face crumpled with despair. "Then if you can't get though the crowd, they're as good as burned."

"Not so fast." All she needed was a plan—she'd been able to destroy her whole village, once she had a plan. "I might be able to get through the crowd. There's a spell that'll make people look right over me. But it's not strong enough to make them overlook me if I step across that chain and lift the goblins down from the tree. We need to distract them. Maybe if we could burn down something else—but it'd have to be important, not just a haystack, and we've no time to lay a fire and have it take hold."

Without looking, Cogswhallop reached behind him, grabbed Oddi's tunic, and hauled the goblin, squeaking, in front of Makenna. "Oddi's a Flamer. He's the lad who's been keeping your fire going nights. He can get anything blazing in minutes."

"Really? How? No, never mind. Oddi, could you set fire to a building?"

"Aye, gladly. What for?"

"For a divers— Oh. But what do you want?" Makenna gestured helplessly. "I left all my gear back by the trail. I could owe you—"

"No, girl, I'll have no owing." Oddi looked shocked by the mere thought. "All I want's a token, to keep us in balance, like. A button would do. Or a small stone or a bit of cloth. Anything, really."

This was how friends traded. Makenna's heart

warmed, despite the urgency and fear. "But what use would you have for one of my buttons?"

Oddi shook his head pityingly. "You're a bit dim still. It's the trade, not the profit, that counts."

"But—"

"They're moving," hissed the littlest goblin, Pimo.

Makenna spun. The crowd had seized the farmer and dragged him back, ignoring his shouted protests. The priest stepped forward, torch in hand, and the older farm boy leapt away from the crowd and tackled him. They rolled over and over, struggling, and the torch went out. Makenna drew her knife and sliced a button off her vest.

"Oddi, burn the church," she commanded. "The rest of you, tell me quick, what can you do?"

As she listened to the goblins' replies, she watched the mob. Beekin and Narri were Makers, supremely clever with their fingers, but slow. Pimo was a Sleeper, but he warned her that his gift worked best on people who were relaxed or tired, and still better on animals. Makenna smiled briefly, remembering all her sudden naps. Cogswhallop, son of a Maker and a Flamer, could work with iron and steel, but he had no other gift.

The mob dragged the farmer's son off the priest and clubbed him into unconsciousness. His mother screamed and ran to kneel beside him, pulling his head into her lap. The farmer struggled harder, but he couldn't break free.

The villagers helped the priest to his feet, brushing off his clothes, restoring his dignity as much as it could be restored until his nose stopped bleeding. Someone brought another torch. The priest started to make a speech.

Makenna sliced four more buttons off her vest. She had her plan. "See that sheep pen, the one that opens into the yard?" she asked quickly, passing out buttons. "It's closed with an iron catch, so that's Cogswhallop's job. Beekin and Narri, can you saddle a horse? The quietest one you can find. Then get out to the pen and get those sheep ready to spook. It shouldn't be hard to excite them; there'll be fire nearby and they're silly creatures."

Beekin and Narri took their buttons and vanished. They were supposed to be slow?

"Pimo, can you keep an animal relaxed and drowsy without putting it to sleep?"

His tiny face screwed up doubtfully. "It depends. I'll try."

"Then go with Beekin and Narri and bring the horse as soon as it's soothed. And remember—"

A roar from the crowd interrupted her. The priest had lit the pyre. Pimo snatched a button and vanished.

"That horse has to stay calm," Makenna hissed after him. "Because"—she turned to Cogswhallop—"I'm not much of a rider. Why are you still here?"

"It's a simple latch. I can undo it in seconds. And since it's in plain view I'd best wait till your diversion has taken hold." He was watching the flames rise around the base of the tree. His face, contorted with anguish and hope, made a terrible contrast to his carefully calm voice. Makenna felt a surge of respect for the little goblin. This was courage.

She hadn't been able to save her mother. Maybe she could save someone else who deserved it.

Hoofbeats clopped on the barn's wooden floor. The horse sounded calm, but it hadn't seen the fire yet. The sheep were beginning to bleat and bounce. "Here's your button, Cogswhallop."

Cogswhallop looked at her oddly. "Keep the button. It's me that's owing you again. More than I'll ever be able to pay, if you bring this off. Do you think we have a chance?"

The horse arrived, a big gray. Pimo rode high on its neck, clinging to its mane, whispering in its ear. Makenna climbed awkwardly into the saddle and settled Pimo on the pommel in front of her. "There's always a chance," she said. The sheep were going crazy. "Now get out there and get ready. Open the pen when I come out of the barn and not before, understand?"

A taut smile flickered across Cogswhallop's face and vanished. "Aye, gen'ral." And he was gone.

General?

The fire was reaching into the lower branches now. Makenna scraped a handful of dried bird droppings from a post beneath a swallow's nest and, rubbing it on the horse's flank, drew the look-away rune. The horse twitched its hide and looked back at her curiously. Pimo's whispering became more intense, his face streaked with the sweat of fear.

Makenna felt the terror, too, rushing like a pulse through her body, but it was mixed with anger and a wild exhilaration that came close to joy. "Steady," she said, to the horse, to Pimo, to herself. "Wait for it . . . ."

Finally it came. A gust of smoke from another direction. Murmurs of confusion. Cries of dismay and outrage. The priest yelled, "My spell books!" and raced for the burning church. Makenna smiled grimly. It seemed that endangering their spell books would distract anyone who made magic, not just hedgewitches. Three-quarters of the mob followed the priest to fight the fire. Makenna kicked the horse into a drowsy amble, out of the barn.

An avalanche of bounding, bleating, wild-eyed sheep rolled over the farmyard, leaving more chaos in its wake.

Makenna guided the placid gray carefully through the shouting crowd that struggled to control the terrified animals. One man, fingers wrapped tight in a kicking ewe's coat, bounced off her horse's rump without even looking around at her. The spell was working.

As the horse stepped over the chain, Pimo turned faintly green and his voice choked into silence. On the high saddle he was almost five feet from the charmed iron, but it still might not have been enough if the horse hadn't carried him past. The horse snorted and started to flinch back from the raging fire, but the goblin coughed once and started to mutter again and the horse calmed.

Makenna caught an echo of the spell—for a moment the fire seemed distant, like something seen in a dream. No need to run, no need to fear; it couldn't hurt anything. She fought the spell like a diver fighting for the surface, and when she won free of it, the fire crackled before her, above her, greedy and dangerous. Heat beat against her face, her arms, her hair. She guided the horse around the tree to the windward side where the flames burned less fiercely.

"Come here," she cried, lifting her arms to the branches. "I'll get you out. Come—"

A furious rustling erupted above her and a tiny goblin boy, no more than a foot tall, dangled above her hands. She stood in the stirrups and grabbed him, propping him on the saddle between her and Pimo. He squirmed in her grasp, staring up into the tree.

A goblin man and a young goblin woman crouched there, shouting over the roar of the approaching flames.

"You get, girl."

"What about Mam?" The flames cast distorting shadows on the girl's long-nosed face. "She hasn't got Bini out yet. We've got to—"

"I'll go get 'em as soon as you're gone! Now—"

The young woman turned to climb back into the tree, and the man, snarling, pulled her forcibly from the branches and dropped her, screaming and struggling, into Makenna's arms. She fought with insane, panicked strength, and it took all Makenna's attention to subdue her.

The gray, distracted by the struggle on its back, began to snort and sidle, and Makenna took a firm grip on the reins.

When she looked up, the tree was a writhing vortex of fire, but she stayed, struggling with the horse as it grew more fearful despite Pimo's efforts.

Then a voice from the crowd cried, "Look! The tree . . . girl on a horse . . . saving the goblins!"

Half a dozen people started toward her. Makenna dropped the reins, and Pimo dropped the spell. The terrified horse bolted, carrying them with it, scattering villagers as it raced toward the cool safety of the woods.

The roar of the fire and the pounding hooves could not drown out the goblin girl's despairing scream.

"There was nothing more you could do, gen'ral." Cogswhallop gazed tenderly down at the hair of the young goblin woman, Natter, who had finally cried herself to sleep in his arms. "That you accomplished this much is a wonder."

"It wasn't enough," said Makenna stiffly. If she was a general, she was a bad one. The demon-cursed priest had won, and she had lost.

The little orphaned goblin boy stirred in her lap, and she cradled him gently, murmuring till he lay still again. His small fingers were curled around her thumb. The tips of Natter's fingers were tinged with green, but the boy's were the same as the rest of his skin—skin the same color as Makenna's. Cogswhallop said that meant he had a different gift. Only Greeners had green fingers. Makenna hoped the boy was warm enough, wrapped in her jacket. It was cold after the sun set, but they hadn't dared light a fire.

"How could they do this, those people, those *humans?*" she demanded. "Natter and Miggy said their family served that farm for five generations."

"And their folk did their best to fight for them. You have to grant that," said Cogswhallop.

"It wasn't enough."

Cogswhallop sighed. "Seems like nothing is enough these days. The priests are determined to get rid of us."

Makenna frowned. "I knew they'd forbidden folk to put out the bowls, that they were trying to drive you out, but . . . this is happening in other places?" She remembered Todder Yon's gossip.

"Aye. Why do you think there's so many of us living wild? Maybe you don't know, but most of the goblin races do better in villages. We're a civilized folk, for the most part."

"Which is more that can be said for humans!"

"You're human, gen'ral. No way around it."

"Maybe not. But this is one human who's going to fight for goblinkind. Cogswhallop, you owe me, right?"

"Aye." He smiled down at the sleeping girl. "More than I can pay in a lifetime's service."

"Then I want you to help me fight the priests. To save

as many of our people as we can—and maybe get some of theirs! Will you do that? I'd have to have help. Much as I want to, I couldn't do it alone."

General. With the goblins' help, she could make it real.

"Are you asking me to be your second-in-command?" His eyes gleamed in the darkness. "Sounds a dangerous job to me. They'll be looking for you now. And someday you'll want to return to your own kind. Don't build too many obstacles in your path."

"I'm never going back to humankind." She said it with no particular emphasis; it wasn't a decision she had to defend, it was simply a fact. As much a part of her as her bones.

"Aye, you think that now, with the smoke stench in your hair. But this will fade. Someday a likely lad will come along, and you'll discover that you're human enough."

"You're wrong," said Makenna. "I'm going to fight the humans. I swear it on my mother's soul. And no one will make me change my mind. No one."

CHAPTER 4

The Knight

FIVE YEARS LATER . . .

Tobin woke up in the middle of the night with an urgent need to go to the privy. He muttered a curse, softly, so as not to wake his brother, and groped for his slippers, but he couldn't find them. The need grew more urgent.

Tobin yawned and crawled out of bed, wincing as his feet hit the cold stone floor. The privy was at the far end of a long corridor. By the time he returned his feet were thoroughly chilled and he was much more awake. As the light from the corridor lamp spilled into the room, he saw his slippers placed neatly at the foot of his bed and whispered another curse, glancing over at Jeriah, for his brother was a light sleeper. The blankets didn't even stir. Jeri was usually a very light sleeper. Tobin frowned and tiptoed over for a closer look.

He swore loudly this time, yanking the covers back. The bed held nothing but artfully stacked pillows.

Tobin took two angry steps toward the door and then hesitated. Did he really need to leave his warm bed in the middle of the night to chase after his brother? Jeri was fifteen, only three years younger than Tobin—by St. Rydan the Teacher, it was time he started looking after himself! Perhaps having his big brother hovering all the time actually provoked him to mischief.

It was a sobering thought, and Tobin's anger lessened. But he'd been careful not to mother Jeri all winter. And this had happened before. This winter had been Jeriah's first campaign, his first taste of the horror, exhilaration, and boredom of fighting the southern barbarians. There had been nights, in the army camp, when Jeriah's bed was empty till nearly dawn. Too many nights? Most boys went a little wild on their first campaign. Tobin had kept a firm grip on the bulk of their funds and told himself that even Jeri couldn't get into too much trouble in the restricted world of the camp. But this wasn't the camp, this was the City of Steps—what could his brother be up to here?

Tobin looked longingly at his own bed. His feet were freezing. He might go back to bed, but he'd never be able to sleep. Promising himself that he'd skin his brother with a dull knife when he laid hands on him, Tobin began to fumble for his clothes.

His soft-soled boots hardly made a sound as he ghosted down the corridors. No one seemed to be stirring except a few men on their way to the privy. Tobin whisked into other men's rooms twice to avoid being seen, and it was only by the Seven Bright Ones' grace that he didn't wake anyone. It would be ironic if he got in trouble and Jeriah made it safely back to bed. But if his brother wasn't in the dormitory, where was he?

The compound that housed knights who had no other lodging was in the second tier of the city, surrounded by a high wall that separated it from the third tier on one side and the even higher wall of the Hierarch's palace on the first tier. All the gates were guarded, so Jeri must be somewhere on this level. And there was nothing on this level except the offices of the civil clerks and the buildings dedicated to the maintenance of the military, the stables, the tilt yard . . . and the armory.

Tobin grimaced. The armory held possibilities for mischief, and so did the tack in the stables.

He let himself out of the dormitory. The late spring night was like silk against his skin; no need for the cloak he'd forgotten. The rising moon gave him plenty of light.

On the southern border now, even the nights were hot, and during the day the desert would be a scalding shield on which nothing could survive. Tobin was always relieved when the onset of summer forced the barbarian tribes to retreat to their distant, stony mountains in the far south.

This winter had been his third campaign. Tobin been knighted at the beginning of the year. Once it had been his dream, to be a knight. But by the time the Hierarch's staff touched his shoulder, Tobin had realized that it was not honor it carried, but a lifelong burden. Tobin was tired of fighting. He wanted to go home, to spend his days helping his father see to their horses and learning the management of the farms and villages in their care.

He knew this war was necessary. The Hierarch's army was all that stood between the southern farmlands and the barbarians. And when those barbarians had broken through the hard-held lines, and sacked a farm or a town, Tobin had seen what they did. But he hated killing them anyway. And it seemed to him, perversely, that the more barbarians the army killed the more there were, more every year, and no end in sight.

It had been six years since the Decree of Bright Magic, which was supposed to induce the Bright Ones to favor the Hierarch's army, but Tobin had seen no sign of the gods' favor so far. Well, it was over for this year. He was free to go home as soon as he saw Jeriah placed as a squire in the Hierarch's service—provided his brother was still acceptable to the Hierarch if tonight's prank came to light.

Tobin approached one of the gates. The guard's only business was with those who wanted to pass through, but he still had no wish to be seen. He heard the guard arguing with someone and crept closer to the shadow of the wall.

"Come now, sir, you're in the wrong place. The guest

quarters are at the north side of the city on the third level down. May I get someone to guide you, sir?"

"Demon's claws, why'd you think I need a guide? *I* know perfectly well where I'm at. Perfec'ly. What you think I am, drunk?" Torchlight gleamed on the rich embroidery of the man's jacket. A lord, probably. At the least, a man of wealth and influence. Tobin sympathized with the guard.

"No, sir, of course you're not drunk. Anyone can get lost in this maze of a place, sir. I'll just fetch you a guide."

"What makes you think I need you t' guide me?" the lord demanded. "Fool like you couldn't guide no one. You don' even realize that I'm drunk!" The man toppled into the guard's reluctant embrace. "I'm going to be sick now," he confided.

Tobin slipped easily past the cursing guard. As long as he didn't laugh, there was small chance of his being noticed.

There was no one in the armory—or if there was, they were quieter than Tobin could imagine Jeri and the wild group of squires he'd befriended ever being. He moved on to the stables. Tobin had thought Jeriah was dropping that lot. Lately he'd seen his brother more often in the company of a group of knights, most of whom were older than Tobin.

Tobin frowned, remembering several heated, low-voiced conversations that had been broken off at his approach. But what in this world could Jeri be up to that included Sir Sharam and Sir Brilan? Master Carderi was a priest! Surely they weren't involved in the kind of mischief that would draw a young squire from his bed. And yet there had been something odd about Jeriah lately. He'd been quieter, almost . . . secretive? Tobin had put it down to growing up, perhaps even a desire to put some distance between himself and his motherly older brother. He'd been a little hurt that Jeri hadn't realized he'd understand—that he was prepared to give a young man freer rein than he'd given a boy. But now . . .

Tobin stared into the quiet stable. The big horses dozed peacefully, a sharp contrast to his uneasiness.

Jeriah wasn't in the stables. He wasn't in the grooms' quarters, or the deserted tilt yard, so unless he was in the pasture, the clerk's offices, or swimming in the lake, he wasn't on the second level at all—and that was impossible because he couldn't have gotten past the gates! The Hierarch's guards might be distracted by a drunken wanderer, but they knew their business. The only way to pass through those gates unchallenged would be to kill them. So where in this world or the Other was Jeriah?

Could he have gone for a moonlight swim? With a warm public bath available? Besides, the lake shore was a blanket of mud . . . .

. . . just like the mud on the boots he'd seen thrust under Jeri's bed only a week ago. At the time Tobin had smiled and resolved to let Jeriah discover for himself that boots under the bed didn't get cleaned. Now he gritted his teeth, furious at his own stupidity. Friends had told Tobin that there was a place you could sneak under the wall between the second and third levels, if the lake was low enough, but Tobin had never used the escape route himself, and he'd almost forgotten about it.

He stamped through the deserted pasture to the place where the lake met the twelve-foot-high wall, and squished along beside it through the muddy lake bed. The ground on the other side was level with the ground here, the water flowing under the barrier through grated pipes, but . . . Yes, here was the pass-through, a muddy dip where the ground beneath the wall had washed away. Even in the moonlight, he could see boot tracks—and they were Jeriah's size.

There was no reason to stand in the mud. Tobin trudged back out of the lake bed and found a large stone half sheltered in a clump of bushes and settled in to wait for his wayward brother. And kill him. And then shake the truth out of him.

He was dozing when he heard the scrape of boots over rock and the harsh panting that heralded an approach. Tobin smiled grimly, peering through the brush until the man scrambled under the wall. His hood was drawn forward over his face, despite the mildness of the night, but Tobin recognized the cloak.

He held quite still as Jeriah hurried past his hideout, then he stepped out and grabbed his brother's wrist firmly. "Got you!"

Jeriah jumped and spun around, moonlight flashing on the knife in his free hand. Only the reflexes developed through three years of combat enabled Tobin to leap aside as the knife plunged toward him.

He grabbed Jeriah's other wrist and forced the knife up. *Jeriah pulling a knife?* The impossibility of it swirled through his mind. Was this his brother, or had he ambushed someone else? The man's hood had fallen completely over his face—it must be blinding him.

The man twisted his wrist, almost freeing the knife, and Tobin braced himself and kicked the inside of his opponent's knee, hard.

The muffled cry sounded like Jeriah, but Tobin didn't have time to think about it. He surged forward, pushing his opponent's wrists up and back, and the man's damaged knee gave, tipping him backward, with Tobin on top of him. He slammed the hand that held the knife against the ground, harder and harder, until his opponent cried out and the knife fell.

Tobin let go of the man's wrist long enough to cast the knife into the bushes. The man's freed hand struck for his face and missed by inches. With a muffled curse the man swiped the hood off his face, and Tobin grabbed his wrist and bore it toward the ground. But the man wasn't resisting. Tobin looked down and met his brother's startled eyes.

"Tobin! What are you doing here?"

"What am I doing here? What are you doing here?

And why did you pull a knife on me?"

"I didn't know it was you. Thank the Seven I missed! Tobin, let me up, I've got to get out of here!" Jeriah's wrists twitched in his grasp.

"Not a chance. Not till you tell me what's going on."

"But you don't understand! They're after me! I think I lost them, but they had dogs and trackers and they might have picked up the trail again. I've got to be in bed before they start looking for missing men. Tobin, let me up!"

"Who's after you?" demanded Tobin, not budging.

Jeriah stopped struggling. "The Hierarch's guard."

"The Hie— By the Bright Gods Jeri, what did you do?"

"Are you going to let me go?" his brother asked quietly.

Tobin released him, and Jeriah sat up, grimacing and rubbing his wrists, then, gingerly, his knee.

"Jeri, tell me what's wrong."

"I can't," said Jeriah. "It's not your business and I don't want to involve you. Help me up."

"Involve me? I'm your brother. I'm supposed to be placing you in the Hierarch's service. How can I not be involved when you do something stupid and make that impossible?"

"Well, if I don't get back to bed, that will certainly be impossible." Jeriah's eyes gleamed with a determination that disturbed Tobin more than anything he'd said. He'd never before seen his impetuous brother so cool and self-controlled.

He grabbed his brother's arm and pulled him up, but when Jeriah put his weight on his injured knee, he gasped with pain and his leg buckled.

"Demon's teeth, I've torn something," he muttered through gritted teeth.

"You mean I tore something," said Tobin remorsefully. "Lean on me. Can you make it, or shall I fetch someone to carry you?"

"You mustn't fetch anyone," hissed Jeriah. He hobbled a few steps, wincing.

"But you have to see a healer priest, Jeri. Whatever's wrong, it isn't worth crippling yourself." Memory washed over him coldly. "Or is it? Jeriah, why did you pull a knife on me?"

"Because if it had been anyone but you, and they'd stopped or recognized me, I'd have had to kill them. Do you still want to fetch me a healer priest?"

"No." Through his stunned shock, Tobin's mind finally began to function and his irritated alarm deepened into real fear. "Jeri, you have to tell me what's going on."

"No, I don't." Jeriah gritted his teeth and tried to move faster. The sickly pallor of his face gleamed in the moonlight. "You know too much already."

"Not by half, I don't! You said the guard was after you! If they'd caught you, what would the charge have been?"

"They'll catch me yet, if you don't get going!"

Tobin slowed his pace even more. "The charge, Jeri."

"I can't tell you."

Tobin stopped and spun his brother to face him. "Of all the—" Then he heard it, and his blood ran cold—the distinctive, high-pitched baying of the Hierarch's tracking dogs, on the other side of the wall and not far away.

Jeriah drew a short sharp breath, but when he turned to Tobin his voice was calm. "Run. You can cross the pasture before they get here. Then they'll be busy with me."

"But—"

"I'll never make it with this knee." The baying sounded closer. "Go on, Tobin. This isn't some prank played with gisap glue and feathers—you can't mother me out of it. Just . . . I love you, brother. Now go!"

Tobin's fear transformed itself into a well of still, icy terror. "Whatever it is, it's not worth dying for."

Jeriah's face contorted. "It would have been," he whispered passionately, "if we'd been able to bring it off, but— Tobin, the charge is high treason. So go now, all right?" Jeriah pushed him away. "There's no time to be stupid. Think what it would do to Mother to lose us both—to Father to have his heir disgraced as well as his second son. Go on, Tobin, run!"

Terror rose and drowned him. A traitor's death. They took an ax and hacked you, screaming, into bits, keeping you alive as long as they could. His little brother. *Never.*

"Jeriah," said Tobin. The dogs were nearer now. Jeriah turned and Tobin swung his fist up, striking the point of Jeriah's chin, just like the master of arms had taught him.

He caught his brother as he fell, limply unconscious, and threw him over his shoulder. The slope of the lake bed was steeper here. There was a small grassy island, just a dozen feet from the lake's shore—even a dozen feet of shallow water was enough to cover their tracks, and the wind was in the right direction to keep the dogs from scenting anything.

Tobin waded out and dumped Jeriah on the island's far side, fumbling furiously with his brother's cloak pin. The dogs sounded as if they'd almost reached the gap beneath the wall. Swinging Jeriah's cloak around his shoulders, Tobin splashed back through the lake and raced away. He was halfway across the pasture when the baying became crystal clear, and he knew the dogs had come under the wall. The shouts of their handlers sent him flying over the rough ground. One quick glance over his shoulder told him they'd passed the island where Jeriah lay and were happily chasing after him. The dogs, drawn by the scent on the cloak, had no doubt of their quarry. *All I have to do now is save myself.*

He raced into the tilt yard and rolled under the fence without a check. Sword posts, jumps, jousting barriers— no place to hide, nothing to stop them. The stables? On a horse he could outrun them, perhaps even get through a gate.

He banged through the door and slammed it, startling the nearest horses, who snorted and stamped. He took a second to drop the latch and pull the string so it couldn't be opened from the other side, then he ran along the corridor. His own horse? No, it might be recognized. He threw open the big doors at the other end of the stables and chose a dark bay that would blend with the night.

No time for saddle or bridle. Tobin looped a rope around the horse's neck, and the animal followed him obediently into the corridor, though it danced nervously, fearful of his strangeness and the barking of the dogs.

Tobin threw himself belly-down across the horse's back. A guardsman smashed into the door. The bay shied and Tobin slid off, staggering to keep his balance and still hold the prancing horse with his makeshift halter. The guard pounded on the door and one of the dogs howled. Tobin leapt for the horse again.

It was too much. The bay tossed its head and bolted for the open doors, tearing the rope from Tobin's grasp. A burst of shouting greeted it, and the horse took off alone, at a dead run. Two of the baying dogs ran after it.

Tobin held his breath. Would they follow it? Surely they could see, as it raced through the moonlit shadows, that there was no rider on its back.

Evidently they couldn't. The barking of the dogs drew away from the stables. Tobin prayed the bay would lead them a long chase.

Shaking now that the crisis was past, he made his way back between the stalls. The horses were settling down again, with the dogs gone.

He opened the door a crack and peered outside—

nothing. With a sigh of relief, Tobin stepped out, and the butt of a pike shot between his legs and sent him sprawling.

He rolled over and started to sit up, but a sharp blade pricked his throat, forcing him back to the ground. His eyes traveled up the pike and met the eyes of a man wearing the sunred tunic of the Hierarch's guard.

"I arrest you," he said formally. "In the Hierarch's name. To resist him is to resist the Seven Bright Ones' will." A fierce grin spread over his face. "And if you give me any trouble, traitor, I'll skewer you here and now, and save the executioner the trouble."

CHAPTER 5

The Knight

T HE CELL WAS DAMP and cold enough to make Tobin glad he had Jeriah's cloak. A stone box with no windows, the cell had a stout wooden door with a barred peephole in the top, a slop pot in the corner, and nothing else. Tobin had become familiar with every stone in its walls because, judging by the changing shifts of the silent guards who brought him meals and emptied the bucket, he'd been there for four days.

He spent most of his time praying Jeriah had gotten away. He had no idea what his brother would do for the rest of his life, as an outlawed traitor, but whatever he did would be better than being executed.

Jeriah had always been the adventurous one. Perhaps he wouldn't mind too much, vanishing into the mass of homeless farm folk the war had created. And once Tobin knew his brother was safely away, he could admit that it had been Jeriah they were chasing, accept whatever punishment they chose to lay on him (surely not too severe—

an impulsive decision to save his brother?), and go home.

A wave of longing for the mellow stone house, the laughter of his young sisters, and the rolling fertile fields washed over him. He closed his eyes. Surely the law wouldn't be too severe. He hadn't even known about the conspiracy until it was over. He still didn't know anything! And he was his father's heir—everyone knew that heirs to lordship got off lightly. It was almost a scandal. No matter how angry his father was at Jeri, he'd surely do his best to help Tobin. Surely. So why had he heard nothing in four days?

He opened his eyes, looked at the stone walls, and sighed. The longer he was here, the longer Jeri would have to escape. It would be better if weeks passed before they came for him. A nervous person might have gone mad by then, with no light, and no news. It was a good thing Tobin wasn't the nervous type. And since he intended to tell the truth the instant anyone remembered him, waiting here, day after day.

He heard voices in the corridor outside and sprang to his feet, apprehension warring with relief. It wasn't mealtime, but they might be coming for someone else. There'd been several false alarms in the past few days. It was ridiculous to assume— A guard looked through the peephole. Tobin leaned against the far wall and tried to look harmless. The door opened. The guard stepped in, set a lamp on the stone floor, and ushered Tobin's mother respectfully into the room.

She was plump and astonishingly pretty—Jeriah had inherited her looks. Tobin, on the other hand, had the kind of face that even his friends described as ordinary.

"Oh, Tobin." She hurried across the small room and pulled his head down to kiss his cheek. The scent of roses, which she always wore, was a ludicrous contrast with the dreary cell. "Oh, Tobin." She embraced him again. "Dear one, you look dreadful! I'm so proud of you!"

"They wouldn't let me shave." Tobin shook his head, trying to get his mind to function. "Mother, what are you doing here?"

"I bribed the guard, of course. It was really quite easy." She sounded surprised.

Tobin winced and glanced at the door. The guard had gone, but he lowered his voice anyway. "Did Jeri get away? I've been going mad, not knowing what was happening."

"Jeriah is perfectly safe, dear." Then why was she avoiding his eyes? "At least, he's safe for now. I left him at home with your sisters. They were hysterical, poor girls. I had trouble persuading him, but he was always like that, even as a child. I remember . . ."

Tobin remembered, too. "Mother," he said firmly. "What are you hiding? What's happening to Jeri? I know it can't be too bad—no matter how angry Father is, he'd have to help him escape . . . at least . . . surely, he would."

"It, ah, it hasn't arisen," said his mother. "Oh, Tobin, you know how your father is. Of course you do. Why, I remember when you were four—"

Tobin sighed. "Where is Father?" Strict, formal, and inflexible, but at least the old man would give you a straight answer. Tobin's father had taught him honor, just as his caper-witted mother had taught him love.

"Your father is here, of course. I know he can be a little . . . stern, but he couldn't stay home with you in so much trouble."

"But you said Jeri was at home? Isn't Father helping him get away?"

"Well, dearest . . ." She looked up at him pleadingly. "Oh Tobin, you know how he is. He'd have been so angry, and Jeri's only a second son, and your father's always been so harsh with him. I was afraid he might not help, and then Jeri would die horribly and I couldn't bear that, so I persuaded Jeriah not to tell him about it!" She finished in a breathless rush and smiled.

"What do you mean, not tell him? If you didn't tell Father anything, why is he here?"

"Why, to help you, of course. I had to tell him you'd been arrested. The only thing he doesn't know, and no one must find out, dear one, is that it was Jeriah who was . . . involved in . . ." Her voice trailed off under his astonished gaze.

"You mean—" He took a deep breath, his voice rising in spite of himself. "You mean Father doesn't know I'm innocent? Mother, how could you? I can't believe you did that! I can't believe Jeri would ever do that!"

Easy tears streamed down her face. "Oh, Tobin, I know how you must feel, but think. Jeriah would die a horrible death, that I couldn't possibly—"

"But if I'm executed, that's all right?"

"No, of course not, dear one. But you won't be executed, because you're the heir. Your father almost has it settled. You'll be punished, of course, and probably deprived of your knighthood or some such thing, but you won't be killed like Jeri would have been. Like those other poor men." She shuddered, genuine horror flickering over her face.

"What other men?"

"The leaders of the—the conspiracy have already been executed. They're trying the rest more slowly. They're not going to kill them all, although most will be stripped of rank and some will be imprisoned for a while. For a long time, actually. But when it's over you could come home and run the estate, which is what you always wanted anyway. As a second son, Jeriah's only possible career is service to the Hierarch, and if he's convicted he can't ever, ever do that!"

"But—" Tobin felt like he was trying to wade through molasses. Conversation with his mother often had that effect. "But surely the other conspirators named Jeri. You'll never be able to pull it off!" Unbelievable that Jeriah had agreed to this.

"Well, that's been very fortunate. One of the guards mentioned you'd been arrested, and the other conspirators must have guessed what happened, for they've all named you as their accomplice. I expect they're trying to keep their real people free. And I must say, they've been very nice about it, for they've been saying you were hardly involved in the conspiracy, and Jeriah assures me that he was in it up to his teeth!"

"Mother, you can't possibly expect me to take the blame for Jeri."

"You've done it before."

"When he was a child! This is different!"

"Yes. It's much more serious."

There was a tap on the door and the guard opened it. "This is all the time I can give you, lady. My watch is almost up."

"Of course. I'm grateful you managed this much," said his mother, giving the guard the lovely smile that turned any man who didn't know her into putty. "Just one more minute, please?"

The guard smiled and withdrew, and she turned back to Tobin.

"I know it's a lot to ask, my dear, but you've always looked after him for me, and the consequences would be so much worse for him than for you, and—"

"It's a lot to ask," said Tobin bitterly. "Is this what Jeri wants?"

His mother's eyes shifted. "No one can force you to do anything. But you were always the one who saw all the sides of everything. I can't think where you get it from.

Perhaps your father, but he's so unyielding when he finally makes up his mind, that it doesn't seem at all—"

The guard's face appeared in the peephole. "Lady, you've got to go!"

"Tobin, please, think of the consequences for—"

"I have to think about all the consequences," said Tobin. "For everyone." He had long since learned to be firm with his mother.

"But—"

She was still talking when the guard pulled her out. The cell seemed quieter than it had before.

Jeriah had always been her favorite, just as Tobin was his father's. Both he and Jeri had accepted that, though hearing it voiced still stung. But she was fighting now to save both her sons. Tobin knew there was nothing she wouldn't sacrifice in that cause, including his own feelings. And his father's.

He had never really understood his parents' marriage. They dealt well with each other, on the surface. But as Tobin grew older, he had realized more and more how they both went their own way—his father wrapped up in the estate, his mother in correspondence with a vast number of powerful friends. It was through her influence that Jeriah had been offered the chance to enter the Hierarch's service. A chance now lost forever. Or was it?

How could she not have told his father? And how could Jeri possibly have accepted that? Jeriah might be impulsive, but he wasn't a coward. Tobin would have sworn Jeriah would never let him take the blame for something like this. But a week ago, he'd have sworn his brother would never be involved in treason, either.

His heart felt as cold as the stones beneath his pacing feet. He would sooner have doubted the sunrise than Jeriah's love.

But in the end, that didn't matter. It didn't matter whether his mother loved Jeriah best, or whether his father believed Tobin had betrayed the principles he'd tried so hard to teach both his sons, or even if Jeriah loved him at all. What mattered was that Tobin loved them. He would save what he could—whatever it might cost.

Tobin found it difficult to concentrate as the court's Speaker announced the charges. He'd been standing for some time, awaiting his turn, and his feet were tired. The light from the windows hurt his eyes, which had adapted to the dark after all these days. At least he was warm.

". . . listened willingly, in his weakness, to those who plotted against the sacred Hierarch himself . . ."

They'd let him bathe and shave and given him clean clothes, but he still felt soiled and weary to his bones. Neither his mother nor Jeriah was here—his father had probably forbidden them to come. His father sat in the first row of the audience, directly behind the seven lords and priests who were judging him, but he'd looked at Tobin only once—a scorching glance that made Tobin's stomach twist sickly.

To his father things were either right or wrong—no middle ground. The muddled mixture of good and bad that Tobin so often perceived under the surface of things was invisible to his father.

"... agreed to work with the Dark One's minions, who sought to bring chaos to our dear land. It was only by the Seven Bright Ones' grace that he had no time to act on his evil intent ..."

His mother had visited him twice in the past three days. On her last visit, she assured him that his father had everything fixed. She didn't know how much of the carefully hoarded savings his father had been forced to sacrifice, what pieces of the estate, as dear to him as his own body. How much honor had he lost, saving a son he believed to be a traitor? *Look at me, Father. I didn't do it. I've kept my honor!* But his father continued to stare into middle distance. The Speaker had reached the evidence now. His words were markedly less florid.

"... seen running away from the meeting where we arrested the traitors. Three guards and three trackers were sent after him. He lost them for a time, in the garden pools, but the dogs picked up his scent again and ..."

... were following Jeri back to the dormitory, where he'd have gotten in safely if I hadn't stopped him. How could my brother have gotten involved in this? Stupid, stupid, stupid. And typical of Jeriah. He was always involved in some sort of wild scheme.

His mother said no one suspected Jeri. Why should they? A fifteen-year-old squire was an unlikely conspirator. Tobin had been wondering all week why the traitors had recruited his harebrained brother. If Jeriah had visited him, he could have asked. He swallowed against the tightness of his throat. There were probably plenty of reasons why Jeri hadn't come to see him. He'd understand his brother's seeming abandonment perfectly—as soon as he knew what they were.

Jeriah's absence had hurt him even more than his father's, for he hadn't expected his father to come, and he had counted on Jeri's support.

None of his friends had come to see him, either, but that had dismayed him less—befriending a "traitor" would be dangerous these days. But surely Jeri—

"Sir Tobin! Do you plead guilty or innocent?" The Speaker sounded as if he was repeating himself, and Tobin, who'd been "Sir" Tobin less than a year and didn't always respond to the title, felt heat rise in his face.

His father wasn't looking at him, but his expression was harder than a statue's. Right and wrong, all mixed together.

"Well, Sir Tobin, do you plea—"

"Guilty," said Tobin hastily. *Forgive me, Father, I have to.* "Guilty, sir."

A sigh rustled through the room. His father's distant stare never wavered, but the flesh of his face tightened until you could almost see the skull beneath the skin.

Sorry, sorry, sorry.

The Speaker consulted briefly with the council of judges and turned. "Then hear your punishment, Sir Tobin."

That hadn't taken long! They had probably decided on his sentence days ago, when his father bribed them. This was a farce, not a trial. Tobin closed his eyes, lest the sudden flare of anger show. Perhaps the traitors had a point—some things needed to be changed.

"Because of your service on the battlefield, because of your youth, and because your involvement with the evil that threatened us was relatively slight, the Hierarch, in his beneficence, has chosen to show you the mercy of the Seven Bright Ones."

Tobin shivered. *How much of the estate—*

"Instead of a traitor's death, you will be stripped of the knighthood you have befouled, and you will know the scorn of your peers."

Tobin's eyes snapped open, a chill racing through him. The "scorn of his peers" would be expressed with the lash. It was the most humiliating punishment that could be given a knight, short of death. He should have expected it, for treason. He was lucky they'd agreed to let him live.

Tobin bowed acceptance. He knew he had behaved with honor. No one else's opinion mattered. At least it shouldn't matter.

"Sir Tarsin, you said you wished to address the court

before we call the next case."

"Yes." Tobin's father rose and met his eyes. Cold, all the way to the bottom. The trial had been real after all, but his father had been the judge, and the judgment had fallen against him. His heart beat faster. *Father, please!*

"I will not suffer a traitor to take my lands—to sit in my house." His father's eyes never left Tobin now, filled with anger, determination, and grief. "I deny this man. He is not my heir. He is no longer my son. And if he ever comes onto my land, I will have the servants beat him off like a thief. Let the Speaker take my words and make them law."

Exclamations of surprise rippled through the room, but Tobin barely heard them. His eyes filled and he lowered them, grateful that he could no longer meet his father's gaze. He could feel it, though, proud and anguished. It never left him until the guards led him out of sight.

Tobin let the tears fall as he walked down the corridors in the guards' grasp. Jeri and his mother should have told his father the truth. They should have *told* him. But if they had, would his father have abandoned Jeriah to face the Hierarch's wrath alone? This went beyond anger, touching the unyielding core of his father's honor. But now—

The guards opened a door, shoved him through, and closed it behind him. Tobin tripped over the fringe of a finely woven rug and looked up, startled.

This wasn't a cell. Expensive rugs covered the floor, their colors bright in the sunlight streaming through the windows. Bookshelves lined the walls, and a tall, lean priest rose from behind a desk and gestured for him to take a chair.

"Sit down, Sir Tobin. Should I be saying 'Sir' Tobin? No, I see I shouldn't, but sit down anyway."

Tobin sank numbly into the chair and the priest reseated himself and gazed at him over steepled fingers. He had the lined, ascetic face of a scholar, but he moved easily, like a man much younger than he appeared to be.

"Let's get the trivial things out of the way," he said. "My name is Master Lazur, and I don't care if you're guilty or not. The conspiracy is crushed, the leaders dead, so it no longer matters. I have no desire to prosecute your brother, either." He smiled and waved off Tobin's attempted protest. "If that's the man you're protecting. If it's not, fine. As I said, I don't care. There are more serious matters at stake."

As Tobin wondered dazedly what could be more serious than treason, the priest leaned forward and said, "Tobin, you just lost your home, your family, your rank, and your honor. Would you be interested in a chance to win them back?"

CHAPTER 6

The Knight

"**W**HO DO I HAVE TO KILL?" asked Tobin, astonished.

Master Lazur's eyes widened.

"That was a jest," Tobin told him swiftly. "I didn't mean . . ."

Master Lazur had composed his expression—but still something gave his thoughts away.

"You do want me to kill someone!" Tobin rose to his feet. "I'm not an assassin. Not for anybody—not for any reason. Find some other traitor to do your dirty work."

The priest neither moved nor spoke as Tobin went to the door and yanked it open. The two guards outside glanced at Master Lazur and shifted to block Tobin's path.

They were both armed, and he wasn't. He couldn't get out. Several seconds passed. One of the guards reached out and closed the door. Tobin stared at it, his back to the priest. He felt almost as foolish as he was furious.

"Come back and sit down," said Master Lazur quietly, "and listen. When I've finished, if you still want to leave, I'll let you. Surely it will do no harm for you to hear me out?"

Tobin returned to his chair and sat down, glaring at the priest.

"It isn't as bad as you think." Master Lazur was smiling, a charming smile of genuine amusement. Tobin didn't respond, and the smile faded.

"I'd best start at the beginning." The priest rose and paced across the room. The sunlight from the window picked out the seven-rayed sun inside five circles on his plain robe. A priest of the fifth circle was powerful—only two levels below the council itself. But Tobin was no one's killer.

"You've been fighting the barbarians on the border for three winters now. Have you noticed a pattern?"

Tobin remained silent.

"Perhaps you haven't," the priest went on. "Not in just three years. Let me give you a wider view. The barbarians have been attacking our southern border every winter for fifteen years now—every year there are more of them, fighting with greater ferocity. Since the first attack, we've had to move our defended border back toward the midlands four times."

The grinding, bloody chaos of the great retreat two years ago echoed in Tobin's memory as the priest went on.

"In the early years, we assumed the attackers were

only bandits. We thought they'd give up if we proved too tough for them."

Tobin frowned. His commander had told him that, just three years ago, but no one believed it now.

"When the attacks increased in size and became better organized, the southland lords were forced to call on the Hierarch for help. We sent spies in among the barbarians and discovered the reason for the attacks."

"But they're cannibals!" Tobin exclaimed. "How could your spies—"

Master Lazur's gaze was cool. "A spy does whatever he must, to survive and complete his mission. You should remember that. Our spies discovered that the barbarians are attacking our land because theirs is dying. A long drought is beginning on the other side of the desert. Each year the rainfall is less, and their soil is poor and easily overfarmed. Each year, more are forced from their homes, to flood our borders. In four or five years, we estimate they will hold most of the southlands. Then they'll be able to fight us all year round. Their magic is different from ours. At first we thought it must come from the Dark One, but the spies say the barbarians worship no gods at all. Wherever it comes from, their magic is very strong. You've probably seen yourself how even strong winds fail to affect their arrows' flight. Or how muddy ground firms under their feet, how strong they are, and how fast their wounds heal. Our battle priests are barely holding their own. And there are too many of them for us to defeat."

"But there must be a way to stop them! Could—could we just give them the southlands? Since you say they're going to take them anyway?"

"It's impossible to negotiate with the barbarians."

"Why? If we sent an ambassador, surely they'd listen—"

"We did. And they may have listened, for all we know. But then they ate the ambassador. And the next one we sent. After that, we stopped asking for volunteers."

Tobin's stomach twisted. "So you sent spies. But surely—"

Master Lazur shook his head. "They regard anyone except themselves as animals. They won't negotiate with animals."

"Then . . ." Tobin's mouth was dry, remembering things he'd seen in border villages the barbarians had overrun. "Then we have to defend the border. We can recruit more troops, if the need is this great."

"We can. And we'll have to. But you've been fighting on the border for the past three years. Do you think, even with more troops, we could defend our present border all year round?"

Tobin shook his head thoughtfully. "We might during the winter. We can take men off the farms then. But in spring the farmers have to plant, or we'll all starve."

"Exactly."

"But part of the problem is that the southern border is

so wide, so open. If we fought in a more defensible place, we might be able to hold them!"

Master Lazur smiled and pulled a scroll off a shelf. "It took the Hierarch's council more than ten years to reach that conclusion. Or at least, to accept the consequences." He unrolled the scroll and a map of the known world lay before Tobin. "You're a knight. Find me a border we could defend against a barbarian force eight times the size of the one you're fighting now."

"Eight times!"

"That's how many there are. When the drought has driven them out, they'll all come here, so find us a defensible border."

Tobin turned shocked eyes to the map. Sea to the east and west. In the far south lay the desert, with the unexplored lands of the barbarians beyond. In the far north, past the vast expanse of the goblin woods, the map trailed off into a great white plain of ice and snow. Between the desert and the goblin woods lay the Realm of the Bright Gods.

First the southlands—rolling, rocky hills, dry and warm and dusty. Poor soil for crops, but the best wine in the realm.

Above them, the midland plains—grassy, flat, and fertile with the great rivers twisting through them and the low-lying wetlands off to the east. The heart of the realm, wider and even less defensible than the south. Tobin's eyes sought the curve in the Abo River that bounded his home, and sickness twisted through his stomach.

North of the midlands were the light woodlands—poorer crops, but they produced timber and furs. The land narrowed here. Fewer miles to hold, but the barbarians could slip an army through those woods, man by man, and nothing could stop them. And that was where the realm ended, at the narrowest point where the great goblin wall . . .

The great wall, stretching right across the narrowest part of the continent, ten feet high and six feet thick—the army could hold that wall against all the barbarians in the world, but . . .

"But that's the northern border of the realm! There's nothing beyond it but the deep woods, and then the ice! We couldn't possibly—"

"Move the whole realm behind that wall over the next ten to fifteen years? It's already begun. What do you think happened to the southern villagers when the border passed over their lands? The ones we were able to evacuate have moved north and resettled. Since we understood the situation, we've been trying to talk them into traveling all the way to the north woods and settling beyond the wall. Most refuse to believe the barbarians will make it that far, and they settle in the midlands. Only a few of them have been wise enough to see the truth and gone all the way, to build anew on the other side of the wall. And these are people who've already been driven out of their homes!" Master Lazur sighed. "Even with the enforcement of the Decree, which consolidated our power, we haven't been able to persuade anyone else to start moving. And we can't really begin to try, until—"

"The Decree of Bright Magic." A chill passed down Tobin's spine. "You didn't pass it because the Bright Ones stopped favoring the army."

"Of course not. How could the Hierarch's army lose the Bright Gods' favor? But peasants who will turn to a hedgewitch for healing, even though their magic is far inferior, just because it's cheaper . . ." The priest shook his head. "You can imagine how they'll react to being asked to pack up and leave land they've farmed for generations. The church's power must be absolute—proven to be absolute—long before that question arises." For a moment, naked steel sounded in his voice. "But there's an even more urgent problem before us."

"I can imagine," said Tobin. "Having to uproot a forest to plant a field must appall the southerners."

"It does," Master Lazur admitted. "But the ones who go that far are determined, farsighted people. Trees wouldn't stop them. The problem, ironically, is goblins. Three centuries ago the church sought to drive the goblins into the north, and failed. But the Decree of Bright Magic has accomplished what those old priests couldn't. A large number of goblins have been driven out and settled behind the wall, precisely where we ourselves must now go."

"But surely goblins couldn't stop us. They've been dwelling in this land for . . . well, forever."

"Yes, but they're extraordinarily hard to exterminate, as we've learned since the Decree passed. Goblins have neither loyalty nor courage, so they're easily discouraged. Even if we couldn't kill them, we could defend our settlers against normal goblins. However, these goblins are different, because a human is leading them.

"There is a powerful sorceress in the northern woods. Somehow she's managed to enslave a vast horde of goblins who drive out anyone who passes the wall. Even our armed exploratory troops have been killed or forced to retreat."

"A sorceress? I didn't think they still existed."

"They're rare, thanks to the Bright Ones' grace. But occasionally someone obtains power from the Dark One. Then we must destroy the sorcerer, which isn't always easy, for they can be very powerful. Make no mistake about that, Tobin; never underestimate her—it's likely she has the power, if not the training, of a high-ranking priest."

"Then she, this sorceress, is the one you want me to kill? I thought it took a priest to kill a sorcerer. I thought you needed magic to fight magic."

"Not necessarily. Put a blade through her heart, and anyone will die. The problem with sorcerers is getting close enough to do it. You're right, though, ordinarily we'd send seven high-ranking priests to take a sorcerer, because one cannot stand against seven. The problem"—irritation flashed over the lean face—"is that horde of goblins she's compelled into her service. They killed two of the seven priests we sent and drove the rest off before they could even find the sorceress. That was four years ago, when we first heard rumors of her existence. Since then we've sent armed troops, with another group of priests, and several bounty hunters have tried for the reward, but all have failed."

"Then what makes you think I could succeed? Even if I agreed to become an assassin, which I haven't."

"Don't you think it would be worth sacrificing your scruples to save this whole land?" Master Lazur leaned forward. "That's what's at stake, Tobin. If we're to get our people behind that wall in time, the early settlement, and the exploration of the outlying woodlands, must begin now. A flood of panicked refugees crashing over that wall would simply starve. It must be an organized resettlement if we are to survive it, and that means it must begin soon. Within the next year, three years at the very latest. So this sorceress who prevents us must be stopped. And she's already earned death, for the deaths she has wrought in the Dark One's name." The passion in his voice sounded sincere.

Tobin, having spent years learning to resist his mother and Jeriah, distrusted passion in charming and persuasive people. And Master Lazur struck him as both. Still, if the sorceress truly deserved to die— "What makes you think

I could do it, when so many others have failed?"

"Frankly, I've no reason to think you could. Your presence is part of my larger plan. I'll send you in, and at the same time I'll arrive with a band of priests and a troop of guards, mixed in with, and disguised as, a large group of settlers. Our presence should distract her from you, and your presence should distract her from us. Your real job is to find where she lairs and plant this nearby." He held out a small, flat, brownish orange rock.

"What's this?" Tobin took it reluctantly. "Is it magic?"

"No, which is why I hope it will work. If it was magic, she'd be able to sense it and would take care to keep it under her hiding spells."

"Hiding spells?"

"You've never had a hiding charm? You must have been a very honest child—most apple-thieving boys have bought one from the local hedgewitch by the time they're ten. At least they used to. It's a simple charm, but even if it's made by someone with very little power, it will shield its wearer from detection by magic. The hiding spell is like a hiding charm, only it covers an area. You put this rock outside that area, and I'll be able to scry for it—to see it in my crystal, or in water if I wish. And, though this is more delicate and might take several days depending on the distance, I can locate it. Planting the stone may take some work. If she captures you, she'll put a hiding spell on you. I'm hoping you can drop it outside her spells, but close enough to her lair to enable me to find it."

"What's so special about this rock that you can find it?"

Master Lazur smiled. "It comes from the Otherworld."

He laughed at Tobin's expression.

"I thought the Otherworld was a myth!"

"Oh, no, it exists. Priests have always been able to open small gates to it. Remember the story of St. Agna's escape?" He ran a finger down the spine of one of the leatherbound books beside the desk, and Tobin realized they must be his personal spell books.

"Have you seen it?" asked Tobin, fascinated.

"Yes. It's a beautiful place, in a strange sort of way. We once considered trying to send the barbarians there— which should tell you how desperate our situation is." The smile flashed again, conspiratorial, inviting. "Only a handful of priests can make a gate big enough for a man to pass through. Those who simply step through and return are unharmed. So we tried some experiments with convicted criminals, but . . . Never mind. What's important is that this rock is the only one of its kind in this world. I'll be able to find it."

Tobin thought that whatever had happened to the criminals was important, too, at least to them. A ruthless man, this priest.

"Suppose she kills me instead of capturing me?"

"Then I'm hoping she'll either take the rock with her, or leave your body close enough to her lair for me to locate it. I can't claim this isn't dangerous. But I can give you something that might help." He rose, took a box from a lower shelf, and set it on the desk. "Open it."

Tobin did. It looked like a loose-woven shawl. "A net?"

"Of a sort. This is magic, of a very special kind—it's drawn to magical power and absorbs it. If you can wrap this net around the sorceress, she'll be completely unable to work magic for as long as it clings to her."

"What happens if it falls off?"

"It won't fall off. I told you, it's attracted to magic. She might be able to peel it off, but it won't be easy."

The priest noted Tobin's skeptical expression. "Watch." He reached into the chest. As soon as his hand neared the net, tendrils of string stirred, rose toward his fingers, and wrapped around them. Master Lazur shivered and pulled his hand away, and a fold of the net followed it. He closed the lid firmly on the fabric and pulled his hand free. As soon as he was out of range, the strings went limp. The priest rubbed his hand as if it was cold. "You'll have to close it," he said.

Tobin tucked the net back into the small chest and fastened the latch. "I've never seen anything like it."

"Such things are made only for the capture or holding of sorcerers. One of the reasons I'm giving it to you is that I'm not . . . comfortable traveling with it in my luggage."

"I might be able to use this, if I could find her."

"My guess is that she'll find you. Or her goblins will. Which reminds me." He reached into a desk drawer and pulled out a small iron medallion on a chain.

"What's that?"

"A charm that repels goblins. They won't be able to get within ten feet of it. It might make it possible for you to reach her, and if you can get that net on her, you've won. Most sorcerers just sit down and shake when you take away their power."

"If I bring down their leader, what will the goblins do?"

"If they were human, they'd probably thank you. But goblins are completely mercenary—they never do anything except for payment, or to avoid punishment. Once her hold over them is broken, they'll probably just run off. But place the stone before you try anything else. Just in case."

In case he died in the attempt. "I see." Tobin drew a deep breath, his gaze wandering over map, chest, stone, and charm. "Isn't there any other way?"

Master Lazur shook his head. "The barbarians are coming. We have no place to go except north. They have no place to come except here. There is nothing in this world I would not sacrifice to get the Bright Realm behind the goblin wall in time. How high do you weigh the life of a sorceress, one who has killed again and again, against the survival of this whole realm?"

Tobin's finger traced the river curve that marked his home. He couldn't imagine living in the woodlands, but he'd seen the barbarian armies for himself. Master Lazur was silent, letting him figure it out. Tobin didn't like it, but surely the priest was right. How many knights, men Tobin knew and respected, had already died? If it would end the war, save the whole realm, then the life of one sorceress was a cheap price to pay.

"All right," said Tobin. "I'll go find this sorceress, and do what I can, though I don't promise to kill her."

"If you plant the stone so we can find her, you'll have done enough. And if you survive, all the honor you've lost will be restored, in the eyes of the law and of the world. In fact, you'll be a hero. Remember that tonight."

Master Lazur took the chest and the charms and put them away. "I'll see that these things reach you later. We won't be able to meet again, for the goblins' eyes are everywhere. This room is protected, but others may not be.

"I think I'll take your brother into my service for a time. It wouldn't be wise to place him in the Hierarch's service until he's had time to become a little more . . . politically sophisticated."

Was this for Jeriah's protection, or was he a hostage for Tobin's good behavior? Either way, if the priest would keep his suspicions to himself, and keep an eye on Tobin's impetuous brother, he could only be grateful. "Thank you."

"Don't thank me. Your mother mentioned it."

"My mother?"

"Yes, she's an old friend of mine."

Tobin knew he should have guessed. Any scheme this devious was bound to have his mother behind it. Her friends were everywhere. Tobin knew what his father had paid; wondering what his mother was trading for these favors was downright unnerving. But he could hardly complain—this scheme might save his future, and Jeriah's as well. He should have known she wouldn't abandon him to disinheritance and disgrace, even if Jeri was her favorite.

"I'll be watching you when I scry for the stone," Master Lazur continued. "I can see and hear what happens around it, so you don't have to worry about reporting to me. Just remember—if you succeed, you can get it all back, and more." He paused, eyeing Tobin gravely. "And remember also that the Seven Bright Ones are watching over you. Whatever happens, you are always in their hands. May their grace go with you."

A whip cracked and someone snickered. Tobin tried to meet their gazes boldly, defiantly, but he couldn't seem to raise his eyes from the wet, torchlit stones of the courtyard. It had rained that afternoon while he huddled in his cell thinking about Master Lazur's offer and trying to prepare himself for this.

His heart pounded sickly, and his hands, bound in front of him, shook despite his efforts to keep them still. It was a sign of manliness to pass through the gauntlet without screaming or fainting, and Tobin had resolved with all his will to do it. Now he couldn't even raise his head to meet the eyes of the men he had fought beside.

Men who had trusted his honor.

His first flashing glance over the courtyard had told him that only twenty of his peers had shown up to express their scorn—a great relief. With enough men, the gauntlet could kill as surely as the executioner. It was an even greater relief that his father wasn't among them. He couldn't have borne that.

The guards tied his ankles with an eight-inch hobble. If he tried to run, or even take a long step, it would trip him. So he'd take short steps, Tobin told himself, trying to quiet the frantic pounding of his heart. He would be free when it was over. Only twenty men. How bad could it be?

A knife cut through his collar, then rough hands gripped it and tore his shirt open. The cool, rain-scented air swept over his exposed skin, making him shiver. Once it was over, he'd be free, he reminded himself desperately.

They were shouting now, taunts, challenges, and strange, animal sounds. Tobin could barely hear them over the blood beating in his ears.

A guard pushed him, and the hobble caught his ankles, bringing him down. They laughed. Anger gave him strength—he'd behaved with honor, whatever they thought! He lurched to his feet, before the guards could lift him, and looked ahead.

The gauntlet stretched before him. Some of the men held the whips still at their sides, but some whirled and snapped them. They were the ones doing most of the shouting. Demons take them.

Tobin lifted his head and stepped between the first two men. He was braced for it, but the crack of the first cut made him jump. He just had time to think that it wasn't so bad, when the pain bit and he clenched his teeth against it. He took a short, hobbling step, and the second blow fell.

It was held to be a sign of manliness to pass the gauntlet without screaming or fainting.

Tobin did not succeed.

He lay on his stomach, staring at the wet grass. There was enough of the gray, predawn light to see droplets of water shivering down the long stems. His clothing was as wet as the grass. The cool wind numbed the throbbing agony in his back, except when he tried to move, so he'd stopped moving.

He had a vague memory of his hands being lashed to someone's stirrup, of being dragged, staggering, down the dark, cobbled streets, through all seven tiers of the city. They'd thrown him out of the main gate at the bottom of the city's hill, and he'd managed to crawl off the road before passing out. When he wakened, he crawled for what felt like a long time but probably wasn't. When he'd wakened again, he'd crawled some more.

A whistle sounded; distant, piercing, familiar. It reminded him of Jeriah, and he blinked back tears. He hadn't realized it, but he'd been hoping that Jeriah would be waiting by the gate at the bottom of the hill.

No one had been there. Not Jeri, not either of his parents, or their servants, or any of the men he'd thought his friends. The whistle again. Was it nearer? It repeated itself, insistently.

He'd really thought that someone would be waiting for him, maybe even Master Lazur. He was beginning to think there was a flaw in Master Lazur's plan, for he felt like dying in this cold, grassy place. He hoped the priest wouldn't be too badly inconvenienced if he did.

Perhaps Master Lazur had assumed his friends would come and pick him up. But it seemed the friends he'd made so easily were easily lost, and the father who'd disowned him would hardly come and save him, or permit his wife to do so. And Jeriah, who hadn't come once to visit him, would hardly come and—

The whistle! It was Jeriah's whistle! The all-clear signal for hundreds of games of knights and bandits, many years ago.

It sounded again, unmistakable now that he'd recognized it. Trust his brother to expect him to remember a signal they hadn't used for years.

He was crying. He took a deep breath, which hurt his back, and pursed his lips. It took several tries to get an answering whistle out of his dry mouth, and it was soft and wavery. But Jeriah must have been listening hard, for the calling whistle sounded again, nearer, demanding, and in just a few moments Tobin heard his brother thrashing through the grass.

"Tobin! Are you . . . ? Bright Ones' mercy." Jeriah's voice had fallen to a shocked whisper. Tobin turned his head painfully. He tried to tell Jeriah he was all right, but his voice wasn't working. A flask appeared at his lips, and he lifted himself slightly to gulp down the cool water. When his head fell again, Jeriah's cloak was beneath it.

"Demon's teeth! Tobin, how could you let Mother talk you into this?"

"It doesn't matter. I'm glad you came." He groped for his brother's hand and it closed around his instantly, warm and strong.

"*Doesn't matter?* Are you trying to prove you're a candidate for sainthood? No, don't answer, I always knew you were an idiot and now I'm sure of it! Don't talk—I'll get my horse and get you out of here before you freeze. You're soaked, do you know that? And your hands are like ice. No, I said don't answer. I don't have time to argue with lunatics." A soft hand stoked Tobin's hair. "We'll talk later." Jeriah rose and ran, swishing away in the long grass.

"How could you let Mother talk you into this?" Jeriah asked again. He sounded furious, but his hands were utterly gentle as he carefully cleaned the cuts on Tobin's back with a soft rag soaked in witch heal.

Tobin lay warm and drowsy on the pallet in the shepherd's hut where Jeriah had taken him. He felt almost too comfortable to answer. After the first sting, witch heal had a numbing effect, and the throbbing pain in his back had subsided. The fire, where broth was heating, combined with the sunlight pouring through the holes in the east wall to heat the abandoned shack beautifully.

"Well?" Jeriah demanded.

"She talked. She cried. You know Mother. Besides, she was right; they'd have been much harder on you."

"Dung!"

"Don't swear," said Tobin automatically.

"All right, but of all the—" Agitation made Jeriah clumsy, and Tobin winced. "Sorry. No, I'm not sorry— you almost deserve this. I've never heard anything so stupid in my life. Give me one good reason why you should take the blame for my actions."

"Because they might have killed you."

"And you think Father couldn't have bribed them for me, just as well as you?"

"Yes, but . . ." He stopped himself, but Jeriah wasn't slow.

"You're not sure he would have? Well, maybe he wouldn't, but he had a right to know the truth, and I always knew I was taking that chance."

When had his brother's voice become so steady? "So how did Mother talk you into agreeing?" Tobin asked. "I . . . wondered about that. Especially when you didn't visit me."

"I'll bet you did," said Jeriah grimly. "Mother didn't

talk me into anything. I know her too well."

"Then what happened?" Tobin turned in time to see a blush wash over his brother's face.

"She drugged me."

"What?"

"She drugged me. She'd just come up with her 'wonderful' plan and I'd refused. I might run off, but there was no way I'd let you take my punishment. She got hysterical, and when she finally started to calm down, she got herself a cup of tea. She said she needed it, soothing, you know? She got me some at the same time, and I didn't want to upset her, so I drank it and—"

Tobin's shout of laughter woke the pain in his back and he gasped, twisting. Jeriah pushed him back gently.

"Don't do that! Anyway, I started to yawn, and the next thing I remember is waking up locked in the attic storeroom with an awful headache. The second in three days, I might add."

Tobin chuckled in spite of the pain. "You thought you knew her so well."

"Yes, but I didn't think she had drugs in her tea cabinet! I should have. She's always been fiendishly effective, our feather-headed mother."

"So what did you do?"

"What could I do? I yelled at the girls every time they poked food under the door, but Mother had them completely mesmerized. Finally I twisted a hinge off a chest and filed through the door so I could lift the latch, but it took days. Then I stole a horse and came straight here. I got in just after sunset, and by the time I found out what was happening they already had you in the courtyard. I knew I couldn't stop it in time, so I got this place ready and went to get you. I could kill Mother for this."

"You don't have to go that far. But when I get home, I'll— When you get home, you'll have to take away her drugs. Where do you think she got them? And why?"

"No idea. But you're the one who's going home, big brother. As soon as I've told Father the truth. You're supposed to be the good son, remember?"

"No." Tobin rolled to his side and seized his brother's wrist. "You're not the bad son, you're just—"

"A traitor?" Jeriah met his eyes steadily.

"Jeri, why did you do it?" How long had he wanted to ask that question?

"Because I believe it was the right thing to do. Tobin, look how much is wrong with the way the Hierarch governs this land. We thought if we could put our own man in his place—"

"The Hierarch is chosen by the Bright Gods themselves!"

"I'd be more impressed by that if the Bright Ones didn't express their will through the council of priests. We thought we could—"

"Don't tell me. I don't even want to know," said Tobin wearily. His father wasn't the only one to see the world in terms of right and wrong, with no middle ground. "Were you going to kill the Hierarch? What made you think you could get away with something like that?"

"We weren't going to kill him. He's an old man, in his seventies now. We just wanted to be sure the man we'd chosen would replace him. My part would have been to keep an eye on the opposition. I was going into his service—who'd suspect me? I was going to report . . . well, it doesn't matter now."

"Jeriah!" Tobin gripped his brother's wrist. "Promise me that you'll stop this. You can't go on—"

"Don't get upset." His brother pushed him down again, the gentleness of his hands a startling contrast to his grim face. "We can't go on with it. The man we intended to be Hierarch was hacked to pieces eight days ago."

Tobin had never seen that bleak determination on his brother's face. It frightened him far more than the old, impetuous wildness. "Promise that you'll stop trying. Master Lazur all but told me that he suspects you. Think things through, for once in your life! Think what you'll cost Father if you try anything else. It would kill both of them to lose you."

Jeriah pulled his hands away slowly. "I can't promise. There are—there are things more important than family. But I promise to think it through, and to be sure as I can that what I do is safe and will succeed. All right?"

"No! Jeri, I'm going to go mad out there, not knowing what you might be doing while I'm gone. Promise you won't do anything. Swear it." He knew he was using his brother's guilt shamelessly, but he didn't care. Jeriah had always been idealistic, but the will and ability to act on those ideals was new and terrifying. To his astonishment, his impulsive brother thought for a moment before answering.

"All right. I won't start anything until you're clear of this mess. I swear it. I'll try to work within the system, until then. Is that enough?"

"No," said Tobin. "But it looks like that's all I'm going to get. When did you grow up anyway?" How had he failed to see such profound changes?

"A long time ago." Jeriah smiled. "You were too busy mothering me to notice. And since I didn't want you to notice too much, I didn't bring it to your attention. Speaking of growing up, I'm going to tell Father the truth."

"Don't. If you tell him, it's all been for nothing. I can make it right myself." Even a few hours ago, he might have hesitated to tell Jeriah his intentions, but this new Jeriah had proven he could keep a secret—and a trust. Tobin told him everything—the barbarians, the sorceress, Master Lazur's plan. Jeriah looked very thoughtful when he finished.

"I don't like it," he said. "It sounds like he expects you to get killed right after you plant that stone—if not before! Tobin, I—I couldn't get along without you to keep me in line. You know that, don't you?"

Tobin gripped his brother's hand. "I would have believed that, this morning. I won't get killed, Jeri. I could have died anytime in the past three years, but I didn't. I'm not a hero. I'll be careful, and I'll come back. I promise."

CHAPTER 7

The Hedgewitch

T HE WOMAN RAN FROM the burning cabin carrying
an armload of blankets and an iron pot. Flames
licked up her skirt and caught in her long
blond hair. She dropped the blankets and ran for the
creek, slowed by her heavy pregnancy. Her man caught
her and pushed her down, rolling her over, beating at
the flames with his bare hands until they were extin-
guished.

Makenna turned her attention to the building—burning nicely, she judged. No chance they could put it out,
just the two of them. No chance to save more of their
household goods, either. She glanced up as Cogswhallop
crept soundlessly into the bushes beside her.

"Got the animals away when they were busy about the
fire," he reported. "The barn's just starting to burn, but
it'll go fast."

Makenna nodded with satisfaction. "They won't be
back."

Cogswhallop cocked his head thoughtfully. "They're a stubborn pair."

"And vicious." The tactile memory of extracting Maddit's body from the human's trap washed over Makenna, sickening her even now. Cold, sticky blood, pouring over her hands, soaking her britches as the iron spikes pulled free of his flesh. She had to take several deep breaths before she could speak.

"The walk back will take it out of 'em," she said coldly. "Two days, no food, no shelter—that's hard on a pregnant woman. My mother said they need lots of rest, when they're big like that. They won't be back. You're certain you found all their traps? The one that got Maddit was well hidden."

"I'll take my lot, and we'll do a thorough search once the humans have gone."

"Do that. And if you have any problem springing them, let me know. If I never have to tell another goblin their life mate died on one of my missions, it'll still be too many."

The shrill, grief-stricken keening of Maddit's wife echoed in her memory, and the thought of the loneliness that lay before the little woman cut even more deeply. For the goblins, life mate wasn't an empty title. But at least she had the children. Makenna discovered that her eyes were wet. She wiped them impatiently.

"You can't save us all, gen'ral," said Cogswhallop. "Not with the best plans. Sooner or later, something will go wrong."

"I've learned that," said Makenna shortly.

"Aye, you just don't believe it. You've hardly lost a handful, in all the battles we've fought. And won! Think how many you've saved—not how many you've lost."

"There is that," Makenna admitted. How many times over the years had Cogswhallop supported her? He could be hard, as hard as any human soldier in the midst of war. Soldiers had to be hard. But his loyalty was truer than any she'd known, except her mother's, and Makenna relied on him more than she'd ever relied on any human.

These humans had gone to the stream and were wrapping wet rags over their burns. Makenna's conscience twinged, but she ignored it with the ease of practice.

She remembered the tiny force she'd started with—only six goblins, for Miggy was too young to help then. Now there were almost sixteen hundred goblins, living in half a dozen villages up and down the wall, who were willing to aid her. She'd actually rescued very few of them—the rest were refugees from human persecution. She could offer them nothing but a safe place to rebuild their lives, but she gave them that, defending the Goblin Wood against all humans who sought to invade it.

She paid her troops in buttons, string—in pinecones if there was nothing else to hand. They repaid her with miracles of courage and cleverness . . . and she loved them. They were her people.

A rustling in the undergrowth made her head snap

around. Erebus joined them, wheezing from the long crawl, spectacles sliding low on his sweaty face. Makenna smiled and began to greet the Bookerie, but Cogswhallop got in first.

"Clumsy ink-finger! Haven't you been told not to blunder in when we're in a fight?"

"The sentry said the fight was over," said Erebus with his usual placid indifference to Cogswhallop's insults. "He assured me it was safe as long as I didn't let them see me. I've got some news, from my cousins in Brackenlee, that the mistress ought to hear." Beaming, he held out his hand, and Makenna pulled off one of her trading buttons and gave it to him.

"There's a big group of settlers moving up from the south, over two hundred, they say. And they claim they're going to settle beyond the wall."

Cogswhallop whistled softly. "That's the biggest lot we've had to deal with yet. That's four times more than that troop they sent."

"Aye," said Erebus. "But remember what happened to them?"

Makenna snickered. She'd sent Spoilers in to rot their tack and weapon belts. Two days later, when she knew the leather would be ready to crumble, she'd sent a mob of Flichters in to spook their horses. The memory of the resultant chaos brought a grin to her face. Even Cogswhallop smiled dourly.

"Have your friends keep an eye on them, Erebus,"

Makenna told him. "I'd like to know what their plans are, and when they'll be passing the wall. It's only fair that they get the warning. Who knows? Maybe they'll be wiser than these two." She nodded in the direction of the young couple. They were gaping at their burning home, instead of starting the long walk while they still had light. Foolish, as well as vicious. Makenna dismissed them and crawled back through the brush. Five years of guerrilla warfare had made her almost as silent as Cogswhallop. Erebus, on the other hand, made enough noise for both of them.

"There's another thing you should know, mistress," he said as they crawled into a small gully where they could walk upright without being seen. "There's a man, all alone like a bounty hunter, asking questions about you and the wood. They say he's got armor, as well as a sword."

Makenna frowned. Most bounty hunters were no problem—but a man covered with steel armor would be harder for the goblins to deal with. "I'll look him over when he passes the wall," she decided. "When's he coming? Do you know?"

"Set out from Brackenlee this morning, should reach the wall tomorrow midday. He'll probably meet those two on the road, now that I think about it."

Makenna shrugged. "Might as well learn what he's in for. In fact—" A sparkle of mischief danced through her. "I'm tired of these foolish, greedy hunters. Let's give him a taste of what's to come, along with his warning, shall we?"

Makenna sat on the goblin side of the wall and waited. A cool spring breeze rushed past the gap where the road ran through, and clouds were building for the afternoon showers. But on the wall's lee side she was out of the wind, and the heat of its magic warmed her back. It took some searching to find it, the magic that all those priests had poured into the wall three hundred years ago, when it was newly built—but the magic was there, still flowing into the long iron plates that rimmed its top and kept goblins from crossing anyplace where the line was intact.

Makenna had wondered what had turned that long-ago Hierarch and his council against the goblins, but even Erebus didn't know for certain—only that their attempt to drive the goblins into the north and imprison them there had failed. You'd think they'd have learned better, in three hundred years. But of course they hadn't.

In her first few years in the wood, Makenna had spent a lot of time with a stolen crowbar, prying out the charmed iron at strategic intervals, so her troops could never be trapped against it.

Now she set her palms against the cool stone and the slow pulse of the old magic warmed them. Amazing. Over the past five years she'd all but memorized her mother's spell books, but she couldn't set a spell on an inanimate object that would last more than a few weeks without renewal. Her mother had been able to make them last for months, and priests could set a spell that would last beyond their own lifetime, but three hundred years? Erebus said that his great-great-grandfather's aunt had counted two hundred and seventeen priests involved in the casting, but even so—

"Mistress," Miggy hissed from the top of the wall. "I see him."

Makenna knew she had several minutes before he reached the gap, so she took the time to stretch and loosen her muscles. Several painful sprains had taught her not to climb while she was stiff.

Here, close to the breach people had made for the road, there were hundreds of cracks and crevices in the stone. Makenna climbed the wall easily and rolled onto its broad top, keeping her head low, where she knew even a man on horseback couldn't see it. She crawled over to Miggy, who pointed.

A lone man on a horse, with a packhorse behind him. Only bounty hunters approached the Goblin Wood alone. After they'd run the first one off, even those tiresome explorers came in packs.

But bounty hunters seldom wore armor, and this man had steel plates on his arms. Was that a helm tied to his saddle? Well, she'd see him up close soon enough. Even from this distance she could tell that he was riding sloppy, all relaxed and careless. She wriggled back and pulled out the small bag of fine dust she always carried. She dumped it on the edge of the wall and blew to make an even layer. "Miggy, let me know when he's in the right place."

"Aye, mistress." The young goblin's face twitched nervously as he turned away. They both knew Miggy was far less likely to be spotted, but he hated making decisions, even something as simple as deciding when the stranger was in position. Still Makenna trusted him, even if he didn't trust himself. Besides, she needed to pay attention to her spell casting.

She drew the rune of the eye and the circle, carefully leaving a gap in the circle just in front of where her foot would be. Then she called up the power that resided in the wall, and it rose sluggishly to invest the rune. More power than she could dream of bringing to the spell by herself. Her magical ability had grown further than she'd ever believed it could, though she knew she would never be her mother's equal. But with the power of the wall to draw on, she could do things even her mother could never have dreamed of. Of course her spell had to be in physical contact with the wall to use its power, which limited its practical uses sharply, but still . . . .

"Almost," Miggy whispered. Sweat stood out on his forehead, despite the chill breeze. "Closer . . . closer . . . now!"

Makenna gave the signal and caught a flash of motion at the edge of her vision as the Flichters swarmed for the horses. She heard a horse snort and the startled thudding of hooves and sprang to her feet, stepping carefully into the circle, ignoring the wind that tugged at her hair and clothes.

The stranger clung desperately to his shying horse. A second Flichter materialized on the beast's rump, pin uplifted, just as another appeared in front of its face, shrieking and gibbering. The pin went down and the panicked horse reared, lashing out at the Flichter, who vanished in a blink. The stranger slipped from the saddle and fell to the dusty road, rolling away from his horse's pounding hooves. Goblin laughter echoed eerily.

Makenna frowned. That was a helm on his saddle, and the horse looked more like a knight's charger than the scruffy, ill-bred beasts bounty hunters rode. But charger or not, he was still a horse—he raced after the bolting packhorse, back down the road to the south. She turned her attention to his rider.

He sat on the dusty road, staring up at her with his mouth wide open. He looked like a landed fish.

"This is the Goblin Wood," she said coldly. "Humans have no business here. I warn you now, go back while you still can."

His eyes widened when she first began to speak. He got his mouth closed, so he looked less like an idiot as he scrambled to his feet. The rim of a chain-mail shirt glittered at his tunic collar, and there were steel plates stitched on the backs of his gloves. Hard, very hard, for goblins to attack this one. Even the Stoners couldn't get a blow through that mail. She'd never seen a bounty hunter who could afford a chain shirt. Was this man a knight? What was he doing here?

"Are . . . are you the sorceress of the Goblin Wood?"

Aye, that was a lord's accent, all right. What was one of them doing here, and alone, too? He'd no armor on his legs, but she'd bet he owned it. The armor he wore looked like it had seen hard use—under the dust she could see old dents and scrapes. But he'd asked if she was 'the sorceress,' just as the bounty hunters did. How odd. Makenna disliked odd things—they usually made trouble.

Irritation swept over his plain face. "Are you the sorceress? Speak up, girl."

Aye, this was a lordling, not used to having peasants ignore his questions. A slow smile crept over Makenna's face. She scraped the toe of her boot through the dust, completing the circle, and murmured the word. Lookaway was her strongest spell—with the power in the wall assisting it, he swiveled clear around to stare over his shoulder.

She dropped quickly, rolled to the edge of the wall, and climbed down. To him, it would seem that he glanced aside for a second and she vanished without a trace. She was grinning as she squirmed into the shallow cave she'd had dug beneath the wall for just this purpose—the entrance was spell hidden. She'd made these caves in many places where goblins could pass the wall, for emergencies. It could hold several goblins, but it was cramped for her, especially when Miggy pressed in to join her.

"He didn't search for you very long," the goblin reported. "He's gone after the horses now—won't be back for hours, the way they were running."

"You did fine!" Makenna told him, and enjoyed the smile that spread over his face. She was working on building Miggy's confidence, but it promised to be a long job.

He climbed back up the wall to keep watch as the Flichters swarmed around her. Half material and half . . . not, only five or six inches high, they were the strangest of the many goblin races. They flew without wings, faster than hummingbirds—you could never catch more than a glimpse of them in flight. It took two or three of them to lift something as light as a key, and the other goblins had considered them totally useless until she'd realized how easily they could spook horses.

They were one of the few goblin races that insisted on real payment, so she unstoppered the small pot of honey she'd brought and let them take all they could.

One, perched stickily on her wrist, told her there was something "nasty" about the packhorse but she couldn't express her impression more clearly. Makenna dismissed her with a shrug and capped the jar, turning to meet Miggy's worried eyes.

"Do you think he'll be back?" the goblin asked.

"Aye, that one's a lordling. It'll take more than a vanishing act to get rid of him."

"And he had all that steel on him, too," Miggy fretted. "I dunno. I don't like it."

"Don't worry. Steel or no, he eats like everyone else. We'll snatch his food, rot his tack and his boots, and send him home, barefoot and starving, just like all the others."

CHAPTER 8

The Knight

Tobin gazed at the charred ruins of the cabin, and his resolve hardened. He would bring the woman who had done this to justice. If he had to, he'd destroy her.

He'd met the young couple on the road yesterday; the pregnant girl, pale and spent, and her worried husband. Tobin had seen enough refugees in the past three years to know he couldn't help them all, but he'd stopped to make them a meal and had the satisfaction of seeing a trace of color return to the girl's face, though she'd hardly eaten anything.

They described their cabin's location and told him all they remembered about the goblin attacks. They added a few more pieces to his growing store of knowledge. Over the past weeks, Tobin had spoken to everyone he could find who'd dealt with the goblins and the terrible sorceress who led them. All those he'd spoken to had lost against her.

But he was prepared, with knowledge and with magic, and he wouldn't lose. He had promised Jeriah, and himself.

Tobin went to search the wreckage, charcoal blackening his boots and hands. He didn't really think he'd find anything. It had become clear that the sorceress and her minions fought primarily with magic—a very dishonorable advantage against poor peasants.

But she was a peasant herself—the round country accent was unmistakable. It had been the third thing about her that astonished him. The first was her youth— she looked no older than Senna, the sister who'd been born just before Jeriah. The second shock had been her beauty.

But it wasn't just beauty—he'd seen many lovely girls. It was the strength and wildness of her, as she stood with the wind swirling through her hair, that had stricken him mute.

Tobin shrugged. If he were a powerful sorcerer he'd make himself young and beautiful—or at least handsome. He wondered why she wore a vest covered with buttons. Perhaps they had some magical significance? He tried to shake off his uneasiness at the thought. As Master Lazur said, a blade through the heart would kill anyone. Superior planning could beat the strongest magic. He knew enough about his enemies to guess what they were likely to do in their first attack. All he had to do was plan a counterattack. And there was ammunition ready to hand—he'd passed several gisap bushes on his way to the burned-out cabin. Tobin's father, who prided himself on being a good hunter, had taught Tobin most of his wood-craft, but it was Jeri who had shown him the uses of this particular plant. Yes, there were things he could do, even against magic.

Tobin knelt beside the fire, finishing the stew he'd fixed for dinner. He'd made camp in a clearing, sheltered on the windward side by an outcrop of jutting rocks, with a stream nearby and plenty of grazing for Fiddle and the packhorse.

It was full dark now, with the moon riding high, barely visible through the lacy canopy of branches. It was late for dinner—it had taken longer than he'd expected to boil down the gisap leaves. At least making camp was little trouble. Once he'd built his fire ring, he'd only had to spread a ground cloth and lay out his bedroll. And of course, hang his food sack so nothing could get at it, just as everyone did in the wilds.

Tobin was still smiling when he heard a scrabbling noise at the far side of the rocks. He reached instinctively for his sword, but the face that appeared at the top of the rocky jumble was anything but threatening. Small, round-cheeked, with spectacles atop its long nose, the goblin's expression was quite friendly. Tobin remembered the lovely peasant girl sneering at him from the wall and drew his sword. Appearances could be deceiving.

The goblin froze. "You're not planning to do anything with that, I hope. They promised me I'd be out of reach up here, even from that nasty steel blade. Aren't I?"

A smile tugged at Tobin's mouth—the creature was a good four feet out of reach of his sword. "I can't reach you up there," he assured it. "Not without climbing the rocks. This is just in case you decide to come down and attack me."

The creature eyed his mail shirt and snorted. "Attack you with what, my teeth?" It seated itself comfortably on the point of a rock with the air of someone settling in for a long chat. A diversion, perhaps? Tobin was perfectly willing to be diverted. He had the Otherworld stone in his pocket, and the net hidden under his tunic, so nothing too serious could go wrong. The repulsion charm was placed where it would do the most good. Besides, if he handled this right, he might learn something.

"What do you want from me?" he asked.

"Why, information." The small creature beamed as if he'd said something clever. "Knowledge, facts, theories even. I am what the common tongue calls a Bookerie, and our trade, indeed our purpose in life, is to collect knowledge of all things and pass it on. And you?" He paused expectantly.

"Umm . . . what?"

"What are you, and what is your purpose in life? When you asked what I wanted, I thought you understood. I've offered you knowledge, and you must now give me some in exchange. Surely even humans understand exchange of knowledge. Look how they introduce themselves, which you, incidentally, have not."

"I'm Tobin," said Tobin, his mind reeling at the spate of words.

"And I am Master Erebus. That's a fair exchange, your name for mine, you see?"

"So—so if you tell me something you expect me to tell you something back?" Tobin grasped at a sudden hope. "Can I ask you for things I particularly want to know?"

"Certainly. Most of our trade with others is in useful knowledge, although among Bookeries, worrying about the usefulness of knowledge is considered vulgar. Almost rude. But with others we tolerate it. That seems to puzzle you?" He whipped out a piece of paper and a quill. Tobin noticed an ink horn on his belt. "Tell me, have I interpreted your reaction correctly? I'm making a study of human reactions and I want to be precise about these things."

"Well, I'm a little puzzled. Humans usually trade money for knowledge. Or just give it away."

"Give it away? Then how do you clear the debt?"

"What debt?"

"Your debt to the one who has given you knowledge, of course. Surely you realize that knowledge is precious!" He sounded utterly shocked.

"Yes, we do," said Tobin thoughtfully. "In fact, I exchanged some food for knowledge just yesterday."

"Ah." The little man began to scribble earnestly.

"You said you were studying humans. Why not start with the sorceress? She's human, isn't she?"

"The mistress? Of course. And I did start with her, but I've come to the conclusion that she's atypical."

"You know her well?"

"Certainly." The goblin paused to beam at him. "I'm one of her closest advisers. I gather knowledge for her so she can make informed decisions. Why do you ask?"

It was not a rhetorical question, and the sparkling eyes behind the spectacles were astonishingly shrewd. Should he lie to the goblin? It seemed a dishonorable exchange.

A chorus of shrieks sounded from the side of the clearing where Tobin had hung his food sack. It was followed by a furious thrashing in the bushes. Tobin leapt to his feet, snatched up his sword, and ran to investigate.

The sack lay on the ground in the little ring of bushes where he'd known it would fall. Even in the moonlight he could see the places in the brush where the goblins had leapt to escape the magic of the repulsion charm. The leaves he'd coated so carefully with gisap glue were all but gone. He'd hoped the bushes would be strong enough to hold at least one of the goblins till he got there, but they'd all escaped. It'd take them hours to peel off all those leaves, though—a fitting payback for his humiliation at the wall. Glue made from gisap leaves dried out in a few days and lost its holding power, but for those few days it was incredibly adhesive. No, he didn't envy his opponents. The first skirmish had fallen to her, but this one was his!

He turned back to camp just in time to see his bedroll vanish into the bushes. With a cry of dismay he dashed after it. He thought he saw several small, scurrying forms, but as he crashed through the bushes, he kept his eyes on the one that had his bedroll. And he was gaining on them. Just a little more—

Something grabbed his ankle, and he crashed to the ground, stunned and gasping. His elbow hurt, and his ankle had been scraped, right through his boot leather. He turned and saw the trip rope.

"Now." Master Erebus' voice came cheerfully out of the darkness. "How would you describe your reaction to this incident?"

Tobin couldn't see him, but he knew the pen was poised. An inarticulate growl rose in his throat.

"Hmm. Would you say that's closest to irritation, anger, or fury? Or something in between? Please, try to be precise."

"Get out of here, goblin, or I'll—I'll roast you alive!"

"Hunger? How very odd. And I thought the mistress was atypical! I must make a note . . . ." His voice trailed away.

Tobin dropped his head to the soft earth and consigned all goblins to the Otherworld.

No doubt they'd try again. And now, thanks to the goblin's boasting, he could use their persistence. If he read

Master Erebus right, the little goblin would be incapable of resisting a chance to pick up more knowledge, and Tobin still owed him several answers. Then he would take her. Not kill her, not unless he absolutely had to. Tobin had begun to consider his mission a good deed, like St. Meriot slaying the monster that had ravaged several coastal villages. But something in him still shrank from the idea of making her helpless with the net and then killing her. This way would be better.

It took him most of the next day to boil down all the gisap leaves he needed. He had to load all his gear onto the packhorse and take it with him when he went to gather the leaves, for he didn't dare leave it unguarded. He painted a thick coating of the glue over all the places he thought a goblin might decide to perch. He had to stop work twice, once to free a bird that lit on a low limb, and once a squirrel that ran over a sticky log. But when the sun set, the animals became fewer.

His camp looked just as it had before, except for his missing bedroll. He kept an ear cocked for Master Erebus' arrival all through dinner, but the goblin never came.

Finally Tobin curled up in his cloak and went to sleep—right under the branch where he'd hung his food sack. He had coated the branch with gisap glue, but he wanted to stay near it. This time of year, when little had grown and nothing had ripened, it was almost impossible to live off the land. If he lost his food he'd be forced to retreat, just like the others.

His cloak was neither as large nor as warm as his bedroll. Tobin wakened several times, cold and stiff, to wrap himself more snugly. The third time he wakened, he needed to visit the privy.

He slept in his clothes, so all he had to do was pull his boots on. The horses were asleep, though Fiddle roused as Tobin walked past, and he gave him a pat. He wandered drowsily away from camp, took care of the problem, and started back.

The dim light of early dawn was creeping through the forest, but he wasn't so thoroughly awake that he couldn't get a few more hours' sleep. He walked on, trying not to wake up more than he had to. He seemed to have come a long way. He yawned, wondering why they hadn't tried for the sack. It wasn't a problem. The sap would remain sticky for several days—all he had to do was keep the animals out of it. Tobin plodded on, not really looking where he was going until a loose rock turned under his foot. He stumbled, regaining his balance with an effort. He looked around and gasped. He was almost a quarter mile from camp!

Racing back, he cursed the sorceress in his mind—he needed his breath for running. He could hear Fiddle snorting and stamping even from this distance. How long had he been wandering in bespelled circles? If they got his food—

As he ran into the camp, three goblins scurried off,

with his food sack on their shoulders. They made good time for small creatures, but their legs were far shorter than his, and they were heavily burdened. He could catch them.

He jumped the first trip rope, but the second sent him sprawling. This time he was ready—he fell rolling and was back on his feet with barely a break in his stride.

He'd almost reached them when they raced into a grove of low-growing trees. Crashing through the branches, he defended his face as best he could while they scampered beneath the worst of the tangle. They had gained almost five yards when he burst from the grove and saw them dashing across a small meadow.

He surged forward in a furious sprint. They were almost into the forest. Willing all his strength into his pumping legs, he laid hands on the bag and grabbed it.

The three goblins shot in different directions and vanished.

Tobin sat down, clutching his prize and gasping for breath. It was several moments before he roused enough to wipe the sweat from his face, and several more before thought returned. How had the goblins beaten the charm? She must have been behind it. Had she cast some sort of spell that negated the repulsion? That meant she must have been in his camp just a few minutes ago!

But Tobin still had his food—that was what mattered. As long as he had that, they couldn't force him back. What else were they stealing? Fiddle would give them trouble, but the packhorse was vulnerable. He'd better get back.

He rose, threw the sack over his shoulder—and something inside it clacked woodenly. There was nothing in his food sack that would make such a sound. A blinding realization hit.

Tobin dropped the sack and tore it open. Bags stuffed with dried leaves to imitate bread loaves. Strips of dried bark instead of meat. A few stones to add weight. Now that he looked closely, it wasn't his sack at all—it was too new, too clean.

His mind filled with the memory of the goblins racing away with the dummy, and fury warred with admiration. They'd been wonderfully convincing. He hadn't even glanced at the tree where his own sack had probably been hanging in plain sight. It wouldn't be there now. He remembered the wild chase through the forest, and suddenly saw himself, smashing through the trees and triumphantly grabbing the wrong sack. Tobin burst out laughing, clear and bright as the sun creeping over the horizon.

"How very odd. Is this your usual reaction to being tricked?" Master Erebus' voice put the cap on the ridiculous situation. Tobin sat down and laughed until his sides ached.

"Hmm. But last time you were angry. I'm certain of it!"

Tobin wiped his eyes and looked around till he spotted the little goblin, in a tree high above him—far from his carefully laid traps. He fought down a fresh surge of laughter.

"Well, last time I was angry at my own stupidity. This time I wasn't stupid, you were simply too smart. You see?"

"I suppose so, but it still seems odd. Are you by any chance atypical in your reactions?"

"Probably. But tell me, how did you get me out of camp? And how did you get past the repulsion charm— you've taken that, haven't you?"

"Of course," said Master Erebus complacently. "It was the mistress' plan. The Charmers led you off with a suggestion that the camp was in the other direction. Being pixie-led, they call it in some parts. Though as far as I've been able to determine, there are no such things as pixies. It helped that the Sleeper kept you drowsy. While you chased after our decoy, we untied the rope, and the mistress herself removed that nasty charm so we could carry the sack off. Before you go, would you mind answering a few questions? You owe me several now, remember?"

"I know," said Tobin, sobering. "But I'm not leaving yet."

"And how will you live with no food?"

"I can hunt," said Tobin. "At least for a while. And I'll answer some questions, but there are some I won't answer. Aren't there questions you wouldn't answer for me?"

"Hmm. I see your point. What questions would you answer?"

"Ah, would you like to learn about the barbarians

who live in the desert to the south? I've been fighting them and I know quite a bit. They have some very atypical reactions."

"Really? I suppose . . ."

But Tobin knew he had him. It had been the most useless knowledge he could think of.

Master Erebus arrived at midday, right on time. Tobin had spent much of the day trying to apply glue without being obvious about it. Now he fought down a surge of guilt as he watched the little man settle himself exactly where he'd sat the night before last, right on top of one of the largest patches of quickstick. Tobin had figured him for a creature of habit. Perhaps he could repay the creature with a lot of knowledge, once his sinister mistress was out of the way. The goblin might even be grateful for his freedom. But somehow, Tobin didn't think Master Erebus' reaction to being tricked would be at all atypical.

"Now," said the little goblin cheerfully, "let's begin with the background. You said you've been fighting these barbarian humans for several years?"

"Three. Where's your mistress tonight? Watching out there in the bushes? With my packhorse, perhaps?"

"Surely you didn't expect us to leave you the horses. We can sell them. We'd have taken that great gray brute you ride, but he didn't want to come, and he was too big to argue with."

"He's been trained not to go with strangers. You didn't answer my question about your mistress."

"I'd guess you don't expect me to. But I'm going to surprise you." The little goblin beamed at him. "She's not here. She has more important things to attend to than watching you starve."

Tobin tried to control the irritation that surged from his empty stomach. All the snares he'd set had been neatly sprung when he went back to check them, and he knew full well who was behind that.

"You really should go," Master Erebus told him gently. "This forest is ours now—which seems only just, since humans were the ones who tried to confine us here in the first place. Why are you doing this?"

Tobin shook his head. "If I tell you, you'll start asking questions I'm not going to answer. Are you here alone?"

"Of course not. I'm not that foolish. But since you'll be leaving soon, we'd better get down to business." He turned, reaching for his ink horn, and a curious expression crossed his face. He tried to stand and failed.

Tobin leapt to his feet and scrambled up the rock. It only took him a few seconds, but Master Erebus was half out of his britches by the time Tobin reached him. He hadn't expected to see Erebus struggle with such furious determination, twisting and biting. Still he couldn't defeat Tobin's superior strength.

When he'd bound the creature's small wrists, he stuffed him back into his britches and carefully fastened the waistband. That would hold him until the glue lost its grip. The forest had fallen silent as they struggled. Tobin could feel the presence of the watchers, but he didn't bother to look for them.

"Whatever you're thinking, it won't work. I'll tell you nothing." The goblin's voice was cool for the first time—cool and fearless. Tobin felt a stab of admiration. Master Lazur had said that goblins had no courage, but maybe Erebus was "atypical" himself.

"I don't need any information," Tobin told him. "If your mistress cooperates, you won't be hurt at all."

The little goblin's eyes widened in alarmed comprehension. His spectacles had fallen off in the struggle—his face looked naked without them. "I'm nothing to her. Completely worthless."

"Really? I thought you were one of her closest advisers." If her power over Erebus was this great, he'd have to gag him when he laid the second part of his trap, or the goblin would warn her. But first he had to get rid of the watchers.

He drew his knife and bent over Erebus, feeling the goblin shrink from the steel. He should probably cut the little creature to prove he was serious, but he couldn't bring himself to do it. Instead he put all the determination he could into his voice. "Tell your mistress that I want to talk to her," he said to the silent trees. "Tell her she must return my horse, my gear, and the charm she stole, and come unarmed—"

"I told you, she's away," Erebus interrupted. "It'll be days before she can get here. You'll be starved to death by then."

"I hope not," said Tobin loudly, "for your sake. Because if she's not here before I fall asleep, I'll cut your throat before I nod off. Tell her that," he called to the trees.

A moment later he felt the watching presence vanish. A bird chirped tentatively, and he knew he and Master Erebus were alone.

CHAPTER 9

The Hedgewitch

MAKENNA WIGGLED UNDER THE screen of bushes and stared at the settlers' camp. She'd chosen her spying spot with care—she could lie comfortably in the shallow, dry hollow for many hours. The brush along its rim would shield her from the sharpest-eyed human, but she still had a fine view of most of the clearing where the settlers had chosen to build. It was even downwind, so the dogs couldn't catch her scent. That was a mixed blessing—the smell of fire, animals, cooking, and waste came clearly to Makenna, and her nose wrinkled. Dirty, smelly, noisy creatures. The stench of humanity was as familiar as a childhood nightmare.

They looked to be well organized, and better equipped than most. Better armed, too.

When she'd risen at the wall to give the warning, half a dozen men had lifted crossbows. If Cogswhallop hadn't done some scouting earlier, she might not have been able to complete the look-away spell in time. And they'd searched around the wall longer than most. She had no regrets about not finishing her warning speech—these people had obviously been warned. Perhaps that was why so many of them had come together.

They looked as if they'd gotten information about other things, too, for they were equipped with woodworking tools, and most of them were busily erecting a large building, probably a church. Why not build cabins first? She cast a curious eye over the herd of horses at the other side of the clearing. Even at this distance it was easy to make out the great plow horses, six of them, towering over the smaller beasts.

They'd need at least three pair to get fields cleared in time for spring planting, and if they worked very quickly, they'd likely make it. But she wasn't going to give them the chance.

Too bad, foolish ones. You should have turned back at the wall instead of wasting all this effort, for all you'll do in the end is get on your horses and—

An odd uneasiness caught her attention. Horses. There were six great ones, but there were also many others, almost . . . fifty? What did a settlement this size need fifty horses for? A few of the others might be big enough to pull a plow, but most looked like riding horses—and surely they'd only need a handful of those. Horses were expensive; expensive to buy and expensive to feed, if you didn't have a grainfield. An oddity—and sometimes those turned into traps. She frowned and turned her attention to the people.

The nearest were the men standing guard around the camp. It was a sensible precaution—another sign that these people had learned something about the Goblin Wood. They wore the rough tunics of hired men or servants, but they stood straight and attentive. They'd be hard for humans to get past, but she was confident her goblins would manage.

Makenna studied the humans for some time before she realized that there were too many hired men for a group this size—unless they were very well off, and rich folk didn't leave their comfortable homes to plow up the wild lands.

Though there were many women and children among the settlers, almost all of the servants were men. This, too, was odd. Not inexplicable, but strange, just like that knight hunter with his charger and his goblin charm.

A smile crept over her face as she remembered his laughter pealing through the woods. She remembered her own fury at being tricked by goblins. That open laughter at his own expense was charming. Makenna scowled and then grinned again at the memory of the leaf-covered goblins. Because of the goblins' fear of fire, the Makers were the only ones who'd known anything about gisap glue, which had to be boiled. Erebus had been fascinated, and Cogswhallop, who'd been caught in the trap, hadn't appreciated his interest.

Makenna continued her watch. The humans' building

began to rise. She had to admit they were fast workers—they got a lot accomplished before they set up kettles to heat the midday meal.

But they weren't miracle workers. A servant near her end of the clearing was trying to make a fire with wood still wet from yesterday's rain. He got the tinder going, but no matter how hard he blew, the soaked wood above it failed to catch. At this rate, it would be tomorrow before the family this man served got a hot meal.

Evidently the servant had reached the same conclusion. He stood abruptly, glaring down at the damp wood. Then he made a single sharp gesture and the wood roared into flame.

Makenna's eyes widened in astonishment. Fire-start was a simple spell, one of the first she'd learned, but no one would take a hedgewitch as a servant. And though she might not have seen him place the pitch-soaked pinecone that was the best essential object for this spell, she was certain he couldn't have drawn the rune without her noticing it.

Only a priest could work magic like that—with will and word alone. And priests served no one but the Hierarch and the Seven Bright Gods. *This man was a priest in disguise.* Probably many of the servants were disguised priests or— Her eyes shot to the perimeter guards. Now that she knew what to look for, their alert posture all but shouted "soldier."

Makenna crouched lower in the hollow. Her hiding

charm was so familiar that she usually noticed it no more than she noticed her navel, but now its hard smoothness was comforting. It was a trap! The whole settlement was a trap. If she hadn't seen that careless priest, she might have fallen right into it, but now . . .

A cold smile crossed her face. Watching closely, she soon spotted all seven of the priests in their hired men's clothes. There were almost fifty soldiers—fifteen of them formed the perimeter guard, and they changed the watch with military precision. Aye, they'd be tough, but her goblins could get past. She'd fight any human who encroached on the goblins' territory, but fighting the priests, who had ordered her mother's death, was her favorite revenge.

It crossed Makenna's mind, as it sometimes did, that her mother wouldn't have used her own magic to do harm.

Her mother was dead.

Try as she might, Makenna couldn't spot the place where their weapons were hidden. The Spoilers would need to know where to concentrate their attack, and there were dozens of covered carts and wagons. It would also be dangerous to try anything without knowing what magical defenses the priests might have set up, and how the soldier's interior guard was organized. She'd—

Something shook her boot, making her jump. It was Cogswhallop. She signaled hastily for silence, and he glared at her, for of course he knew better than to speak, but with this crafty lot she wasn't prepared to take the slightest chance. She followed him back into the woods, down one of the narrow, twisting paths the goblins favored, ducking when the branches were too low.

"Well?" she asked when they were safely away. "What is it?"

"You won't like it." Cogswhallop scowled. "That clumsy pen pusher went and got himself caught."

"Dung! By who? The knight? Is Erebus all right?"

"Oh, aye," said Cogswhallop laconically. Makenna fought an impulse to shake him. "He's fine so far—just held. The knight fellow wants his stuff back. The charm, too. Me, I'd let him slit the worthless scribbler's throat and whistle for it. Do you know what he went for? Information about those barbarian humans in the south-land deserts! Of all the worthless—"

"Cogswhallop," said Makenna through gritted teeth, "would you do me the favor of telling me exactly what the man said?" She knew full well that despite the rivalry between them, Cogswhallop would never abandon Erebus, or any goblin, to die at human hands. But this was no time for private quarrels!

The goblin sighed. "You're to come yourself, unarmed, bringing his charm and all the rest of it, before he falls asleep . . . or he'll cut the pen pusher's throat."

Makenna took a deep breath and calmed herself. "Feel later" was the first rule of combat. "How long ago was this?"

"About four hours."

"What!"

"Well, the scribbler only took two others to watch after him, can you believe it? They were Bookeries, too, all primed to take notes in case he missed anything. They're not quick travelers—it took 'em several hours to get back to the village and find me, and I came straight for you, but it's not a short trip."

"And it'll take the same amount of time for me to get the charm and get back." Makenna was already walking faster. "I hope he got some sleep after we robbed him. If he hurts Erebus, by St. Maydrian's hand I swear I'll kill him."

"I hope you're not planning to just walk in there," said Cogswhallop, trotting beside her. "It's a trap, gen'ral."

"Of course it's a trap. There's a lot of those about lately. I wonder— Well, no matter. I'm an old hand at springing snares, Cogswhallop. He'll get no meat from this one!"

The setting sun was dyeing everything red when Makenna approached the knight's camp. He looked tired, dark circles ringing his eyes, but the knife at Erebus' throat was steady. Carefully—she must go carefully. She eased forward a step.

"I've brought all your things." She gestured with the bundle she held. "Even the charm. I'm unarmed, just like you asked."

"What about my packhorse?" He sounded wary. His helm was plain, just a dome and nose guard, but it concealed his expression. He was wearing all his armor, protecting everything but his legs, which would make it harder for the troop to seize him. Erebus, on the other hand, was completely unprotected. His throat, bare beneath the knife, was unmarked, but he twisted like a creature in torment, squeaking something behind his gag, over and over. He didn't seem to be hurt.

"The packhorse?" Impatience crept into the knight's voice at her silence.

"I'd already sent him to be sold in Brackenlee when I got your message. He's days gone, or I'd have brought him, I swear it. The horse is nothing to me—I've got money here," she shook the bundle hard enough to make the coins jingle, "for you to buy him back." She eased forward a few more steps.

Erebus had stopped wiggling. Just as well. A Maker, with their clever hands, might have worked free, but the Bookerie didn't stand a chance. He was speaking as clearly as he could through the gag—it sounded like "ah ret." All wet? She took another slow step. "Will this content you?"

"No," said the knight, and she stopped, shocked.

"But I couldn't get your packhorse, truly!"

"Then you will have to give me something else, won't you?"

"What do you want?" It was coming now—she was

about to learn his purpose.

"I want you to swear a binding oath, by all the Bright Gods and the Dark One, your master, that you'll leave the Goblin Wood and never return, or ever trouble those who seek to live here."

Contempt for the stupid lordling welled within her. Did he think he was in a heroic ballad, where oaths were as binding as chains? She bit back her eager agreement. He was a fool, but that didn't mean he was an idiot. Carefully.

"But that would mean I must leave my home!" She tried to sound pleading, instead of mocking. "All I care for is here. Will nothing else content you?" Another step. Another.

"Nothing." He was watching her intently. She was near enough now to see his expression in the shadow of the helm, even in the dim light.

"Then I have no choice but to give you what you ask." Another step.

"Stop there," he commanded, his face suddenly twisted with disgust. "And tell me why I should believe your oath when you've already lied to me."

Makenna froze. "What are you talking about?"

"You said you had the charm with you, but no goblin can stand to be within ten feet of that charm. You're only six feet from Erebus, and he's unaffected. So you've already lied."

"The charms only keep goblins about six or seven feet

away," Makenna stalled, trying to gather her wits. Not so foolish after all. He'd been perfectly aware of her slow approach and permitted it so he could make his test, St. Spiratu the Truth Giver curse him.

"You don't have the charm," he said. It wasn't a question.

"Not on me, but I did bring it. I can get it in moments."

"Do so." His grip on both Erebus and the knife tightened.

She turned and hurried through the gathering shadows to the small bush where she'd hung the charm. So much for her plan to get Erebus away and let the goblins overwhelm the fool. On to the secondary plan. It would be harder if he had the charm, but they'd prepared for this. Once Erebus was free, they could attack.

She went back to the camp, walking more slowly as she approached him, the charm held out before her. At about six feet away, the color drained from Erebus' face. She took another step and Erebus writhed in his captor's grasp, throwing himself back and forth in a futile effort to break free. The knife nicked his throat.

"All right," said the knight coldly. The last of the sun was sliding away—she could barely see his face now, in spite of his nearness. "Step back and put the charm on that flat rock over there." He gestured with his head and she did as he asked. It was ten feet away. When the charm was removed Erebus went limp, whimpering behind his gag.

"If you kill the little man, I'll see you dead, human."

"I won't kill him, if you do what I say. Stand over there, by the fire pit."

That was more than fifteen feet from Erebus, but she trusted her own quickness and the weight of his mail to make up the difference, so she didn't protest. As soon as she reached the fire pit, he started backing away from Erebus and she stepped forward cautiously, matching his pace.

When he was closer to the charm than the goblin, he leapt for the rock and she sprang for the small captive, drawing her concealed knife as she ran.

She slit the side of Erebus' britches with one stroke and hauled him free, tossing him onto the grass where he could run for safety despite his bound hands. Then she whirled to face the knight. She expected a blow, even a sword cut, and had lifted her knife to block, but instead of an attack, a mass of string fell over her face and arms. What in this world?

She tried to yank it off, but it resisted her as if it were alive, and her sense of the world around her dimmed. But she could see clearly. She could hear just fine. What . . . ?

Then she understood, and panic hit her like a blow in the stomach. It was her power, her magic, that was dimming, draining away. She tore frantically at the net, but it clung like the web of some terrible spider. She didn't even notice the knight until he stepped forward, jerked the knife out of her hand, and grasped her wrists.

Magic or no, she could still fight. And he was the one who'd done this to her!

She pulled back to put swinging room between them and kicked him in the groin as hard as she could. The long skirt of his chain mail took most of the force from the blow, but he hadn't expected it, and he doubled over, grunting.

She got one wrist free and twisted the other, kicking for his face. He ducked, avoiding the blow, and straightened up. She tried to claw his eyes with her free hand, but the net hindered her and he grasped her wrist again. She twisted her body, trying to pry herself out of his grasp, but that was a mistake—he hooked his foot expertly around her ankle, tripped her, and then lunged forward to land on top of her.

Makenna saw the log, half buried in the new spring grass, as she started to fall, but there was nothing she could do.

CHAPTER 10

The Knight

TOBIN BARELY GOT THE sorceress's hands and feet bound before she began to moan and stir. Good. That meant the blow that had stunned her wasn't serious. He hadn't even seen that log. Well, it was her fault anyway—he still ached from that vicious kick.

Master Lazur had said she probably wouldn't put up a fight once he got the net on her. Tobin wondered what else the priest had been wrong about.

The net clung to her, but Tobin still gagged her, just as a precaution, and whistled for Fiddle. The woods were utterly silent, not even a breeze to stir the branches. The only sound was the thud of Fiddle's hooves. The moon wouldn't rise for several hours, but the road was only a few miles east, and Fiddle was more accustomed to night riding than most horses. They might reach the road before moonrise.

Tobin saddled the gray and threw the sorceress up to the horse's back, grunting with effort, for she was muscular—

heavy for her size. She glared hatred at him, then her eyelids drifted down again. Tobin didn't care how she felt. He'd been disgusted by the ease with which she lied and her obvious willingness to swear falsely. This one had no honor at all. He'd take her to Brackenlee, see her in gaol, and send a message to Master Lazur, who was the proper person to deal with her.

Tobin mounted behind the sorceress, whose bound legs forced her to ride sidesaddle like the lady she wasn't. He pulled Fiddle's head away from a tempting patch of clover and turned him to the woods. It was black as a cannibal's cook pot where the branches blocked the starlight. Should he stay here till morning? Master Lazur had said the goblins would probably run off when their mistress was powerless. Master Lazur had also said that goblins had no loyalty or courage. Tobin, remembering Master Erebus, was beginning to doubt that.

The silence felt more ominous than barbarian war drums. No, he'd better get out of the Goblin Wood as soon as possible. He kicked Fiddle into motion.

The second trip rope almost brought the horse down. Fiddle stumbled, snorting, and then planted his feet and refused to go forward. Tobin could hardly blame him.

He dismounted and, after a few moments' thought, retied the sorceress's hands to the saddle in front of her. Her eyes sneered at him, but Tobin ignored her. He could lead Fiddle and cut the trip ropes. After all, the moon was beginning to rise, and he couldn't be too far from the road.

He walked for perhaps half an hour, and the trip ropes stopped appearing. He began to feel safer. Goblins were little more than vermin—though it was hard to think of Master Erebus in those terms. Still, how persistent could vermin be?

The only warning was a split second of furious rustling in the undergrowth, then a rope whipped tight around his ankles. His body hit the ground, dragged a few feet, and hurtled into the air. With a startled shout, Tobin crashed into the trunk of a young tree and hung there, upside down, bruised and stunned. Leaves clung to his face and hair, for his helm was gone. He clutched the trunk to steady himself, and his wits returned. The goblins had—

The goblins! They'd free the sorceress!

He drew his knife, hauled himself up, and hacked through the rope that held his feet. He managed to grab a branch with his other hand before the rope parted, so he fell feet first, but several branches hit him and he landed in an awkward sprawl. Half a dozen tiny, dark forms were advancing on Fiddle, and the sorceress was working at the knot that tied her to the saddle.

Tobin staggered to his feet, shouting and drawing his sword. The goblins vanished in a blink, as if they'd never existed. He might have doubted his eyes if it weren't for the mockery on the sorceress' face.

"It won't work," he said loudly, more to the silent forest than to her. "I've got you, and I'm keeping you. They might as well give up."

No one replied. Tobin shrugged and checked the knot that held her to the saddle before he assessed his own damage. He'd picked up several painful bruises and scrapes, especially on his legs. His armor had protected the rest of his body. Perhaps he should have brought his leg greaves as well, but they were uncomfortable for walking and he'd thought this mission would be less dangerous than full combat. Tobin sighed, picked up his helm, and reached up to brush the damp leaves from his face and hair. They didn't come off. "What in this . . ." He yanked off a glove and tried again. His fingers recognized the sticky resistance. The leaves had been coated with gisap glue.

The woods echoed with ghostly, goblin laughter.

They were leading him astray. The moon rode high now—it had provided enough light for him to avoid the last two traps, but it also told him he should have reached the road hours ago. His aching feet reinforced the message. Exasperating, that he had to walk while she rode.

Tobin leaned wearily against Fiddle's sweaty flank, closing his eyes. If he walked away from the rising moon, he could hardly fail to cross the road eventually. But eventually had passed, and passed again, and he still wasn't there. Surely no spell was so powerful it could affect the moonrise! So how—

Fiddle shied, almost pulling the reins from Tobin's grasp. He grabbed the bridle, soothing and commanding. He caught a flicker of movement from the corner of his eye. It was the thing that had spooked the horses at the wall!

One appeared right in front of Fiddle's face, shrieking, and the horse jumped again. Tobin swung at it and was astonished when it vanished in a spatter of blood— he'd felt almost no resistance when his blow connected. At least the things could be killed, if you could hit them.

Several more appeared, but now they kept out of his reach. Fiddle stamped and pranced. A stone flew out of the darkness to strike the horse's hindquarters, and he tried to rear, despite Tobin's grip on his bridle. The sorceress clung to the saddle with both hands. If the horse bolted they could free her at leisure as soon as he stopped running.

The goblin things swooped and gibbered. Another stone came out of the dark. Fiddle lunged, shaking his head. Tobin yanked out his knife, one handed, and slashed at the rope that held the sorceress to the saddle. Fiddle was trotting now, trying to break into a run in spite of Tobin's weight pulling his head down. It took Tobin three tries to cut the rope, and he cut her, too, in the jouncing struggle.

Stones whirred though the dark. Fiddle screamed and reared. Tobin dropped both knife and bridle and grabbed the sorceress, dragging her from the saddle as Fiddle bolted into the forest.

He fell to his knees, scrabbling for the knife. He cut the gag and pulled it free.

"Call them off," he commanded. Another thrown stone made his helm ring.

She looked into his eyes, smiled, and said nothing.

Stones stung his ribs, even through his mail shirt. Tobin grabbed her hair and laid the blade against her throat. "I'll kill her!" he screamed. "I'll kill her, if you don't leave me alone!"

As the crashing of Fiddle's escape faded, the silence returned, impenetrable. Tobin could feel the anger, the burning determination of those who watched him from the shadows, and he realized with sick dread that his threat was worthless. If he killed her, he would never leave the Goblin Wood alive.

Tobin plodded wearily on, following Fiddle's tracks. He'd cut the rope that bound the sorceress' ankles and made her a hobble that let her walk, but not run. He'd tied her hands behind her again, and he used the small amount of rope that fell from the knot as a leash. His precautions seemed excessive—she walked meekly where he directed. But her lovely, dirty face held neither meekness nor defeat, and he understood her triumph. He knew he was being pixie-led, but he couldn't think of any way to prevent it. Only the small orange-brown stone in his pocket gave him hope.

The tracks crossed a stream. Even in the branch-sifted moonlight, Tobin could see the hoofprints coming out the other side. Were they Fiddle's tracks or some sort of illusion? The sunrise would give him direction again. If he had Fiddle he might still escape, but without the horse's strength he would never make it. He rubbed his throbbing forehead wearily. There was no reason to think Fiddle hadn't crossed this stream. It was shallow and not very wide—no challenge for a horse. Tobin could do it himself. He sighed. It was those clear tracks on the other side that made it look so much like a trap. He was so obviously meant to follow them.

"If you're going to take all night thinking about it, I'd like to sit down." It was the first time she'd spoken since he'd removed the gag. Her voice held the same mockery as her eyes.

"Don't bother," said Tobin. "I've got a better idea." He could search for the trap. He might even be able to spring it without getting caught, but there was a simpler way. "You go first," he told the sorceress.

She shrugged delicately and stepped toward the stream. At the edge of the bank she paused, probably trying to figure out how to step down into the water without tripping.

Tobin was just hoping that she'd fall and get thoroughly soaked when a springy branch whipped over the ground and knocked her feet from under her, pitching her into the stream.

Smiling grimly, Tobin waded in and dragged her up the opposite bank. Cold water streamed from her hair and clothing, and she snorted to clear her nose. She glared at him from beneath the wisps of soaked hair that straggled over her face.

"It was your turn," he told her. The small victory was immensely cheering. Tobin looked at the tracks leading into the forest. Why should he follow the trail they laid? Sooner or later this stream must join the Abrin River, and that would lead him out. He hauled the girl to her feet and set off, away from the hoofprints, walking downstream.

"You won't make it," said the sorceress.

As if she had summoned them, a flurry of stones flew out of the darkness, striking his mail, pinging off his helm. One hit his unprotected leg and he yelped and clutched it. That was a mistake. The second barrage was entirely directed at his legs.

The sorceress laughed. Tobin grabbed her arm and tried to run, but the stones were a constant stream, all but crippling him. He noticed that the stones never hit the sorceress and tried to use her as a shield, but the stones came from all sides and he could only use her to block one. The sharp blows were agonizing and his muscles knotted in protest. Tobin gave up and turned, dragging his prisoner back to the stream. He was hoping to find cover along the water-cut bank, but as soon as he reached the creek the hail of stones stopped.

Tobin's legs gave out. He fell to the ground, gingerly rubbing his bruises and trying not to cry in front of the enemy. By the saints, that hurt!

"I told you so."

Tobin looked up. Most girls that bedraggled would have lost all dignity, much less the power to intimidate, but nothing could detract from the look of cold satisfaction in the sorceress' eyes.

"The net stops your magic," he said. "How are you controlling these goblins?"

"You think they have to have me around to come up with a battle plan? Taking me was your first mistake, human. On their own, they're even nastier than I am."

"I didn't ask who came up with the plan, I asked how you're controlling them. How you're keeping them enslaved without—"

She began to laugh. It sounded like genuine amusement, but Tobin couldn't think of anything he'd said that was funny.

"You think they're doing this because my magic enslaves them?" she asked.

"Well, since goblins have no loyalty—"

"Who told you that? That goblins have no loyalty?" She sat down beside him, without asking permission, but Tobin was too tired to care.

"A—A man I know. A wise man."

"Priest, was he? Never mind, you don't have to say.

But let me tell you a story my mother, who was also a wise woman, once told me."

Tobin scowled, but he had no way to stop her. Listening was better than being stoned.

"It's about a farmer, who owned an apple tree and a grapevine. His grapes were good, but the apple tree, ah, the apple tree produced the most, and the biggest, apples of any tree in the village. He was a wise man, this farmer, or so he thought. How could he not be, when his tree produced apples so fine?"

Her voice had softened, its country lilt pronounced. Chattering about apples, she sounded more like a farm girl than a mighty sorceress.

"Is there a point to this?" Tobin asked.

"Patience, lordling. For the time came when the grapevines grew high and shadowed the apple tree. The farmer, being so proud of his fine apples, uprooted his grapes and burned them. Only then did he discover that the reason the apple tree had done so well was because the grapevines shaded it in the hottest part of the summer. That, and the mulch from the grape squeezings, which he'd spread around the tree's roots. Without the grapes, his apples were just like everyone else's."

Tobin snorted. "So the point of this story is that humans need goblins? We've done fine without them for the past six years."

The sorceress smiled. "That's likely the point my

mother would have made with the tale. My point is that the farmer was a fool, who knew as little of apples or grapes as your priest knows of goblins. And if your priest's a fool, what does that make you for following him?"

Tobin looked away from her smug expression. Apples and grapes. Perhaps she was mad—madness might account for a lot of things. But the goblins she led were altogether too sane. The hoofprints lay before him, their message as clear as if someone had posted a sign. He couldn't leave the trail.

If he stayed there, all they had to do was wait until he fell asleep, and he was tired enough to do that right now, in spite of the pain in his legs.

If he killed her, he would die.

But if he went on . . . Tobin touched the stone in his pocket and made up his mind. "All right." He hauled himself to his feet, dragging the sorceress up after him. "We'll do it their way."

As long as he followed the tracks, the goblins gave him no trouble, but his bruised legs were unsteady and he kept his eyes mostly on the ground, not looking up until the hoofprints vanished into a wall of dry brush.

"What in . . . ?"

The brush pile extended to his right and left, curving gently back behind him. Tobin spun to flee, but it was already too late. They'd closed the ring. How had they done it so quietly? Too late. He was in the center of a clearing, about ten feet across, surrounded by burnable wood.

Small fires sprang to life all around the circle. Tobin released the sorceress and leapt for the wall, to claw his way through before the flames took hold. A hail of stones drove him back, and he had to sink down so his mail shirt could protect his legs. Even then the stones didn't stop, bouncing off his armor, forcing him to use his arms to protect his face. When the rain of stones finally ceased and he lowered his hands, he was surrounded by a ring of fire.

"But you'll burn her, too!" he cried to the darkness beyond the flames. "She'll—" A gust of smoke caught his throat and set him coughing.

The sorceress had laid herself flat in the center of the circle, where the heat was least and the smoke rose above her. With her water-soaked clothes and hair, she'd last far longer than he would. That, no doubt, was their plan. She was laughing, demons take her.

Tobin had to get out. He had to break through that flaming wall, or he would burn. If the smoke didn't kill him first. He was coughing again. He sank down beside the girl, drawing his knife, and cut open her vest, not caring that he sliced through strands of the net as well.

She turned to glare at him, but he didn't care. The goblins would save her, and burning to death wasn't part of Master Lazur's mission. Jeriah would never forgive him if he died.

His commander had taught them how to deal with fire. If he ran fast enough, he could probably break through the barrier without being too badly burned—if his clothes caught fire, he could roll to put them out. Of course, if the burning brush was stronger than he thought, he might get stuck in the middle and go up like a torch. Tobin pushed the thought aside. He cut off a large strip off the girl's wet shirt and pulled off his helm to wrap it around his face. The sparks stung, and the smoke seared his eyes. He never even saw the stone coming.

The first thing he became aware of was a headache so intense it made his stomach heave. Vomiting would only make the throbbing worse, so he took several deep breaths of the clear, cold air and his nausea gradually calmed. His throat was raw and his mouth tasted of smoke. A fire? He opened his eyes, wincing at the morning light, and a clearing holding a pile of blackened brush spun dizzily around him. He closed his eyes quickly, and took more deep breaths.

As he lay there, he became aware of two voices speaking nearby, one deep and gruff, and one higher. Female. That voice was familiar. The sorceress. Memory returned, and he groaned.

"He's awake, mistress." A new voice. Nervous. He heard footsteps approaching and tried to open his eyes again, but his vision still spun and he shut them.

There was no sound for several moments. He supposed she was inspecting him. He heard her thanking someone called Miggy. A hand lifted his head, not too gently, and she spoke a word he didn't understand. His head dropped with a thud that almost made him sick again.

But then the pain began draining away, lessening with every throb. He stirred and discovered his hands and feet were bound. No surprise. She had resumed her conversation with the gruff voice, but now he was alert enough to follow it. They seemed to be bargaining. "Five deer," she said. "Five deer is more than the weight of a horse."

"There was fire. We went right up to the fire to throw our stones, and we did not do it for deer. We can always get deer."

What were they talking about? Tobin opened his eyes carefully. The world no longer spun. He was lying just outside the ring of burned brush. A young goblin, a stranger to him, hovered anxiously. In the damp earth before him, he could see the edge of a circle and several runes, no doubt the reason his headache was receding. His armor was gone, and he could feel a chain around his throat—probably the hiding charm Master Lazur had warned him about. Fiddle was tied to a tree.

He had to twist his neck to see the sorceress, for she was standing some way beyond his feet, talking to a creature almost as strange as the horse-spooking things.

It was almost four feet high, tall for a goblin, with

long, dirty, wild-looking hair. He had thought that most goblins dressed in imitation of humankind, but this creature wore nothing but skins, short furred, except for what looked like . . . yes, it was a horse's mane running down the back. It was wearing horsehide.

The goblins had freed her from the net. She offered six deer. The creature declined. Tobin shut his eyes. Who cared that six deer were almost half again the weight of a horse? Then he realized what they were bargaining for.

He sat up with a shout of protest, which was a mistake, for he did get sick. To his surprise, the strange goblin helped him lie down again when his stomach was empty, but he didn't take time to thank the creature. He was listening with desperate helplessness to the debate over Fiddle's life.

The gruff-voiced horse eater finally settled for seven deer, and tears of exhausted relief crept down Tobin's face as they discussed the time and place of delivery.

When the sorceress came back to him, he opened his eyes. Whatever happened, he owed her for this. "Thank you for saving Fiddle. He's—he's a good friend."

She scowled. "I didn't do it for you. To kill the wild things is bad enough. To slay a trusting servant like that big fellow is an act of betrayal only a human would commit."

"Or a goblin, if I understand the original bargain. And you're human, whatever else you are."

"Insults," she snapped, "will get you nowhere.

Offering the horse was the only way Cogswhallop could get them to come in time. Stoners like horse meat, and with goblins, you have to trade something for what you want."

"Because they aren't capable of love," said Tobin. "I understand."

The corners of her mouth turned down. "You are a fool. The goblins repay kindness with kindness. Humans repay kindness with death. How dare you look down on them?"

Tobin's head hurt too badly to debate it. "Anyway, I thank you. I've had Fiddle since he was a colt."

"I thought knights' horses were all named for a virtue?" she asked casually.

Tobin sensed a trap in the question, but he was too tired to cope with it. "His real name's Fidelity, but he doesn't always keep his mind on business. A good-looking clump of grass, a butterfly, anything can distract him, so . . . Fiddle."

He thought her lips twitched, but the motion was too slight for him to be sure.

"I see. We'll be moving out soon, so you'd better rest."

She turned away, and Tobin let his eyes fall shut. But before he fell asleep, he made certain the Otherworld stone was still in his pocket.

CHAPTER 11

The Hedgewitch

MAKENNA PAUSED OUTSIDE THE door of the earth hut where the knight was imprisoned. "You've got everything?" she asked Cogswhallop.

"All but the bell, and the pen pusher'll be along with that soon enough. Stalling, gen'ral?"

"Don't be silly," she snapped. But she had to admit it was true—trust Cogswhallop to see it. She opened the door and strode in.

There were several windows, but the little sod room, its ceiling barely high enough for her to stand upright, felt cramped and gloomy. He was sleeping on a pallet by the far wall, free except for the copper chain that dangled from the roof beam to his ankle. Made by goblin smiths, it wasn't as strong as iron, but plenty strong enough to hold a man who had no iron or steel tools. It wasn't a trap, she told herself fiercely. And even if he was trapped, her strange compulsion to set things free didn't extend to humans.

As soon as Cogswhallop stepped inside, she slammed the door and he sat up, blinking sleepily. The bewilderment on his face changed in seconds to mulish stubbornness. Good thing she could work the lying spell, or they'd get nothing out of this one.

Without a word (let him sweat), she gestured to Cogswhallop, who handed her the small bag of silver chains. She laid the first circle on the floor at the north side of the room, opened one of her mother's battered books, and began to trace the elaborate runes around it. Working magic from these books still brought her mother's memory back, but now it carried love as well as sorrow.

The knight watched in silence as she completed the same process at the south and west points, but when she drew near him to lay the east circle he spoke up, apprehension clear in his voice, despite his effort to sound casual. "What are you doing?"

"Setting a spell."

"I can see that! I mean—" He broke off, frustrated.

That's right, lordling. I don't have to tell you anything.

The chain rattled as he leaned back against the wall, trying to look composed and in control.

"It's a spell that'll tell me if you lie," Makenna admitted. She didn't want him too nervous, or he'd refuse to open his mouth. "A bell will ring."

"What bell?"

"Erebus is bringing it."

He looked more suspicious than ever. "If that's all it is, why don't you just put a truth spell on me?"

"Can't."

"What do you mean you can't? Why not?"

She snorted. "I don't have half the power to cast that. This one is complicated enough. Do you mind letting me work?"

"But priests cast truth spells all the time."

"I'm not a priest."

A polite tap on the door proceeded Erebus' bustling entrance. "I've got it, mistress," he announced. "Bocami didn't have one, so I started asking all the likely folk and found one at Wintle's house. She was using it to store dried nettles in, which silver's good for, but she says glass will do as well, if you want to trade for it." He beamed at all of them, including the knight. Cogswhallop scowled.

"Aye, give her this when you get the chance." Makenna passed him two buttons. "The second's for your trouble."

With both goblins' help, she rigged a stand and hung the bell in the center of the room. Cogswhallop glanced skeptically at the complex runes. "Are you sure this'll work, gen'ral?"

"Of course I'm sure—"

Ping. The silvery note echoed in the cramped room. Makenna felt her face turn scarlet.

"Well, we know it works," said Erebus cheerfully.

The knight began to laugh. Makenna glared at him

and he sobered, but she wasn't displeased. It'd be easier to catch him off guard if he was relaxed. Would she have the courage to laugh like that, if she was a prisoner? She doubted it.

"What's your name, knight?"

"What makes you think I'm a knight?" he asked pleasantly.

"Your horse's name. What's yours?"

The lingering laughter fled from his eyes as he realized that he'd given himself away. "Where's Fiddle now?"

"Safe and cared for. Safer than you'll be, if you don't answer my questions."

Ping.

He managed not to laugh, but it looked like a hard fight.

"Dung," Makenna muttered. The knight's expression changed to startled disapproval. A prig, was he? Maybe she could use that.

"I said you should let me handle this," Cogswhallop told her. "I'd have meant it."

"His name is Tobin," said Erebus. "At least, that's what he told me."

They stared at the knight, who nodded reluctantly. "It is. Will you tell me your name, ah, in trade?"

Why not? He wasn't going to take his knowledge to the fair. "Makenna, Ardis' daughter." She saw his shock at the implication of bastardy and smiled. Priggish lordling.

"And will you tell me of your family, Sir Tobin?" He winced at the title, and she wondered why, but he said nothing. "In a way," she continued, "it doesn't matter. Your silence tells me there's something to conceal, and my goblins are everywhere. With your name and rank, I can get your life's history in a few weeks."

"Then why bother with this?" He gestured at the runes and the bell.

"To be sure I have the right name," she answered promptly. "I don't want my spies chasing a trail of rotten fish."

"But why all the trappings? A sorceress of your power should be able to cast this with a wave of her hand!"

This time she laughed. "And what makes you think I'm a sorceress?"

"Master L— But you cast spells. You're certainly not a priest. What else could you be?"

"I'm a common hedgewitch. And you're a knight. What's a knight doing hunting for me, Sir Tobin?"

He said nothing. He looked at the runes, the sign of someone too weak to work magic without aid. The bell hadn't rung, but if she was a powerful sorceress, she might be able to keep it from ringing. She took a vast, malicious pleasure in his dilemma.

"I thought hedgewitches helped people," he protested.

She had thought herself indifferent to any human opinion, but it still stung. "Why should we? People have surely given no help to hedgewitches."

It was his turn to wince.

"What's your connection with the settlers?" she continued.

He tensed, a flash of alarm crossing his face. A trace of color followed it. He was a pitifully poor liar. Who could have been fool enough to send him after her?

"Did the priest you mentioned tell you about them? Or did he send you out to blunder along on your own? They're an odd lot. Half of them are soldiers, or priests in disgui— Ah. Is your priest with them?"

"No!" he snapped.

Ping. He jumped. He'd forgotten the bell.

"I mean, I don't know." *Ping.* "There is no particular priest." *Ping.* He bit his lip and fell silent.

Cogswhallop grinned. Erebus shook his head mournfully.

"So, there's a priest behind both you and the settlers, and he's important enough to make you lose your head. He'd be the one who knows so little of goblins? Still, I'm glad I got the hiding charm on you fast. What's his name, this Master L—?" No reply. He'd probably say nothing more, but she'd learned enough. She took down the bell and began picking up chains.

His face was red with anger. "Who are you?"

"A hedgewitch named Makenna, just like I told you."

"He—" a furious gesture indicated the silent, satisfied Cogswhallop, "—called you general."

"Well, I lead the goblins here."

"Why?"

"They needed someone. The different races won't accept another kind of goblin as their leader, but they don't mind me."

"You turned them into killers! I saw what you did at that cabin—I've heard about the others. You're not just a hedgewitch, you're a killer!" He sounded almost hysterical, but his eyes were observant. Trying to turn the tables and provoke something out of her? A good idea, but he'd picked the wrong target for his jibes. She cared nothing for humans killed.

He must have seen it in her face. His own expression changed, chilled and wary. "How old are you, anyway?"

It mattered even less than her name. "Seventeen."

"Seventeen!" He glared wildly at the dismantled bell as if expecting it to ring. "Seventeen and you're— you're— Bright Gods! Does your mother know what you're doing?"

It was a ludicrous question, but it cut through her defenses as his accusation of murder never could. "My mother's dead. Drowned by the very humans she spent her life helping. If she was alive, she'd be proud of me!"

Ping. The tone was muffled by her grip, but clear. Makenna jumped. It shouldn't have rung, with the runes dismantled. But this was an intricate spell. She'd never really understood it.

"I'm sorry," the knight said gravely. "I can't imagine what that must have meant to you. But surely abandoning the Bright Gods and taking power from the Dark One isn't the answer."

"Pigdung," Makenna snorted, enjoying his shocked scowl. "There is no Dark God. Likely no Bright Ones, either."

"That's blasphemy! Besides, if there are no gods, where does your power, and the priests', and the goblins', come from?"

"From the same place." She gestured to the meadow outside the windows. "From nature, from inside ourselves. The only reason I'm not a priest is that the chooser said I hadn't enough power. 'Her holiness is not sufficient.'" She mimicked the chooser's voice, remembering her mother weeping in the night.

"But. . ." He fell silent and then spoke quietly. "Jeriah said something like that once. That the priesthood was the Hierarch's way of keeping people with powerful magic gifts in his service. Father was furious."

"Who's Jeriah?"

He realized he was giving away information and his mouth snapped shut.

She shrugged. "It makes no difference. He sounds a sensible man, whoever he is. But if you're interested, these days I swear by St. Maydrian the Avenger."

She smiled and left him to think it over.

◆　◆　◆

"Please, sir, all I want is work." She stood before Master Lazur, eyes downcast, her shaking knees concealed by the unaccustomed skirt. Cogswhallop and Erebus had both hated this idea—and they never agreed on anything. But she needed more information about the settlement, and according to the knight, they believed their enemy was an ancient and powerful sorceress. They shouldn't suspect an ordinary peasant girl.

She'd been confident she could deceive them . . . until the guard brought her to this tent and addressed the sharp-eyed priest before her as Master Lazur. Well, what if he was her enemy? He couldn't know who she was, for they'd only caught a glimpse of her at the wall, and she looked very different now, with her drab skirt and properly braided hair. She took a calming breath and steadied herself to meet his eyes. Unlike the knight, she was a fine liar.

"Things are hard this time of year," she said pathetically. "Goodman Branno, he couldn't afford to keep me, and since then I've worked only a few days at a time. In Brackenlee, when I heard about your people, I thought there'd be lots of hands needed in a new village, so I came to ask. I'll work for bed and board until you can pay me."

"I think we can do something for you." His words were kind. He probably was a kind man, unless you got in his way. Then you'd be uprooted and burned, along with the rest of the grapevines. Makenna knew all about ruthlessness in defense of your own. She wouldn't underestimate this man. Just now, for all his kindness, he looked as if most of his attention was elsewhere. Good.

"But first you must answer a few questions, so we can be sure we can trust you," the priest went on. "May I cast a truth spell on you? It's a standard precaution—we've done it with all our settlers here." Makenna's heart lurched. His expression held nothing but a trace of boredom. It probably was a standard precaution, just like he said. Sensible, too, so why hadn't she thought of this possibility?

"Of course you may." To say anything else would arouse his suspicions. She drew a deep breath. "I have nothing to hide."

He stood for a second, gathering power while she strove desperately to gather her wits. Unlike the weaker spell in her mother's books, the truth spell forced you to tell the truth, but perhaps . . .

He laid his hand against her throat, and she felt the power swirl though her like a churn paddle. She gasped and he glanced at her, startled. Should she not have felt it? She blinked innocently. He withdrew his hand, and the power wrapped around her stomach like a giant fist and settled there.

"What's your name, girl?"

The fist squeezed and she felt the answer welling up in her throat. She couldn't stop it. "Makenna, Ardis' daughter." He accepted the indication of bastardy with visible indifference, and she thanked St. Spiratu the

Truth Giver that she'd not yet told anyone the false name she'd intended to use.

"Where do you come from?"

"The wetlands, originally." The name of her village rose in her mind, and she added quickly, "But that was years ago. I've traveled a lot since." It was all true. The alien power in her belly stirred restlessly but forced no further answer. Good lies came from truth, like butter came from cream. If she could keep talking and always tell the truth, would that work?

The priest shrugged. He evidently cared little for her travels. "What do you want here?"

Need it be the whole truth?

"To work for some good family," she said. The words "to spy" surged in her throat, but she swallowed them down and babbled on rapidly. "It's a long time since I had a proper job, and I haven't much money left." The pressure was subsiding. She'd answered and spoken the truth—evidently that was enough.

"Have you heard of the sorceress of the Goblin Wood?"

"Aye, in Brackenlee." And from Sir Tobin and many others, but she managed not to say it.

"Have you ever seen her?"

"No, sir. To tell the truth, I didn't believe much of what they told me." And still don't.

"Do you serve this sorceress?"

"No, sir." For she doesn't exist.

He nodded acceptance, then thought of a final question.

"Do you intend harm to anyone in this settlement?"

The compulsion to answer squeezed her gut and her mind raced. "As long as they mean no harm to me and mine, I mean no harm to them," she blurted, trying to sound pert, then looking down as if embarrassed. The power roiled, dissatisfied, but the compulsion to speak wasn't overpowering. Someone entered the tent, but she was too busy controlling her expression to look around.

"Very well." The alien power drained out of her and she suppressed a gasp of relief. "Goodwife Garron has a new baby—she might need an extra pair of hands. Jeriah will show you."

She glanced up, startled by the name, and saw a handsome boy, younger than herself. The knight's Jeriah? It wasn't a common name. He nodded to Master Lazur and smiled at her.

"I thank you, sir." Makenna curtsied unsteadily to both of them and Jeriah showed her out. She wished desperately for a few moments' privacy to recover from her narrow escape, but Jeriah walked on without pause. She wiped her sweaty palms, gritted her teeth, and followed him.

After one shrewd glance, he didn't speak—did she look that shaken? But probably many did, after their meeting with Master Lazur. She'd have plenty of time to ask questions later, so Makenna fell in with his silence, and used the time to compose herself before meeting Goodwife—what was the name? She felt a moment of panic, but Jeriah introduced them carefully.

Goodwife Garron was a thin, quick-moving woman, still pale and tired from the recent birth. But tired or not, she never wasted time. Almost before she knew what was happening, Makenna found herself up to her elbows in a tub of dirty laundry, where she finally had a chance to relax, after a fashion.

With a host of goblins willing to work for buttons and bowls of milk, she'd forgotten the incessant grind of housework. Even though there was no house, for the cabin they would live in was only half built, cooking, laundry, firewood, and dozens of other chores had to be done. By the end of the day, when the family came back to the big tent where they all slept, Makenna's muscles ached as if she'd been pulling a plow.

There were six in the family. Goodman Garron was as slow moving as his wife was quick and seemed a quiet man, but perhaps that was only because he couldn't get a word in. Along with the new baby boy, there was a boy of twelve, Dacon, who took after his father, and a seven-year-old boy, Mardin, who grinned impudently at her. Ressa, the only girl, was five, and Makenna never found out much about her because her thumb never seemed to leave her mouth. Mardin and Ressa were too young to be much help, so Goodwife Garron sent them off to pester the men during the day. The children giggled when she told Makenna that, and Dacon beamed with pleasure at being classed as one of "the men."

◆ ◆ ◆

Makenna gained a bit of useful information that first night.

She was laying a pallet for herself in the already crowded tent, protesting that she could very well sleep outside.

"Nonsense, Makenna," said Goodwife Garron. "Suppose it rains? The last thing we need is to have to nurse you through a chill. Or suppose the alarm rings in the night?"

"Then she'd be closer to the church than we are," Mardin piped up, and then giggled as Dacon buried him in the blankets.

"What alarm?" Makenna asked Goodwife Garron, who was smiling at the uproar.

"Didn't I tell you? By the saints, I suppose I didn't! All the folk who've tried to settle in this wood have been attacked by goblins—"

"Led by a sorceress, seven feet tall, with flaming eyes," proclaimed Mardin, shaking off his brother.

"Well, not quite that, perhaps. But that's why we've all these soldiers and priests—to catch the sorceress. If the alarm bell rings, you and I and the children will go straight to the church, Makenna. The menfolk, in fact most of the men in the village, plan to stay out and guard the stock and the supp—"

"I could help guard, too!" Mardin informed them. "If I had a medal like father does, I'd—"

"What medal?" asked Makenna, interrupting in turn.

"It's a charm to keep goblins away," the goodwife explained. "The same kind of enchanted iron they've got around the doors and windows of the church. We'll be safe in there, and the men'll take care of the rest." Her frown told Makenna she wasn't quite as sure of that as she sounded. But Dacon told Mardin he was too young to guard a hamster, let alone a cow, the resultant fracas made the baby start to cry, and the subject was dropped.

Makenna slipped out of the tent. The noisy jostling of these humans disturbed her, and she stood a few moments, staring up at the starry sky and trying to ignore the settlement around her. How was she ever going to sleep in a tent full of them?

At least she was getting the information she needed. How easy it would be to have the Flamers set the church afire—no need to cross charmed iron for that. And when the men rushed to save the women and children, their goods and gear could be stolen or destroyed. Of course, something must be done about the priests and soldiers first. She still had much to learn.

These people had been kind, but their kindness was for a human servant girl. For a hedgewitch, for her goblins, they would have no mercy at all. With a weary sigh, Makenna turned back to the crowded tent. In spite of her fears, she was so tired she fell asleep immediately.

As Makenna grew more accustomed to the Garron family, her very lack of unease around the humans began to trouble her—they were, after all, the enemy. If she got too comfortable, she might make some slip and give herself away. She hoped the need to gather information would keep her wary enough.

One bright morning, her hands covered with bread dough, Makenna asked Goodwife Garron who Jeriah was.

She laughed. "Don't set your heart on that lad, dear, he's a lordling or I've never seen one."

"I noticed that," said Makenna, kneading more flour into the dough. It felt strange to perform this task outside, in the sunlight. Perhaps it was the familiarity of these ordinary household chores that was draining her defensiveness. "That's why I asked about him. What's a lordling doing here?"

"He's some sort of assistant to Master Lazur, who seems to be a pretty important man, judging by the way the other priests act around him. It's not that odd."

"Aye, I guess that's right," Makenna admitted, and turned the subject. There was no other priest whose name began with L, so Master Lazur was almost certainly the priest the knight had mentioned. If Jeriah was his assistant, it made sense that Tobin would know him, though it seemed strange that a priest's assistant would have such heretical opinions.

She found out a lot about the soldiers by eavesdropping on their conversations. Though they were civil, the soldiers cared little for the settlers—their one ambition was to capture the sorceress, destroy the goblin army, and get out of 'this wilderness' and back to the City of Steps to spend their reward. That chilled her, for the City of Steps was the Hierarch's city, which meant these men were from the Hierarch's own guard.

They all wore goblin repulsion charms, just like the knight's, and many of the settlers had them, too. In addition, all the priests and some of the soldiers had extra charms to help them resist goblin spells. She tried to learn which of them carried these charms, but it was impossible, for they changed hands nightly when the soldiers gambled. Along with the charms, many of them wore steel armor beneath their rough tunics, but they carried no swords for fear of compromising their 'disguises.'

Their plan was to let the goblins overrun them and flood into the settlement. Then they would close ranks to hold and slay them. The thought of her goblins dying in their trap sent a wave of hatred washing over her, and Makenna took several small risks trying to discover where their weapons were stored.

But it wasn't until she entered the nearly completed church for the priests' First Day Speaking that she found them, stacked neatly in crates along the back wall and protected from the goblin's interference by the charmed windows and doors.

She'd avoided Master Lazur since their first meeting, fearing his sharp intelligence. Now she watched him curiously, but there was little to see. Although his eyes were fixed on the speaker, he looked as if his thoughts were elsewhere. Thinking of her? Makenna shivered and looked away, and her attention was caught by a young woman with tears pouring down her face. She seemed familiar, but Makenna couldn't remember having met her in the settlement.

Goodwife Garron had spent most of the Speaking whispering threats to her restless children, instead of watching the priest, so it was easy to catch her eye and nod at the weeping girl. The goodwife's cheerful face darkened. "Lost her baby, poor thing," she murmured. "Stillborn. It came early when the goblins burned them out."

The girl at the cabin! She looked diminished now, with her lank hair and reddened eyes. Makenna thought of the small, unformed creature that Goodwife Garron cherished so—she'd hardly let anyone else touch the child. Makenna's mother had healed and helped pregnant women. "Magic comes from life and is part of it," the long-dead voice whispered in her memory. But it was different from her mother's voice—silvery, like the chime of the liar's bell. A cold chill crept around her neck and shoulders. Her mother would not have approved of this, of her.

Makenna looked down. But her mother wouldn't have approved of the slaughter of the goblins, either. She'd been forced to choose, and she had no regrets. But . . . magic comes from life. Perhaps it was because of the voice that she did what she did next.

174

◆ ◆ ◆

It started simply enough. The afternoon clouds had blown off without producing rain for once, and the family sat around the dinner fire, wrangling as usual. Goodwife Garron had just told Mardin for the third time not to talk with his mouth full or he'd choke, when the boy stopped talking and wheezed loudly.

At first Makenna thought it was a joke—Mardin had a seven-year-old's sense of humor. Then the strangled choking began, violent and obviously involuntary. Goodwife Garron laid down the baby and rushed to him. His father reached him at the same time.

"Slap his back," said Dacon.

"No, don't," said the Goodwife. "You might drive it deeper!" She pressed her hands against Mardin's stomach, trying to squeeze the air out of his lungs, but nothing happened. His face was turning blue. "Dacon, go for a healer priest, hurry!"

The boy took off like a bird. Mardin's father laid him down. His frantic thrashing was weaker. Soon he would be unconscious. The priest would be too late.

Before she was even aware of moving, Makenna found herself kneeling beside the child. She snatched a piece of charcoal from the fire and drew the runes of loosening and freeing on his chest, then grabbed a pot of butter, since no oil was available for the essential object, and rubbed it on his throat and spoke the words.

His lungs heaved, and he began to cough—loud, clear

coughing, his lungs inflating time and again. He spat out a piece of half-chewed meat. His mother pulled him into her arms and met Makenna's eyes.

"What's happening here? Is the child all right?" It was one of the priests, an older woman with a sharp hatchet face.

Makenna froze, hiding the piece of charcoal under her skirt. *Useless.* Her mind screamed, *Fool, they'll know you're a hedgewitch, and then the rest of it will come out! You've traded it all for that brat's life!*

"There's nothing wrong now." Goodwife Garron stood, holding Mardin against her, pulling his shirt over the smudged runes on his chest. "He was choking, but he brought it up himself, by the Bright Ones' grace! I'm very grateful for your coming, though."

There was a frozen pause as if the entire noisy family was holding their breath. Then Mardin began to sob, and Ressa and the baby joined in, and in the tumult of getting them all settled down, the priest was thanked again and politely dismissed.

As soon as the others were asleep, Makenna stole from the tent. No one had mentioned the spell she'd cast, and she knew Goodwife Garron and her husband never would. But the children were another matter. The sooner she was away, the better.

She wished that she hadn't been forced to put her hiding charm on the knight. She'd put off making herself a new one—she couldn't bring it into the human village, and she hadn't had time for the complex spell. There was no reason for them to use magic to search for a runaway hired girl, and she couldn't imagine they'd ever suspect her of being "the sorceress." But she'd make herself a new one as soon as she could, just in case.

A simple look-away spell took her past the perimeter guard, and soon she was walking through the darkened woods. The relief of being free of the human settlement lightened her heart. She now had enough information to make a successful plan. Soon she'd be back with her own, and they'd drive these humans away.

But at the thought, a cold chill touched the back of her neck. It took her several minutes to shrug off the knowledge that her mother would not have approved.

CHAPTER 12

The Knight

TOBIN PACED BACK AND FORTH, head bent so he wouldn't hit the roof beams. The sod cottage was too small—it had seemed larger, somehow, when the sorceress was here.

He should have told her he'd been convicted of treason, and that he had no desire to hurt her, or any of her goblins. The silly bell wouldn't have rung at that!

His chain was more than nine feet long, but six of those feet stretched from the ceiling where it was fastened, to his ankle on the floor. It only let him pace five steps before bringing him up short. He'd tried pacing in a circle, but that made him dizzy, so now he paced in short lines.

He should have told her he knew nothing of the settlers, except that they intended to live in the Goblin Wood—that was true, too! He could have created a fortress of misleading truths, if he'd been smart enough. Failing that, he could at least have kept his mouth shut.

But he'd lost his head and started to babble, and now she knew everything. Almost everything.

Tobin sat down wearily against the one wall he could reach, clutching the Otherworld stone in his pocket. He had only vague memories of the ride to the goblins' base, maybe because of the headache, which had returned rapidly when he was lifted out of the healing circle, or maybe because the goblins had bespelled him. He'd remained in a daze throughout the ride and slept afterward, until the slamming door woke him and she'd launched into her questions, giving him no time to devise a story that could trick the spell.

Only when she'd gone had he been free to take stock of the situation. The stone was still in his pocket, that was the most important thing. But everything he carried of iron or steel—armor, weapons, even his belt buckle and his boots with iron nails in the heels—had been removed. They'd replaced his belt with a thin rope, and his boots with soft leather slippers, slightly too big, that slid off his heels as he paced.

The only metal on him was the copper shackle around his ankle and a slim chain around his neck that held a medallion—no doubt the hiding charm Master Lazur had warned him about. Tobin couldn't see it. The chain was so tight he could only slip two fingers between it and his throat. Half an hour of careful feeling had discovered no clasp, and the chain was too strong for him to break. The Otherworld stone was in the very center of the goblin's base—but useless because it was with him, and he was under a hiding spell.

Tobin considered throwing the stone out the window, but Master Lazur had said she might have a hiding spell covering the whole camp, and if that were true he probably couldn't throw it far enough. On the other hand, a lot of the things Master Lazur had said weren't true.

Was it possible the girl really was a common hedge-witch? If it was, then how had she defeated all the forces that had been sent against her? A small force could defeat a stronger one, but only if the leader of the small force was a very good tactician. To defeat stronger forces again and again, the leader had to be not merely a good tactician, but a truly great one. A general, in fact. Tobin scowled. A seventeen-year-old peasant girl? She was a year younger than he was. Tobin couldn't believe it. But he found it no easier to believe that she was a mighty sorceress.

The door opened and sunlight streamed into the room, almost reaching the wall where he sat, which meant the sun was low, and the door was in the west wall. Tobin noticed this, but most of his attention was concentrated on the goblin woman who carried the tray in. She was almost two feet tall, what he was coming to think of as average height for goblinkind, with lank brown hair and the longest, sharpest nose he'd ever seen. The tips of her fingers were green tinged—he hoped she wasn't the one who'd prepared whatever was in the bowl she carried. Then the smell of rabbit stew reached him, and his mouth started to water.

"Hello." He smiled tentatively. No use being on bad terms with the gaoler who brought food. "It looks like a nice evening out there."

"Humph." The soft snort was her only response. She came forward, set the tray within his reach, and stepped back quickly. Rabbit stew in a wooden bowl, wooden spoon, bread, and a wooden tankard containing fresh water. Nothing he could use as a tool or a weapon, unless he wanted to hit her with the tray, which he didn't. He was far too hungry.

She stood with her arms folded, watching him eat. His attempts at conversation met with no response. Even his thanks, when he set the tray away from him, went unanswered. She took the tray away and returned with a large clay pot, whose purpose was obvious. Tobin was grateful that she didn't insist on staying to watch him use it.

When she'd gone, he investigated the room. His chain wouldn't let him reach the windows, but he could still see parts of a clearing with trees not too far off. The walls were made of stacked sod bricks. He could probably dig through them with his bare hands, but since the chain kept him prisoner he saw no point in trying.

The ceiling was made of wood planks, supported by thick beams. It was easy to see why they'd attached the other end of his chain to a ceiling beam; aside from the door and window frames, they were the only wood in the hut. His bed, which consisted of a rough mattress stuffed with straw, several blankets, and his cloak, was the only furniture.

Tobin sighed and turned his attention to the chain. It was linked to a spike driven deep in the beam. Tobin grabbed the top of the chain and tried to work the spike back and forth, leaning all his weight on it. It didn't budge. He might be able to loosen it—in about a week.

He sat down and studied the shackle around his ankle. There were hinges on one side and a lock on the other, but he had no tool that would either break the first or pick the second.

His headache was coming back, but he took advantage of the last of the light to study each link in the chain. They were as thick as the tip of his little finger and welded solidly.

Tobin sighed again and went to bed. He was exhausted now, and his head throbbed. Perhaps morning would bring some opportunity to escape.

Morning brought the green-fingered woman with his breakfast. She served him in silence, and he ate again, uncomfortable under her angry gaze. He was almost finished when he heard a slight scrabbling at one of the windows. Glancing up, he caught a glimpse of half a tiny face and two wide hazel eyes.

"Be off with you!"

Tobin jumped at the sound of the little woman's voice—he'd almost decided she was mute. She hurried out the door. "Didn't I tell you to leave the human alone? Tadpoles eat your toes!"

Tobin set his food down and went as far as he could toward the window. He couldn't see her, but he heard her voice scolding, and a childish voice replying.

"Your child?" he asked when she came back for the tray. "I don't mind if they're curious."

"She's not mine. And I do mind." She said it coldly, but at least she'd answered.

"Why?" he pressed on. "All children are curious."

"Not about humans. I don't want them having anything to do with humans, ever!" Bitter passion filled her voice.

"Have you been injured by humans?" he asked cautiously.

"Aye." There was a world of irony in the soft word. "You might say I've been . . . injured." She met his eyes and he flinched at her pain. "The only reason I let you live, human, is that the mistress insisted." She picked up the tray and left then, and he was glad to see her go.

When the knock fell on the door, he was delighted. "Come in, Master Erebus."

The door opened on the little goblin's astonished expression. "How did you know it was me?"

"Because you're the only one who'd knock," Tobin told him. "I'm glad to see you. Come in and sit down. We can talk."

"Oh, no," said Erebus ruefully. He closed the door and sat carefully, several feet beyond Tobin's reach. "I've gotten into enough trouble talking to you. Not that I blame you, mind. You have your duties and loyalties, just as I have mine. But I'm telling you nothing of the mistress or anything else."

"You mean I'll have to rely on my talkative gaoler for information? Thanks a lot."

"Not speaking to you, is she? Well, she's bitter. She has reason."

"Why? Oh, all right, don't tell me. I just hope she's not the one who's fixing the food."

"Oh, Natter wouldn't poison you, if that's what you're thinking. She's a gentle sort, for all her sharp tongue."

"I'll believe that when I see it. Speaking of seeing, I'm going mad in here. Is there some way I could go outside? Just for a bit of exercise? I'll give my word . . . ."

Erebus was shaking his head. "I'll not be taken in by you twice, Sir Tobin. May I call you Tobin? And even if I could be, others wouldn't. You're going to stay right here until the mistress decides what to do with you."

Tobin rubbed his thumb over the stubble of his beard. "In for a long wait, am I?"

"Sorry, I'm telling you nothing this time."

"Will you at least tell me how Fiddle is? If you're having trouble taking care of him, perhaps I could help?" He didn't really believe they'd let him out, but it was worth a try.

Erebus' eyes shifted guiltily. "Well, I suppose I could tell you about that. The mistress sent your horse to be sold."

"Sold!" Tobin's voice spiraled up. "To who? What's happened to him? He could be whipped! Starved! I've got to—"

"Calm yourself," said Erebus serenely. "He won't be abused, he's too valuable. Todd— Ah, the mistress' agent is a tinker. He knows the worth of a good horse."

"But why?"

"The mistress said you'd be less likely to try to escape on foot than on horseback, and—"

"But he's my horse! How dare she sell my horse?"

Erebus shrugged. "At least she didn't sell him to the horse eaters. You can always buy him back, if you get free. Think of it as a small payment for our hospitality."

"But . . . but . . ." There was nothing he could do, curse her! And Erebus was right, a horse as good as Fiddle would be well treated. The humor of it began to strike him—protesting wildly at the sale of his horse when his life was threatened!

Erebus beamed, sensing his change of mood. "Speaking of payment," he continued, "I'd like to get the information you owe me now." Paper, pen, and ink appeared as if by magic. "About those barbarians . . ."

Outrage warred with humor . . . and lost. Tobin laughed and told him what he wanted to know.

◆ ◆ ◆

The next time Tobin heard the scrabbling at the window, he was ready, glancing up cautiously, not wanting to startle them. But as soon as they saw him looking, the eyes vanished. He heard muffled giggling outside the window, but it soon faded away.

On the morning of his fourth day of imprisonment, he wakened to the growling of thunder. The sky was gray, and he couldn't guess the time. He thought it might be late, for he'd worked on loosening the spike far into the night. The spike was beginning to shift just a little as he pushed and pulled at it. The shackle was turning his skin as green as Natter's fingers.

Natter seemed disturbed by the weather when she brought his breakfast and nodded absently when he remarked that the storm would be a bad one.

The thunder grew louder. Tobin had thought the goblins would be busy preparing for the storm and was astonished when the door opened, revealing a rectangle of writhing dark clouds and a tiny goblin girl, hardly more than a foot high. She was slender, her nose quite short for one of her kind, and she looked very young in spite of the determined set to her jaw. Her eyes were a familiar hazel.

"Hello," said Tobin softly, trying not to startle her. "I believe I've seen you, but we haven't met. I'm Tobin."

"My name's Onny." She took a wary step forward, and then jumped as the thunder crashed.

"It's getting closer," said Tobin. "Are your people ready for the storm?"

"They're doing that now." She inched forward, wary and graceful as a hummingbird. "They're all busy, so now seemed like the best time to—"

"To come see me? Then you aren't supposed to be here? I'm glad you are," he added hastily. "I'm don't like being alone with the storm coming in."

It thundered again and the girl flinched, then wrinkled her nose. "That's a lie. You're not scared of the storm."

"Well, not a lot," Tobin admitted. "Are you?"

"Of course not. Only babies are afraid of thunder."

"I see. And I see you're not afraid of the mistress, either."

She looked puzzled.

"Because she told you not to come here, and you have," he explained.

"Oh, the mistress didn't say anything about you." Thunder crashed again and she winced. "That was just Natter. The mistress is away now." She edged toward him.

"Really? Where is she?"

"She's off spying on the human village," said the girl. "Fa was upset about it, but she wouldn't listen."

A brilliant flash lit the windows, and thunder exploded right on top of them. The child jumped and clapped her hands over her ears, her face white beneath the scattered freckles. Then she leapt forward, touched his knee, and darted back to the door like a fish out of a net. "It was a dare." She flashed a smile at him and ran out as the first heavy drops splattered down.

The spike was beginning to shift. Working it grimly back and forth, Tobin wondered how much the girl had learned about the settlement. Everything, if she was as clever with them as she'd been with him. She'd have been there for days by now. And what would she do with her knowledge? He had to warn them. If he could get there in time, perhaps they could—

The spike came loose. Tobin, in the act of pulling back on it, lost his balance and fell, the chain rattling down around him. He stared at it stupidly for a second, then a shout of joy welled up in his throat and he had to struggle to suppress it.

Grinning triumphantly, he jumped to his feet, slinging the chain over his neck to keep it out of the way. He snatched up his cloak and hurried out the door, closing it behind him. If he was lucky, his escape might not be noticed until Natter brought his dinner.

Stepping into the storm was like stepping into a waterfall—he had to pull up his hood to protect his face or he'd have been unable to see at all. At least no one was likely to see him.

Soon the ground began to rise and Tobin climbed rapidly, exalting in his freedom after days in the cramped hut. At the top of the small hill, the trail ended in a cleared space where an ancient pine had fallen. Then the woods began.

Tobin plunged thankfully into the trees. Soon he'd be far from the goblin's base—but wait! He'd almost forgotten the Otherworld stone.

Tobin looked back. The rain fell in torrents. He could only see about ten feet, but considering the rise he'd climbed he guessed the small clearing would give a good overview of the goblin camp. It might not be out of range of any spells she'd placed, but if he left the stone among the trees, whoever found it wouldn't know what direction to go next. If he left it here, when they found the stone they'd find the goblin base without fail.

The great fallen pine lay across the back of the clearing, near the forest. Tobin darted into the rain and tucked the stone out of sight beneath the huge tree. Done! He'd accomplished his mission. Now all he had to do was warn Master Lazur that the sorceress knew about him, and he'd be free to go home.

He climbed to his feet, hindered a little by the weight of his wet cloak, and entered the woods again, heading south.

Tobin tramped wearily through the darkness, wishing he still had his boots, for his soaked slippers offered little protection from the stones and branches that littered the forest floor. He stepped on the sharp end of a branch and hopped, cursing.

Then the ground disappeared and he was falling, striking things. He flung out his hands, shouting, then hit the bottom, his left ankle twisting beneath him. Pain shot through his leg.

Tobin blinked, but he couldn't see anything but darkness until he thought to look up. There was a lighter patch in the blackness above him. He'd fallen into some kind of pit.

He thought about moving around, exploring the area by touch, but he didn't have the nerve. Suppose this was just a ledge and another, deeper, pit lay right at his feet— he'd heard of such things. No, no exploring. He'd told Jeriah he was no hero, and it was true. He would stay right here until daylight.

His first awareness was that every muscle in his body was clenched and shivering. He then realized that this was because he was wrapped in something cold and heavy—it was his struggle to throw it off that woke him.

He opened his eyes and for an instant thought he was back in the hut, for the wall before him was also of earth. But there were stones embedded in this wall, and higher up, roots poked out of it. At the top he saw, not planks and beams, but green boughs and a snatch of sky. Of course, he had fallen into a pit.

Groaning, for his bruises had stiffened during the night, Tobin unwrapped his wet cloak. The chain rattled as it slid off his shoulders. The pit was roughly circular, about eight feet across and twelve feet deep. The floor was littered with fallen debris.

The air, heavy with the scent of fresh rain and damp earth, woke a raging thirst. Several nearby rocks had puddles in the hollows. Tobin rose to go to the closest, but as soon as he stood waves of pain shot from his left ankle, and his vision darkened.

When it cleared, he saw his ankle was mottled with bruises and swollen to twice its normal size. Tobin couldn't tell if it was broken or only sprained. Either way, he couldn't walk let alone climb out. Would it be worse to be recaptured by the goblins, or to die of starvation? Tobin surveyed his dripping surroundings. At least he wouldn't die of thirst. He crawled painfully to the nearest puddle and drank.

Tobin sat and gazed at the top of the pit. He'd tried to climb out several times, and failed. Now the sun was getting lower, not setting yet, but casting a tint of gold across the sky. It was pleasing, and he gazed at it for several minutes before he became aware that a familiar pair of hazel eyes was gazing back.

"Onny?" The eyes jerked away, and he heard a muffled yelp.

"See," said a piercing whisper. "I said he'd see you if you stared like that!"

"So?" said the girl, defiantly loud. "He can't do

anything. I think he's stuck down there."

Five pairs of eyes popped over the edge and looked down.

"I dunno," said a doubtful voice, also familiar though he couldn't place it. "He could be faking, or something."

"Don't be silly, Miggy." Onny's whole face came into view as she leaned forward. "Are you stuck down there?"

"Yes, I am," said Tobin. "And if you want to recapture me, I'd like that very much. Have you got a rope?"

"No." Five faces peered down at him now. Besides Onny, there were two goblin boys, another girl, quite small, and an adult Tobin vaguely recognized from when they'd captured him. Miggy, yes, that was the name. "We didn't know we'd need one when we found your tracks. You can't get out without one?"

"If I could," said Tobin reasonably, "I wouldn't be here. I fell in last night and hurt my ankle." He held it out so they could see the swelling. They gazed down at it for a moment, then the heads vanished. Most of their discussion was muffled, but he could hear mournful protests from Miggy, and a very young voice piping "Me, too!"

After several minutes Onny's face returned. "We're sending Miggy back for help, while we stay here and watch you. As long as you're down there and we're up here, it'll be perfectly safe."

"You shouldn't tell him that, you nit," said one of the boys. "You might give him ideas!"

"What ideas? He can't do anything to us from down

there." She turned back to Tobin. "But Miggy won't be back till morning. You came an awfully long way," she added accusingly.

Soon they all joined the conversation. The boys were Daroo and Regg, and the baby was Nuffet. Daroo was Cogswhallop and Natter's son and had "his father's gift," whatever that was—it seemed very impressive to them. Regg was a Charmer, which sounded odd to Tobin since he hardly said anything, charming or otherwise. Onny was a Finder, which meant she could sense the direction of something she wanted.

"It works best with plants, but I'd watched you enough that I knew you a bit, and I touched you, when I won the dare." She grinned at Daroo, who frowned back. "So when I thought about it, I was pretty sure you'd gone south."

Miggy was a Tracker, and since he was supposed to be watching out for them it had been easy to get him to follow Tobin's tracks, though they'd all get into lots of trouble for it. They didn't seem much alarmed by the prospect.

The sun was setting, and a biting chill began to creep into the pit. "Did you say Miggy wouldn't get back until morning?"

"Yes, why?" Onny frowned at him.

"It's a little cold down here, but I'll be all right. I'll move around and keep warm." And he would, in a minute, but he was too tired now.

"Your cloak's hanging on that rock," said Daroo suspiciously.

"Yes, but it's wet."

He closed his eyes and heard them arguing. Then Onny's angry voice. "—any good to capture him if he's dead. You're just a coward!"

"I am not. It's foolish to—"

"Coward."

"Am not!"

"Are, too!"

"Am not!"

"Then prove it. I'm going down."

Tobin looked up in time to see her climb over the edge. He crawled over hastily, to catch her if she fell, but she scrambled down easily as a squirrel and then stood, regarding him warily.

"Are you going to be able to climb out?" he asked.

"Of course," she said loftily. "It's not hard. You could probably do it if your ankle was whole. Even a boy could do it."

That fetched them. There was a furious scrabbling above, and within moments Daroo and Regg stood beside her.

"Me, too!" But Nuffet was too small. With a muffled squeak, she fell, and Tobin barely managed to catch her, colliding with the others as he lunged. When they straightened themselves out, the two boys stood at a safe distance. But Nuffet looked at the damp ground and settled herself in his lap with the confidence of a child who has never been unwelcome. She was no bigger than one of his sisters' dolls, and he stared at her with fascination.

"You're cold," she said accusingly, and snuggled closer.

Onny stepped forward and touched his hand. "He's freezing," she announced. "Just like I said."

"You don't need to worry about me. I can't die. I promised my brother I wouldn't."

Onny and Daroo exchanged dismayed glances. Regg felt Tobin's cloak. "Wet through. We need a fire."

They all gazed at Tobin expectantly.

"A fire would be nice," he agreed uncertainly.

"What'll you give for it?" Onny demanded.

"Oh, you mean a trade?" Tobin remembered what Master Lazur had said about the goblins' mercenary nature. "But I don't have anything." He looked around at the empty pit.

Daroo sighed. "We'll trade you for buttons, like the mistress does," he announced.

"He's a prisoner," said Regg. "Not a friend."

"Do you want him to die?" Onny demanded. "Go with Daroo and find some wood. I'll help him get some buttons off his shirt. He's going to need them."

By the middle of the night he'd traded all his buttons, the laces from his slippers, and his belt, for they were small creatures, and could only carry small loads. He was wondering how he'd pay for the next bundle of wood when Regg silently reached down and handed him a smooth stone. They tried to explain their theory of debts and equality, but he'd had trouble understanding it because about that time feeling began to return to his numb hands and feet, and pain came with it. At least the buttons on the sorceress' vest were now explained. Had she really traded for their services, instead of enslaving them? Yet another thing Master Lazur had been wrong about? Apples and grapevines.

He smiled down at Nuffet. His cloak had finally dried and she snuggled beneath it, sound asleep on his lap. They'd brought him water as well as wood, and he was sleepily content. The pit was almost warm with the fire blazing in it, and the three older children made surprisingly little noise as they climbed in and out. He yawned and was hoping they wouldn't get into too much trouble as he fell asleep.

When he opened his eyes, the rim of the pit was surrounded by a ring of goblin faces. He'd never seen so many at once. He moved abruptly and discovered four small, warm bodies pressed against him, under his cloak.

The fire had died, but warmth still radiated from the embers. He gazed at the goblin children, who were stirring and rubbing their eyes, and wondered how long they'd worked to keep that fire going before they finally rested.

And he knew, beyond any doubt, that if he was able to keep his promise to Jeriah, it would be their doing. They had saved his life. That was a debt that couldn't be repaid in buttons and stones, whatever the goblins might think.

CHAPTER 13

The Hedgewitch

"I DON'T LIKE IT," SAID COGSWHALLOP. "I don't like not setting any fire around the doors, and I especially don't like you going alone to lead off the soldiers."

"But they'll follow me," Makenna explained again. "I'm the one they want. Once they're gone, there'll be no one but the settlers to defend the gear and seed grain. And as soon as they see fire at the church, they'll go to put it out, and the Spoilers will have a free hand."

"They'd go to put it out quicker and stay there longer if there was fire around the doors and windows," said Cogswhallop shrewdly. "Getting soft, gen'ral?" A rumble of agreement came from the troop leaders.

Makenna leaned against the base of the fallen log and gazed out over the goblin village. It was so well camouflaged that most humans wouldn't even have seen it, at least at a casual glance. But Makenna knew the look of every house, field, and craft yard. This clearing, backed by the old fallen pine, was one of her favorite places, both to come alone and for briefings—it reminded them, and her, of what they were fighting for.

She sighed and turned to face the troubled frowns of her troop leaders—old friends, tried in combat after combat, every one of them. Could she tell them she was being haunted by the ghost of her mother's disapproval? "Aye, maybe I am soft. But there's no need to kill these folk. If their seed is spoiled and their tools start to rot, they'll have to go home—and the priests and soldiers will follow. If they don't go with the settlers, at least we can fight them without hurting other folk." She put a note of finality into her tone and they nodded reluctantly.

"All right," Cogswhallop conceded. "But what about you leading off the soldiers, all by yourself?"

"Demon's teeth, Cogswhallop, let it go! Do you think I'm such a bungler I can't lose a troop of mounted men in a dense forest? They're all wearing pounds of steel! Off their horses, they'll be wheezing before they've run half a mile. I told you about the course I scouted. Do you really think they could follow me through that?"

A reluctant grin crossed his face. "Well, likely not. But you haven't said where we'll regroup."

"That's because I don't know where you'll end up. I'll show some Flichters a place to meet me when it's over and they can guide me back. Have I answered all your doubts?"

"Almost."

Makenna groaned.

"There's that knight fellow. We told you he almost escaped while you were gone. His ankle's sprained and Natter says he's got a fever coming on, so he'll keep for a few days—but you're going to have to do something about him, gen'ral, once those others are gone."

"If he'd had the sense to stay healthy, we could have sent him off with them," Makenna grumbled. "We can't turn him loose till we've beaten them. He's learned too much about us."

"Might be he's learned too much to ever go free."

Makenna suddenly felt cold. She rubbed her arms to warm herself and shook her head. "I don't think so. You're certain he doesn't know how to find this village?"

"Aye. He went a fair way, but he was good and lost."

"Well, that's what matters. For now, we'll keep him here."

"I don't like it, gen'ral. I think he's a danger to us."

"You never like anything." Cogswhallop's level gaze never wavered, and she sighed. "All right, I'll talk to him and see what I can learn."

As she went down the hill to the hut where they kept the prisoner, Makenna found she was looking forward to seeing him. At first, the presence of a human in the goblin village had disturbed her, but now it seemed . . . pleasant? Surely not. It was just the challenge of playing her wits against his that she looked forward to, for she'd enjoyed their last conversation more than she wanted to admit.

It was fun trying to trick him out of his secrets. But no lying bell this time. That spell had cut both ways.

She pushed open the door, and he sat up, staring at her. They'd dispensed with the chain, since Natter swore he wouldn't be able to walk on that ankle for at least a week. Makenna could have healed it, but given his knack for uprooting chains she'd decided it was safer not to. Her lips twitched as she remembered Bocami's dismay as he apologized for his "shoddy craftsmanship" driving in the spike. Bocami's work was never shoddy; he'd simply underestimated human weight and strength. And determination. The knight had told the children it took him three nights to work that spike out. There was more character behind that ordinary face than she had thought.

"I hear you've been spying on the settlers." He was trying to sound casual, but he didn't succeed. "Learn anything?"

"Oh, this and that." She leaned back against the wall. She did casual much better than he did. "Who told you what I was doing?"

Two spots of color flamed in his cheeks. "I'm not saying." The color didn't fade as fast as it should. Natter was right; he was starting a fever. Would it make him loose tongued? Possibly. "Onny, was it?"

The deepening flush on his face was answer enough. "Aye, she's a good girl," Makenna went on. "But she keeps trying to top Daroo. He's the eldest, mind, and it leads her to do silly things. A dare, likely?"

"She won't get in trouble, will she?"

"Not from me, but I'm not her mother. And I won't answer for her hide if Natter finds out she was talking to you. Speaking of hides, I didn't think they flogged lordlings."

He said nothing, but more betraying color flamed in his face. Keep pushing. "You've got nerve, calling me a killer. I can't imagine what you did to get those stripes."

"I didn't do it," he burst out. "I have never been less than honorable!"

Yes, the fever was weakening him. Good. Keep him talking, keep him off balance. "I met your friend, Master Lazur." She hoped the name would startle him, but he only nodded.

"I thought you might."

"And Jeriah, too. He was younger than—"

"Jeriah's there? But he . . . Of course. I should have guessed. What are you going to do?" he demanded.

Now why would Jeriah's name provoke such a violent response?

"What are you planning to do about the settlement?" He looked utterly alarmed.

"Suppose I said I planned to kill them all?" she probed. "What would you do?"

"I wouldn't believe you," he shot back. "We've never known you to commit wholesale slaughters."

"Aye, but I've killed before, and you know it. The only reason I let you live is that Natter's taken a liking to you."

Now why should that make him laugh? It was a pity, for laughter calmed him.

"Please tell me," he said. "What do you intend to do?"

She thought about lying, but the memory of the blond girl weeping in the church filled her mind. He was sick, helpless. Why not give him the truth? "Lead off the soldiers, cause a distraction to get the farm folk away from their seeds and gear, and let the Spoilers in to rot it. With no tools or seed, they'll have to go back."

"They won't." He met her eyes steadily. "Master Lazur means to drive you out, whatever the cost."

"Whatever the cost? Pigdung. Nobody trades a good sow for skin and bones. If I make the cost too high, he'll back off."

"He won't. He believes the good of all the people of the realm outweighs the good of individuals—and that includes both the settlers and himself. He won't back off."

Makenna laughed. "And I thought the farmer who cut down his grapes was a fool. That's like saying the good of the apple crop outweighs the good of the apples! Who does he think the people of the realm are, if not folk like those settlers? But I can hear him saying it. A dangerous man, that."

"Then don't fight him." He leaned forward, putting force behind his words. "Give up now. There's no honor in leading these goblins to die for your vengeance. In spying and lying and trickery. Please, give it up and go, before more are hurt or killed!"

"Before more humans are killed, you mean? Goblins have been dying for six years now, but there's no dishonor in that, is there?" She was standing now, stiff with anger. "Aye, your conduct has always been honorable—I believe it! No mud on your shining armor—no blood, either. You think I lead these people for my own whim? I lead these people, honorable knight, because they have no one but me. Because they came to me when the humans slaughtered their families and drove them out. And I'll keep this place safe for them no matter how much spying and lying and killing it takes. You've never been a commander, lordling, or you'd know that it's easy to prate about honor when you're not responsible for others' lives. But let me tell you a bit of truth—sometimes honor doesn't get it done."

She turned and went out, slamming the door in his astonished face. She stalked through the village, searching for calm. Why let that ignorant lordling anger her so? He knew nothing of her or her goblins. And she couldn't afford her anger any more than she could afford his honor. She had a job to do.

Makenna watched as Oddi and Tama crept forward. It made her nervous, having the Flamers go into the settlement before she led the soldiers off, but Cogswhallop was right—the timing was crucial. They'd have only a few minutes before the settlers got the women and children out of the burning church and returned to defend their gear.

Tama leaned forward, staring intently at a young woman carrying a bucket back from the stream. Makenna recognized her face, but she hadn't learned her name. She didn't know which of the guards had the spell-resistance charms, so they'd decided to take no chances.

The girl shrieked and dropped the bucket. Water poured over the ground. She leapt back, staring at the bushes by her feet.

The guard frowned. "What is it?"

"There's something in that bush." She backed away from it with short, nervous steps. "Something grabbed me."

The guard picked up his spear (a decidedly unfarmer-like tool, Makenna noted critically) and went to investigate the bushes. As soon as his back was turned, Oddi scampered silently past him, into concealment behind a pile of lumber.

"I don't see anything," said the guard, poking his spear into the empty bush.

"But I know it's there! Something pulled on my, ah . . ." The girl blushed.

The guard grinned. Makenna glanced down and saw his humor echoed on Tama's face. She was a skilled Charmer, able to create almost any illusion, but she had a wicked sense of humor.

In less than a minute the guard was back at his post, but now his back was to Oddi. The little Flamer made two more quick dashes before Makenna lost sight of him. She sat watching the bustling settlement. They'd thought about doing this at night, but Makenna knew the guards were more cautious after dark. "And besides," she'd told her troop leaders, "they've got to chase me a fair way. If it's dark, I might lose them before I'm ready to." So they'd chosen daytime, in spite of the risks, for she knew her goblins could remain unseen even in the sunlight.

She waited, fretting, for almost half an hour, giving them plenty of time to get into position. It worried her not to be there to supervise the attack, but she was the only one who could draw off the soldiers.

The inner stillness that always filled her when the waiting ended crept in, and she realized it was time to make an entrance. No spells of look-away now. She waited until the guard glanced aside, then simply stood up and waited for him to notice her. It took several minutes, for her rough clothes blended with the woods.

When he finally saw her standing there, his eyes widened and he blinked rapidly, obviously wondering if she was real. What would he say later? That she appeared out of thin air? That she'd formed out of the shadows before his eyes? Who needed magic anyway? Makenna smiled.

That broke the moment. The guard shouted, inarticulate at first, then finding words. "It's her! The sorceress! Arms! She's here!"

Not very military. Makenna turned and ran lightly away from the camp. Looking back, she saw that the guard waited until several of his fellows had joined him before coming in pursuit. She knew most of them would go for their horses while a few followed her on foot to guide the mounted ones.

She was far swifter than the armored guards and had to slow down several times to keep from losing them. She laughed aloud when she heard the hoofbeats pounding closer, drawn by the shouts of her pursuers. Let them come—she was ready!

Her chosen entrance to the dense patch of woods was a fallen tree, almost three feet thick. Makenna dropped and rolled under it, losing no more than a second. It would take the mounted men far longer to find a way around, and if some decided to leave their horses and try to scramble over it . . .

Only a moment later she heard a startled shout and the crash of a fall. The moss on top of that log was very slippery.

The dense woods slowed her, but she still had to wait for them as they thrashed through the branches.

One of the smarter ones realized the horses couldn't make it through and abandoned his animal, running after her on foot. It took a bit longer for the stubborn ones to follow suit, but Makenna couldn't wait for them. She had to keep ahead of the leaders, so she ran swiftly now.

A bruising scramble through a shallow ravine, under another log, up a small rock face—easy for an unencumbered girl, far harder for men wearing steel plates beneath their clothes. Makenna laughed when she heard them cursing, and her laughter made them curse again. She felt light with the exhilaration of the chase. When she worked magic, botching some spell her mother had cast with ease, she felt incompetent. But she never botched a fight, or a chase, or a battle plan. She was born for this.

She broke out of the dense forest and started the sprint through the lighter woods that bordered this part of the deep ravine. She was hundreds of yards ahead of them now.

She had to wait again at the top of the cliff. It was almost a hundred feet down to the river, but only the first twenty feet were sheer. The wait gave her time to recheck the knots that held the rope she'd tied there last night.

They shouted again when they saw her, and an arrow whistled past as she grabbed the rope to climb down. Arrows might be a problem—she'd hoped they'd abandon the bows with their horses, but she'd long since learned that nothing went exactly as planned.

She scrambled down the long, steep slope and made it to the riverbed by the time they reached the cliff top.

A few more arrows hissed past as she splashed upstream among the boulders, but the archers had to aim quickly and they weren't too close. Still, she breathed easier as she hurried around the river bend that took her out of sight.

The roar of the waterfall greeted her like a benediction. She'd chosen this place carefully. There was another patch of dense woods to keep them from following her up above, and climbing down the rope and the scramble (or better yet, the fall) down the long, rocky slope to the river would take a man in armor quite awhile.

Nonetheless, she hurried as much as she could. Ordinarily this part of the riverbed was dry, but now the river was swollen with spring rain, and she splashed over rocks and around the boulders. She tripped once in her haste and almost got a soaking—not that it mattered. Getting into the hidden cave behind the waterfall always drenched her.

She spotted the second rope she'd hung in the shadow of the cliff. It didn't matter whether they tried to climb after her, or gave up and went back, for she'd no intention of continuing the chase. The cave behind the falls was completely invisible when the river was full, and only a goblin could have found the hand- and footholds needed to climb to it.

She reached the cliff, wet with the mist from the waterfall, and stopped by the rope, gazing up. If she were them, she wouldn't even try— A face peered over the cliff top, saw her, and vanished. A human face. They were waiting for her!

How could they have gotten there so fast? No, no time for questions. Makenna took a deep breath and tried to calm her pounding heart.

They were waiting at the top of the rope. They'd know she hadn't escaped that way and would tell her pursuers when they came around the bend—probably quite soon now. If they knew she was there, they'd find the cave eventually. Perhaps they knew about it already. How? No time.

She had to get out of the ravine, fast, unseen. The river? It would be risky, but all her options were dangerous now, and she'd grown up by the wetland lakes and was a strong swimmer.

She scuttled under the shelter of the cliffs, where she couldn't be seen from above. It took only seconds to strip off her boots and fill them with rocks, keeping a careful eye on the river bend. If her pursuers appeared, she'd have to swim.

Clinging to the shadow of the cliff, she worked her way to the deep pool at the bottom of the fall and pitched her boots in. Like St. Agna escaping to the Otherworld, the mighty sorceress would vanish from their trap without leaving a trace.

The water was up to midthigh. Makenna took a moment to study the current, planning a course that would keep her well away from the pounding falls. She took several deep breaths, forcing all the air she could in and out of her lungs, and then dove.

Cold water searched through her clothes, dispelling the warmth of her body. At least it wasn't the numbing cold of the high rivers that could kill a swimmer before she realized she was in danger.

She swam for the bottom and stroked along, having learned as a child that if you didn't stay close to the bottom, the buoyancy of your lungs would drag you up. Her hands deflected several rocks, but she missed one that scraped her cheek. Then the current took her.

It was far more powerful than she'd thought it would be, dragging her over the rough riverbed like a runaway horse, rolling and twisting her. She slammed sideways into a rock, bruising her ribs, forcing the air from her straining lungs. Was she out of their sight? She tried to orient herself, but she couldn't be sure, and she had to breathe now!

Bracing her feet against a stone, she poked her head into the air, gasping as quietly as she could, clinging to the rock. She dashed the water from her eyes and looked around. She'd come farther than she thought. The rock was between her and the cliff top, but there was the bend—and the soldiers were coming around it!

Ducking under the surface, Makenna felt her way carefully around the rock, surfacing cautiously this time, just her eyes above the river until she was sure neither the soldiers on the cliff top nor the ones on the riverbed could see her. She risked a glimpse upriver. They'd almost reached the rope, and the men at the top were standing, calling down to them. She couldn't make out the words over the roar of the falls, but they weren't pointing down the stream to where she was.

The wet, moss-slick rocks and the hidden cave would keep them busy for a time. Makenna silently wished them a merry hunt and dove again, not surfacing until the current had carried her around the curve and out of sight.

In the end, she let the current take her all the way to the place where the river broadened and the ravine walls fell away. Swimming on the surface, she could avoid the rocks. Once she was accustomed to the chill, it was comfortable to let the water carry her, though she took care to stay out of the deep, fast current.

She staggered, dripping, out of the shallows and found the small glade where she'd told the Flichters to meet her. A warming spell took care of the worst of the cold, but her wet clothes promptly chilled her again. She took the risk of sitting in the afternoon sunlight to dry off while she waited. And thought.

There was no way the men on top of that cliff could have been part of the group that originally pursued her. They'd been waiting for her, perhaps even before the chase began.

A chill that had nothing to do with wet clothes made her shiver, and she wrapped her arms around her knees.

They had known, in advance, that she would be there and had planned to pin her in the ravine. A good plan, too—now that she had time to be frightened, she was terrified at how nearly it had worked. If the men on the cliff top had been a little more cautious, she'd have been trapped in the cave. If the men who were chasing her had been just a little faster they'd have seen her dive in, and they could have caught her easily in the river. But they'd probably seen no reason to hurry, since she was running right into their trap. No wonder it had been so easy to outrun them—they were driving her, not chasing her. She shivered again.

Had someone from the settlement found the ropes and guessed about that part of her plan? It seemed the only possible answer, though she'd concealed the ropes as well as she could. And there was no reason for the settlers to go near the ravine. They got water from the stream, and their stock was pastured on the other side of the camp. Perhaps some children out exploring? Once the ropes had been reported, she thought Master Lazur was capable of figuring out how they might be used. But still . . .

The chill of dread was growing. Even before the time the Flichters were to have met her came and passed, before she saw the bruises on Cogswhallop's face when he finally emerged from the bushes, Makenna knew in her bones that something had gone wrong.

CHAPTER 14

The Knight

TOBIN DEVELOPED A NAGGING COUGH, and his fever came and went.

"Aye, they'll do that," Natter informed him.

"But when will it go away completely?"

"When it does. You'll be lucky if it doesn't get worse before it gets better."

Tobin sighed. At least she was speaking to him.

"Don't pull that long face on me, human. You're lucky to be alive. I'm nursing you only because the mistress wants it."

He started to laugh, which made him cough, and she slammed the door behind her.

His ankle was all right as long as he kept it propped up on pillows with a cold compress, but if he lowered it, it started to throb. Putting any weight on it was excruciating.

"I'd rather have the chain back," he grumbled to Erebus when the goblin came to visit him.

"Well, likely the mistress will heal it for you when . . . ah . . ."

"When she gets back? When will that be?" Erebus was shaking his head. "She already told me she planned to attack the settlement. She even told me how—that she's going to draw off the soldiers and let the goblins in to wreak havoc."

"We all fight with the weapons at hand, Sir Tobin. Even you."

"I know, but that lunatic girl is going to get all kinds of people killed if she's not stopped. Goblins, too!"

"Ah, but the goblins being killed was the reason she started—or, at least, one of them."

"So when will she be back?"

"Since you know so much already . . . I'm guessing two days there, a day to finalize plans, the day of the attack, a day after to heal up and rest, and two days back. Throw in a day for things to go wrong, and you've got just over a week. Mind, I'm just guessing."

"A week? I'm going to be stuck in bed for a week? Couldn't someone else heal me?"

Erebus snorted. "You were a much better prisoner than a patient!"

Now he was both. Tobin fought down the irritation that seemed to come over him so easily these days. "I'm sorry."

Erebus reached out and pressed a small palm against his face. "Aye, that's all right. Being sick makes us all cross. But you'll have to wait for the mistress to get healed, for no one else can do it."

"If I promised not to escape—"

"I didn't say won't, lad. I said can't. The mistress is the only human here. Therefore she's the only one who can heal."

"But I thought healing was one of the simplest spells. Can't all goblins work magic?"

"Ah, you don't understand. And no reason why you should, since it hasn't been explained. But as I understand it, human magic is an unformed talent to manipulate almost any aspect of nature. Some have none of this talent, some have much, and some in between. And it must be trained in order to be useful. Have I got that right?"

Tobin thought of Jeriah's theory that the choosers selected children to be trained as priests for the degree of their magical talent instead of their holiness. "Possibly. Yes."

"I'm going to want some information in trade for this, mind, but goblin magic is different. We're all born with a gift, but it's to manipulate only one aspect of nature, and it's as much instinctive as trained."

"You work magic by instinct?" asked Tobin skeptically, remembering Master Lazur's rows of spell books.

"Aye, exactly. Why not? Though it's not entirely clear whether all gifts are magical. Take the Stoners. They can work stone in any way stone can be worked and they always hit their target with a thrown rock, unless it's far out of range. But is that magic, or just the result of generations of practice? Or even faith? For they believe stone is a god.

"Then there are folk like the Charmers, whose gift is to confuse their prey and even make them see or feel things that aren't there. Their gift is clearly magical."

"Prey?" asked Tobin nervously.

"Then there are those like the Trackers. You see them following a set of tracks and you think, why, anyone with eyes could do that—but then the trail crosses a stretch of solid rock, leaving no trace at all, and the tracker keeps right on as if the tracks were plain as print! No way to know where the skill leaves off and the magic begins." He shrugged.

"Prey?"

"Aye, all the goblin gifts, at least the older ones from before we became civilized, were used in the wild to hunt animals, or find or grow plants. That's why the Finders' ability works best on green things—finding edible plants was its original purpose. Some of our abilities are still very close to the need that created them, like the Spoilers, whose gift is to rot anything organic and who can only digest rotten food."

"I think I see," said Tobin slowly. "But none of you has a gift for healing?"

"Useful, I grant, but not useful for hunting or harvesting. Odd gifts do appear, like Cogswhallop's gift to work with iron or steel as the Stoners do with stone. He's the son of a Flamer and a Maker, but whether that has anything to do with it, we don't know. Often the new gifts aren't passed on, but Daroo has his father's gift, so perhaps this ability will stay with us."

"Is that how new gifts develop?"

"Aye, though it's rare. Why, my own gift, that of long memory and the ability to learn reading, writing, and languages easily, must have developed long after the others, for it's only useful for trade with civilized people."

"Doesn't your history record when different gifts came into being?"

"Well, it does now, but before Bookeries there was no history! At least none remembered or recorded. And speaking of history"—the paper and pen appeared—"do you know . . ."

Erebus' visits were cheering, but Tobin spent his empty hours worrying about what that crazy girl was doing at the settlement. It would be just like Jeriah to decide to do something heroic and get himself killed while his brother was laid up by his own clumsiness.

That night Natter pronounced his fever worse and gave him an herbal brew to drink. He recognized the bitterness of willow bark, but there was something else in it that made it taste even more awful.

"If you don't like the dose, then don't fret," she told him sharply. "It's all this fussing that's wearing you down."

"If you want me to stop fussing, then let me out!" he snapped back. "Being stuck in this hovel is like being buried alive!"

"Humph!" She flounced off, and Tobin cursed her before rolling over to try to lose his worries in sleep.

The bitter medicine did some good, for he slept well and felt more cheerful the next day. He was delighted when the door opened and Onny's bright face peeked around it.

"Come in! I was afraid you'd gotten into trouble."

They all pushed in, grinning. Nuffet came to sit in his lap. Only Regg stopped in the doorway, smiling shyly.

"Well, we did," Onny confided. "A little bit. But Fa said it mostly worked out in the end. And just last night Natter said we could take you out and show you the village, if we could think of a way you could move, and Regg did." She gestured at the door like a showman, and Regg blushed and dragged a pair of crude crutches into the room. Tobin almost wept with joy.

"You're not supposed to get tired," Onny told him firmly. "Or we *will* be in trouble."

"I won't," he promised, standing in the doorway and gazing happily out at the sunlit clearing. "How far is this village you're going to show me?"

They looked at one another and burst into giggles. Even Regg.

"What?"

"It's here." Onny laughed. "All around you."

Tobin frowned, suspecting a joke, and Daroo took pity on him. "Come out, and look back at where you were."

Tobin hobbled forward on the crutches and turned. The night he'd escaped during the storm he hadn't looked back at his prison, but now he saw that the hut's exterior was covered with grass and brush. It looked like a small hill with a door in it.

"The mistress lived here the first year," Daroo told him. "Until we built her a proper house. That's why it's so big. Now we use it mostly for storage."

"I see." He turned and examined the meadow. Now that he knew what to look for, he saw dozens of small hills, some taller, some long and flat. They'd deliberately shaped them to match the contours of the land. Sometimes only a shadowed doorway or the glint of light on a windowpane showed the presence of a dwelling.

"Come on," said Daroo. "I'll show you my house."

"Then mine!" said Onny.

"Me, too," Nuffet piped.

Tobin saw few goblins as he hobbled through the village. Some were walking along the paths, some working in the cleared patches by their homes. Most of those he saw simply nodded a greeting, but some smiled, and a few wished him good morning.

"It's kind of empty right now," Onny told him, a shadow crossing her face. "When everyone's here there's more than a thousand of us. But almost half went with the mistress." Then she brightened. "Here's Bocami's house."

Tobin wondered which of their parents were among those who'd gone, but they offered no information, and he decided not to ask.

They introduced him to Bocami, the metalsmith who'd made his shackle—he held no grudges against Tobin over his escape. Then he met Varbo, the weaver, and Regg's mother, who was a leather worker, and Wintle, the herber.

"It's mostly Makers and Bookeries who live in the open meadow," Daroo explained. "The Trackers and others who hunt live more in the woods, and the Greeners are on the edge of the meadow, by their fields. And outside this village there are others, but they don't help the mistress like we do."

"Other villages?" asked Tobin. "As big as this one?"

"Oh, no," Onny bragged. "We're the biggest."

"How many goblins are there, living in the wood?"

"Not very many," said Daroo. "Fa says only about five thousand or so. But more come all the time. Why do you want to know?"

"Oh, just curiosity." Tobin hoped he didn't look as guilty as he felt. It wasn't a long walk, but he was sweating when he reached Daroo's house.

"There it is," the boy told him proudly. "It's the only one like it. Fa likes to live on the ground and Mam likes the trees, so they compromised."

Starting on the earth, the low grassy mound grew into the lower branches of the tree like a live thing. Tobin could barely make out the woven walls behind the screen of leaves.

"It's beautiful," he said sincerely.

"I'd ask you in," said Natter's voice unexpectedly from behind him, "but . . ." She gestured at the roof, which was no higher than his waist. Tobin laughed and started coughing, doubled over on his crutches.

"He's tired! I told you not to wear him out!"

Tobin joined in the children's chorus of protest, but he was secretly relieved to end up sitting in the shade. Natter went in through a side door and brought him a cup of something cool with herbs in it. She watched him drink, wearing her familiar scowl. "As soon as you've rested, you're going right back."

Tobin bowed to her judgment and let her cope with the children's arguments, which she settled by sending them off.

"It's a beautiful place," Tobin told her, after Onny tossed her head and stalked away. "I think there are more flowers here than anywhere else in the meadow."

"Aye." Natter spread her hands, displaying her green-tipped fingers. "This is my garden, at least a part of it. And my home."

Master Lazur had said goblins were incapable of love or loyalty, but it was love that showed in her small, sharp

222

face as she looked over the green meadow. And they seemed to be as loyal to their peasant mistress as any human could have been—maybe more.

"You know," said Tobin, "in spite of the grass and the size, it's very like a human village. I mean, it's just . . . I guess we're not as different as I thought."

"Insults will get you nowhere, boy. But I know what you mean. When you think about it, my kind and yours have dwelled together since the beginning of the world. I guess we've both shaped each other."

She sat in silence after that, gazing at the peaceful meadow, and Tobin found no answer to her words.

He dreamed that night.

The moon was shining through his windows, shining down on the goblin village, but it was brighter than any moonlight he'd ever seen. Still, he knew it was the moon, for it was silver, and it illuminated the village in shades of black, silver, and gray.

He thought what a lovely night it was and wandered out to find the children—they wouldn't want to waste a night like this in sleeping.

He was wandering among the grassy mounds of the houses, trying to figure out a way to reach the children without waking their parents, when horses appeared on the edges of the grove—horses with saddles and battle harness on their bodies, but no riders. One of the horses stamped, nervously, and flames the color of moonlight flared around its hoof.

Tobin looked up at the moon. It was a strange orangish brown, but it gave off silver light. He didn't understand it, but he guessed what was about to happen, and horror twisted through him.

He tried to cry warning to the sleeping village, but no sound came from his throat. He began to run, to try to find the children and warn them, but the horses charged.

They rode down on the goblin homes. Their moon-flaming hooves broke through the roofs, and goblins ran from the doors like rabbits from a flooding burrow. When the horses trampled them, the silver flames licked up around their hooves and the goblins screamed.

He tried to find Onny's house, but he didn't know where it was. When he found Regg's house, the roof was broken in like a smashed shell, and he decided, shuddering, not to examine the nearby bodies.

He wanted to find Natter's house, but realized by the time he did, it would be too late. He had to stop the horses!

He ran among them, trying to find a rider, someone in charge, someone he could order to put a stop to this, but he found no riders. He grabbed one horse's bridle and tried to talk to it, but it tossed its head, throwing him aside. He sat, listening to the pounding hooves and the screaming, staring at the orange-brown moon . . . and suddenly he recognized it.

Tobin woke, gasping, his throat tight with the effort

to scream. He stared frantically at the windows, but there was no moonlight, only a lighter patch of darkness and the drip of recent rain.

No moonlight! He wrapped his arms around his knees and buried his face in them, rocking, trying to calm himself. A nightmare, only a nightmare.

The Otherworld stone! How long had Master Lazur had to locate it? Three days? Four? Tobin reached for his crutches, but Natter had taken them. He cursed and pressed his foot tentatively against the floor. Pain answered, and the harder he pressed, the worse it grew. He couldn't walk.

But he couldn't leave the stone unshielded, either. Could he wait till morning and send Natter or one of the children? He looked at the windows, remembering the eerie dream light gleaming on the floor. No. Master Lazur could be searching for the stone right now. He wouldn't leave it there another hour.

He pulled off his blankets and crawled to the door. This time he left it open. If someone woke and noticed it, so much the better. They could reach the stone faster than he could.

It had rained earlier, and tiny drops were still misting down. He could see only vague humps in the darkness around him, but the familiar scent of rain, the wet earth, and the cold grass under his hands gave the goblin village a solid, reassuring reality, and the nightmare began to fade.

Tobin kept crawling.

He recognized the irony of working so hard to retrieve the stone when he'd gone to so much trouble to plant it. He wondered if he was now actually committing the treason for which he'd been convicted before. If he was, at least he'd already gotten the punishment out of the way.

Right or wrong, treason or not, he couldn't aid in the destruction of these people. There had to be another way. And he'd find it, but first he had to get the stone back.

There were stickery weeds in the wet grass, and he stopped, cursing, to pick thorns out of his palms. It seemed much farther crawling than it had walking, but he didn't want to stop and rest. He was panting by the time he reached the bottom of the rise, and gasping by the time he crested the top and brushed damp hair out of his eyes.

There was the log, at the far side of the clearing. He crawled to it eagerly, ignoring the pain when he jarred his sore ankle. Fumbling in the dark with stinging hands, he found several other stones and was beginning to panic before his fingers closed over one of the right size and shape.

He pulled it out. He could barely make out the color in the dim light, but his fingers, remembering the smooth flat curves, confirmed it. Tears of relief filled his eyes. It was safe, back under the shield of the hiding charm chained to his neck. By Master Lazur's own admission, no priest would be able to find it now.

He'd never let it off his person again, he vowed, slipping

it into his pocket and closing his fist on it. Not until he had a chance to grind it into dust. Perhaps Bocami could help with that, though it would be very awkward to explain this to the goblins. Natter had just begun to trust him, and many of the others still didn't.

He was too tired to decide now. His head throbbed, and the cool grass felt good against his heated body as he lowered himself down. He'd rest here, and then go back to the hut. He could decide whether or not to tell them about it in the morning, when his head was clearer.

He never remembered the goblins finding him there, for by then he was lost in a nightmare world where villages were about to be attacked and he could prevent it, if he only knew how.

Sometimes the moonlight horses trampled the village, but sometimes it was the desert barbarians who attacked his own people—his home on fire, his sisters fleeing.

In one dream the goblins were mounted on the moon-flame horses, destroying a village of mice.

Occasionally he would wake, recognize the familiar walls of the earth hut, and check to be sure the stone was in his pocket.

Natter was always there when he wakened, with cold cloths for his forehead and bitter herbal drinks. When he was lucid he tried to explain, but it came out muddled and Natter hushed him in a gentle voice that worried him more than all her scolding.

He had no chance to explain until he wakened, aching in every muscle, with afternoon sunlight streaming through the windows, illuminating the circles and runes that marked the floor around him, and realized that she, the sorceress, the general, was back.

CHAPTER 15

The Hedgewitch

"THEY KNEW," SAID COGSWHALLOP FLATLY. "They knew exactly what we planned, in advance."

Makenna, perched on the log, stared out over the village. It was serene in the afternoon sunlight, but today the sight gave her no peace. She'd decided to hold this meeting here, where she had held so many others, hoping it would give her the strength to face what she had to, but there was no strength in her, just the weary pounding of guilt and loss.

"It's my fault," she told them. "I should have listened to you, should have let you burn the church from rafters to foundation. I—" *I let them divide my loyalties. I should have known this would happen. You can't fight a war half-heartedly, especially if you're outmatched in every way.*

Nine dead and more than thirty wounded. There'd been casualties in the past, but never this many. It was the first time one of her plans had failed. Divided loyalties.

I'm their commander—how could I have forgotten my responsibility? My fault.

"You're not listening!" snapped Cogswhallop. "They knew all our plans in advance! Most of the soldiers followed you off, but the rest were in hiding, waiting for us. They'd set traps exactly where we were attacking. I even heard one of them saying it was a good thing they'd been warned because we 'little demons' were so slippery. They knew!"

"Aye. I figured that out when I saw them at the ravine. I just didn't want to admit it. I told the knight about our plan. I didn't see any harm, because I didn't think he had any way to pass the information along."

There was a shocked murmur from the troop leaders. The remaining troop leaders. Makenna closed her eyes against tears.

"But he doesn't have a way to pass information," Cogswhallop protested. "He's been here the whole time since we left, with a hiding charm welded round his throat."

"I know. But he must have some way, because he was the only one who knew our plans. And they knew them, too."

Dismay grew in the faces around her.

"Gen'ral, if he's got some way to tell things to those priests, then we've got to find out how much he's told them and how he does it," said Cogswhallop. "Now!"

"I know," said Makenna. "That's why I ordered all

but the wounded to come back fast. That's why I set the healing spells first thing, when I found him raving. We can't get sense out of him till his fever breaks. I've posted guards, two miles out. We'll keep them there till we find out how much information he's passed on. If he truly doesn't know where this village is, we may still be safe, but we can't take chances on that."

"But that little bell only works if he talks," said Cogswhallop. "Suppose he just keeps his mouth shut?"

"Oh, my friend. Your folk are good people." She smiled bitterly. "There are plenty of ways to force a man to talk. Humans do it all the time."

She stood outside the door, taking deep breaths, trying to calm her stomach.

Cogswhallop stood beside her, carrying the brazier full of hot coals they'd borrowed from the troubled smith. Bocami had almost refused to lend it when they told him what it was for. He liked this human. Many of them did. Erebus had argued so passionately she'd finally put a guard over him, fearing he'd do something foolish.

Natter hadn't argued, but her small face turned white as bleached linen, and she'd gone off to find the children and take them far away.

"There's no use putting this off, gen'ral," Cogswhallop told her. "It'll only get harder."

She couldn't read the expression on his face. He'd supported her decision—at least, he hadn't argued against it.

It didn't matter if he supported her or not. She was their commander, and she owed these people safety. Sometimes mercy, like honor, didn't get it done.

No doubt passing her plans on to the enemy was a fine, honorable act. He was probably a hero. The thought made her furious, and she opened the door and went in.

The knight was sitting up, bound as she'd ordered, and there was no guilt on his face, the bastard. He looked more puzzled than frightened. Well, she'd change that!

"There's no need for this." He twitched his bound arms, his expression growing uncertain as he looked from one of their grim faces to the other. *Make you nervous, do we, lordling?*

"I wouldn't attack you. In fact, I—" He caught sight of the brazier and stopped, the color seeping out of his face.

She'd had to explain this to the goblins, but her fellow human understood it at once. How horrible, that this should be a thing she shared with them.

"Why?" His eyes searched her face, all baffled innocence.

"Oh, that's good, lordling. That's wonderful." She opened the spell book and began tracing runes on the floor. Cogswhallop set the brazier in the corner and started hanging the bell. "It wouldn't even cross your mind that we might want to know how you got word to the settlement about our plans. Or what else you've told them. Or—"

"What?" His voice was loud, indignant. "How could I pass on your plans? I was here all the time!"

"Aye, that's what we'd like to know." She bent to the second rune. When she opened the spell book, a familiar chill brushed her neck, the cold disapproval enveloping her like a damp cloak. Makenna forced the memory of her mother from her mind. This wasn't abuse of magic; this was plain human brutality.

"Wait." He tried to sound calm and controlled, but he didn't succeed very well. His face was white and strained. "Please, explain this to me. You say the settlement found out about your plan? How do you know?"

"Because nine are dead and thirty wounded." She crossed to begin the third rune. "Because they were waiting for us, with clever little traps, everywhere we went."

"But that doesn't prove I—"

"Pigdung. Cogswhallop heard them talking. He heard them say they'd got warning in advance."

"But . . ." He swallowed and visibly mustered his courage. "You shouldn't use language like that, it's . . . demeaning. Why do you think it was me?"

Language! The prissy fool was fussing about her language! Cogswhallop was tending the brazier now, turning the small poker and tongs, heating them through. She shivered and turned on the knight in sudden fury.

"Because, O proper and honorable lordling, you were the only human besides me who knew those plans. Well? No protests? You're not going to say that one of the goblins could have betrayed us? Sold us out for a bowl of milk?"

"No." He gazed at the brazier, sick dread on his face. But there was thought there, too. "No, they wouldn't betray you. They're loyal."

Some thought seemed to strike him, for he fell silent as she completed the last few runes. She turned and faced him. "I believe you're innocent," she lied.

Ping.

He jumped at the sound, and she smiled coldly, wishing she didn't feel so sick. "No point in silence this time, human. You'll talk, sooner or later, and we'll know truth from lies. The sooner or the later, that's up to you."

He took a deep breath. "I didn't tell anyone but Erebus about your plans."

The bell was silent.

"I have no idea how they found out, but—"

Ping.

Color surged into his pale face. "All right, I have an idea, but it's just a theory, and I was going—I was thinking about telling you anyway!"

The bell was silent.

"Then you'd best tell us."

His eyes lowered. He was frowning.

"Now would be a very good time, lordling."

Silence.

"Because you're in our village right now. You may not know where it is, but we can't be sure of that, not anymore." Was she demanding or pleading with him?

"So now we have to know it all. Especially if you're not sure how the information got out. Because if your friends find this place, it's not just nine lives that might be lost, but hundreds."

She thought he flinched, but she wasn't sure.

"I understand that," he said slowly. "And I want to keep this village safe—as much as I've ever wanted anything! But I have other duties, too. There are some things that, in honor, I can't tell you. I want to help you! Please . . ." He stopped, seeming to have run out of words.

"You'll find you can't afford divided loyalties, lordling." Pity for him. Pity for herself. She made her voice harsh and cold. "I'm their commander. To keep these people safe, I must know all you know."

He shook his head, pressing his lips together. He'd said all he was going to . . . voluntarily.

"They've been driven from their homes, trapped and slaughtered!" Was she trying to convince him, or herself? "They have no one but me!" And they were all she had. She swallowed sickly and glanced at Cogswhallop, but his face was blank, giving her no help.

The knight was trying to look calm and determined, but his face was taut with fear. The pulse in his throat flashed like a weaver's shuttle with the pounding of his heart.

Trapped. He was trapped as surely as the goblins had been. And she was the trapper.

"No." Every muscle in her started to tremble, and she

wrapped her arms around herself. "I won't do this." To torture a trapped creature because she feared others might be trapped and hurt in the future was madness. It was destroying the grapes for the sake of the apples. And she had no wish to be a destroyer. Not even of humans.

"This is wrong," she said aloud. "And nothing it might buy us in the future could make it right."

The knight blinked, astonished confusion in his face. But in Cogswhallop's face she saw relief, and a glimmer of respect.

"I didn't think you were that human," the goblin said with satisfaction.

"Well, you might have said something!" Her body's trembling had spread to her voice.

"Why? I knew you'd work it out. To kill in battle, to defend yourself, that's one thing. This is—"

He stopped abruptly and cocked his head. She heard it, too—the deep thuds of someone beating frantically against a hollow tree. She felt the blood drain from her face. Another pounding joined it, and another.

"What's that?" the knight asked.

"The alarm!"

She was reaching for the door when it flew open and Miggy burst in, wild eyed and gasping. "Soldiers! On horses, with swords and armor. They've all got torches. They're coming from all around us, mistress. They know right where we are. They'll have us surrounded in minutes!"

236

"No!" It was the knight's voice, filled with a horror threats of torture hadn't put there. Makenna barely spared him a glance. The calm of battle filled her, decisions and plans flooding her mind. First things first.

"It's the evacuation plan, Miggy. The leaders will be at the center of the village in just a few minutes. You're the one who sounded the alarm?"

"Aye." He nodded jerkily. "I thought it was best to start it as soon as we could. I thought—"

"You did fine. Perfect." She put all the reassurance she could into her voice. "Now go to the center and tell the troop leaders I want three of them to gather their troops and wait there. Tell everyone else it's the evacuation plan. Hurry!"

He shot away. "Cogswhallop, go scout for me. I need to know how many, where they're coming in, and when, and I need it now."

"Aye, gen'ral." His eyes flickered to the bound human.

First things first. She had perhaps five seconds to spare. "We're in battle now, lordling. The rules have changed. Give me one good reason why I should let you live to fight against us."

CHAPTER 16

The Knight

❦

ER VOICE WAS COLD, the way his old commander's voice was cold when he ordered a charge. Tobin took a deep breath and answered carefully. "Because I'm not the goblin's enemy, not anymore. I've seen . . ." There was no time to explain the things he'd seen, things he was only beginning to understand. He put it into the simplest terms he could manage. "You should let me go, because I'll be more useful protecting the children than bleeding to death on the floor. I won't hurt the goblins."

She glanced at the silent bell, then at his face. Tobin had no idea what she read there.

"I swear it," he said.

She looked at the bell again, then, impatiently, out the door. "Very well." She pulled a bronze knife from her belt and tossed it to the ground at his feet. "Natter took the children. I'm not sure where." She turned and strode out, her small lieutenant following.

It took Tobin several minutes, fumbling behind his back with bound and shaking hands, to pick up the knife and brace it with his feet so he could slide the rope on his wrists against the blade. Once his hands were free, he slashed quickly through the rope on his ankles. Her healing spells had cured his sprain enough for him to stand. He lurched stiffly to his feet, hobbled to the door, and stepped out into his nightmare.

Late afternoon sunlight blazed over the meadow. He couldn't see the horses yet, but goblins raced frantically about, shouting the names of family and friends.

Where would the children be in this turmoil? The only place he knew to start searching was at Natter's house, on the other side of the clearing. Could he even find it without a guide?

A shouted command rang out, the harsh human voice overwhelming the goblins' thin cries, and fires sprang up in a ring around the village, bright orange in the sunlight. Tobin began to run, racing across the clearing toward Natter's house.

He could see the horses now. They all had riders, and footmen walked beside them. Gusts of smoke blew over the edges of the meadow, obscuring his vision.

A horse screamed. Tobin turned and froze as the girl and several dozen goblins rose from cover right in front of the line of soldiers and charged. The Flichters' assaults drove the horses mad, but the footmen were less vulnerable. The goblins attacked them—humans more than twice their size—with bronze axes and shovels against steel armor. As Tobin gazed in horror, the goblins began to die under steel swords.

Then the girl shouted, wordless, mocking, triumphant. She'd gotten through the line and, as the soldiers turned to look, she raced off into the woods. She shouted again, and every soldier on that side of the meadow ran after her! As soon as the line broke, hundreds of goblins rose from cover, pouring like a darting river through the gap she'd made.

Shouts of rage from the remaining soldiers drowned Tobin's shout of triumph. Then the commanding voice rang out again, ordering them to close up the line, close up the line, and the nearby troops ran forward, but most of the goblins had already gone.

Most, but not all. Had the children escaped? Natter? Erebus? Tobin ran.

The horses' hooves didn't break through the goblin's roofs, as they had in his dream, but picks in the hands of the footmen did, tearing the houses open like bodies ripped by a sword.

He was still some distance away when he saw them, one on horseback, two on foot, attacking the earthen part of Natter's house. The rooms in the tree were already in flames, and Tobin hoped for a moment the house would be empty. But as soon as the pick smashed through the roof, the older children shot out of the side door, with Natter behind them, running more slowly because she carried Nuffet in her arms.

Tobin redoubled his speed, heart pounding. Thank the Bright Ones they were running in his direction!

The soldiers had been watching the front door, so it took them a second to notice their quarries' flight. Then a shout rang out and the horseman turned his mount and set it galloping after the fleeing goblins. Tobin hurtled forward and grabbed the bridle, dragging the horse to a prancing stop.

"Demon's teeth! What do you think you're doing? Let go of my horse!"

"Your commander! I have to see your commander!"

"Later," the horseman snapped, and kicked Tobin's wrist, breaking his grip.

Natter darted out of a small gully and the horseman let out a hunting whoop and raced after her, but she was far ahead of him now, alone and unburdened. At least she had a chance.

Where were the children? Somewhere between Tobin and the gully in the meadowland from which she'd run. He walked forward, slowly, carefully, but the open meadow held little cover even for creatures as small as goblin children. The gully was better, about four feet deep with a house on one side and several clumps of bushes nearby. They wouldn't be safe in any house.

Tobin found a small door and knocked, calling quietly for the children to come out. No reply. He called that they wouldn't be safe inside, that the soldiers were tearing all the houses open. No answer. But they had to be there! He was thinking about trying to crawl in when something tugged at the leg of his britches. Glancing down, he saw a small hand disappear into the brush. Staring through the tangled twigs, he met Onny's eyes. She gestured away from the house, and he walked beside her as she crawled through the undergrowth.

He didn't look down again—if anyone saw him it might betray the hiding place. Since he was no longer looking for the children, his eyes wandered over the battlefield.

He could tell it was almost over from the way the soldiers moved, relaxed and confident, as if the destruction of the goblins' peaceful home was just a job. Like hunting vermin.

Smoke obscured parts of the scene, but the sight of the gutted houses sickened him. He saw a rider with three dead goblins tied to his saddle like pheasants, and a wave of hatred burned through him. He understood Makenna now. He hated these people for their casual violence. They didn't know anything about the people they killed, didn't even bother to find out about them, for they were only goblins. Now he understood the anger in Makenna's eyes when he'd said she was human too, for the thought of being one of them sickened him.

Three soldiers appeared at the top of the gully.

Onny froze, flattening against the earth. He couldn't see the others, but he guessed they were hidden in the bushes between him and the soldiers. One of the men carried a torch.

"I want to see your commander," Tobin told them. It was easy to make his voice cold. He tried to keep his anger out of it, but some of it got through and they exchanged uneasy glances.

"What do you want with him? Sir," the mounted man asked, belatedly polite. A peasant, thank the Bright Ones—not likely to argue with a lord for long.

"That's my business, goodman. But Master Lazur won't thank you for keeping me waiting."

They exchanged glances again at the name. "Well, sir, we'll get in trouble if we break the line. We've got strict orders to open all the houses and search them."

"I'm sorry." He let his tone make it clear that he wasn't sorry at all. "I can't wait for that. You." He gestured to the man with the torch. "You'll guide me. You two can stay and carry out your duties."

"But with just two of us, we'll get behind," the mounted man protested. "We're supposed to open and burn everything—"

"Then I suggest you get started," Tobin told him. "There's a house right in front of you, another just ahead, and another past that one. If you stop arguing and get on with it, you should keep up. I'll need your horse as well, for my ankle is injured. Now, goodman."

A wave of relief washed over him as the man slid glumly from the saddle and took up a pick. The two of them attacked the house vigorously. Tobin kept the man with the torch beside him while he limped forward and made a fuss adjusting the stirrups till the other two men cast him a final glare and moved out of the gully and on to the next house.

Tobin mounted carefully—his ankle really was throbbing, now that he had time to notice it. The sun was about to set. With the line of searchers safely past, the children could stay where they were and escape under cover of darkness. Tobin had to fight against the impulse to look back as he rode away.

There were several delays, for no one at the small camp they'd set up a few miles from the clearing had any idea where Master Lazur was. They settled Tobin outside the big tent to wait. Through the open flaps he could see a desk, several traveling chairs, and the familiar row of spell books, their rich bindings out of place in the spartan command post. He thought there was another room behind the one he could see. It hardly mattered.

They gave him water and offered him food as well, but the thought turned his stomach. He was grateful when they left him alone. The sun set, and torches were lit. They reminded him of things he'd rather have forgotten.

He thought the children had gotten away safely, and Natter, too, but what about Erebus, who was slow and clumsy? And what had happened to Bocami, and Regg's mother, and the others he had met? His imagination produced a vision of Erebus' body tied to a saddle, and he hugged himself, shivering.

Suddenly another set of arms went around him. "You did it!" Jeriah's voice proclaimed. "I knew it! I knew you could do it."

"Jeri?"

He staggered stiffly to his feet, and his brother embraced him again, pounding his back. It was a terrible relief to hug him, to let loving arms wipe out the horror of the afternoon.

"Jeri, thank the Bright Ones you're safe! When I heard— What were you doing at the settlement? Why are you here?"

"I'm serving Master Lazur now, remember? You were the one who set it up."

"No, Mother arranged that. It worried me. What with him being a priest and you . . . and everything."

"There were priests who were with us. I've been talking to Master Lazur a lot. He's an interesting man." Jeriah released him and looked him over anxiously, making certain he was all right, and Tobin scanned his brother in the same way. His last trace of concern over Jeriah vanished—he was bright eyed and energetic, obviously well. He was also clad in armor, dirty and scraped, as if he'd been in battle. Breaking open houses, perhaps?

"Jeri, you didn't— Ah, I didn't see you in the attack this afternoon. Were you there?"

"No," said Jeriah cheerfully, and Tobin almost wept

with relief. "I went with Master Lazur and the priests after the sorceress. She led us a demon's chase, but we finally got her."

"What!"

"We caught her. Look."

They were pulling Makenna off a horse when Tobin's searching gaze found her. Blood from a scrape above her eye had run over the gag and dried, gluing strands of tangled hair to her face. Her clothes were torn, and she was more filthy and battered than he had ever seen her, even when he'd captured her himself. And since he'd done it himself, he should have known it was possible for others to do it, but the sight of her, bound and surrounded by guards, stunned him, for he had come to think she was invincible. He had worried about the others—but it had never even crossed his mind that she might be caught.

She stumbled as they pulled her from the saddle, and half a dozen hands grabbed her, as if they feared she might break away from them even now. She straightened up, defiance in every line of her dirty, tattered figure. Her eyes, meeting Tobin's over the stained gag, gleamed with courage and hate.

"We could never have done it without you, Tobin," Jeriah told him. "When Master Lazur couldn't find you—for days!—well, I was beginning to worry. But then he found the stone again, and we knew you must be all right. How did you manage to plant it where they made their battle plans? It was incredible. You're incredible!"

Without you, we could never have found or beaten them. You're a hero, brother! You've done it!"

Tobin closed his eyes, closing out Makenna's hate and Jeriah's joyous pride.

It was late before he finally got to see Master Lazur, for the priest was very busy. But when the flaps of the big tent opened, and the last group of men left, the priest drew him in and embraced him. Tobin didn't flinch. Half the men in camp had slapped his shoulders and shaken his hand. Why not? He was the hero who located the sorceress' base for them. For the dozenth time he choked down hysterical laughter, for he knew that if he started laughing, he wouldn't be able to stop.

"Well done, Sir Tobin. Oh, don't wince, my boy, you've earned that title, and it will be yours again officially as soon as we return to the city. And everything else I promised will be yours as well."

"Yes. Ah, when will that be?" Carefully now. Tobin had never underestimated Master Lazur's intelligence, and now was not the time to start.

"Probably in a few days. I think we'll keep the sorceress alive for a bit. I'm hoping some of the goblins will attempt a rescue so we can exterminate them. Far too many escaped this afternoon." He shook his head over the foolishness of the soldiers who'd broken the line. Tobin had already been told several times how the plan was supposed to have worked.

"I doubt we'll get many," the priest went on. "They have no loyalty, after all. They'll be a nuisance to our settlers, I'm afraid, but without human leadership that's all they'll be. We'll kill them off eventually."

Tobin knew, with a sick conviction, that his last statement was right. Jeriah and his father weren't the only ones who saw things in terms of right and wrong, with no middle ground.

"But what will happen to Ma— the mistress herself? That's what they called her, you know."

"Really? Interesting. I must find out how she enslaved them. We'll use her as bait for a few days, then drown her. Dying curses and all that. We were worried when I couldn't find you in the crystal for so long. Jeriah was frantic. Are you all right?"

"Oh, yes. I was ill for a while, but I'm fine now."

He needed the details of Master Lazur's plan—where she'd be kept, how she'd be guarded. But how to ask without making him suspicious?

"Yet I notice you're limping." Was there a trace of wariness in the kind gaze?

"I twisted my ankle when I tried to escape. It's better now. Are you certain she can't escape? She's very tricky."

The priest dropped to his knees and touched Tobin's swollen ankle. "St. Saraday's healing eyes, sit down!" He helped Tobin to a chair and knelt again, clasping his ankle. Tobin felt a chill touch his skin, and the pain drained away.

"You needn't worry about her escaping—I know she's

clever. Do you know she came right into the settlement to spy on us? But she's shackled with charmed iron. No one wearing it can work any spell, and no spell can be cast on it. Which meant we couldn't bespell it against goblins, but we've got half a dozen guards around her. She won't get away. Not this time."

"No, I suppose she won't," said Tobin, keeping the despair from his voice as best he could.

"But what happened to you, boy? I was checking on you every day. I saw you capture one of the little demons, and the next time I checked, I couldn't find you. Did they take you prisoner?"

Tobin opened his collar, revealing the hiding charm.

"Ah!" The priest spent a moment searching for a clasp, then went to the door and sent a messenger to fetch some metal shears.

"Tell me all that happened, Tobin."

So Tobin told him the facts. How he'd captured Makenna and she'd taken him in turn. That he'd been held prisoner and escaped, planting the stone. That he'd fallen and been injured and recaptured.

As he spoke, the messenger came back and the hiding charm was clipped from his throat. It was the first time Tobin had seen it, and he stared at the twisting loops of bronze, wondering why the loss of something he'd never seen made him feel naked.

Master Lazur listened, nodding occasionally or asking a quiet question.

It was amazing how convincing the facts sounded, stripped of the truth. But truth lay in the bright eyes of tiny goblin children, and a fire that had burned all night; a cheerful scholar, and a sharp-tongued nurse—and Tobin knew this man, who listened so well, was impervious to the truths he'd found.

There was silence for a time when he finished.

"You've done very well, Tobin. People are already calling you a hero, and I've noticed you don't care for it." *Careful, careful. This man saw far too much.* "But even if you don't think you're a hero, you should understand how important the help you've given us has been. The barbarians attacked the southern border again, shortly after you left the city."

For a dizzying instant Tobin's mind swept back to another time, another war. "But how? They'd withdrawn for the summer!"

"That was what we thought, but their first withdrawal was a feint. They attacked shortly after our troops had gone and seized a large piece of the southlands. We sent our forces back to the border, of course, but there are several thousand refugees coming north right now. Thanks to you, they'll be able to make new homes here, in peace, and the resettlement can begin in earnest.

"So you see, if we survive this as a people, it is in some part your doing. Whether you wish to be a hero or not, you should remember that, always."

◆ ◆ ◆

Tobin tossed restlessly on his pallet. Master Lazur had healed all his aches and bruises—so simple for him. Tobin remembered Makenna's painstaking runes, and her prickly defensiveness about her lack of magical skill, and he turned over again.

He'd wanted to share a tent with Jeriah, but Master Lazur had offered him a private tent as a courtesy and he hadn't cared enough to argue about it.

What could he do? She was caught and guarded and would be killed for her crimes—and she had committed crimes! Tobin wished them all—goblins, priests, Makenna, the lot of them—to the Otherworld and shifted again.

What could he do? It was over. He was free to go home, regain his rank, tell his father the truth. Well, some of the truth. It was too late for the most important truths. He could go home and spend the rest of his life being lauded as a hero—and remembering the creatures he had betrayed to their deaths. No wonder he couldn't sleep.

He started to turn again, but a light weight dropped onto his chest and something sharp pricked his throat, right over the artery, freezing him instantly.

Cogswhallop's whisper was clear in the darkness. "We heard them talking. We know it all. How you planted a charm so they could learn our plans and find us. I know what you've done." The knife bit down. "So give *me* a reason to let you live, human. And it better be good."

CHAPTER 17

The Hedgewitch

I N THE MORNING THEY undid the chain and took her to the priest's tent. They'd given her some water but no food. Combined with a wakeful night, it had left her light-headed. If her head was light, it should be easier to hold high, shouldn't it?

The big tent was unoccupied. As Makenna gazed around it, her eyes lingered on a row of beautifully bound books. They showed use, despite the care he took of them. She thought of the tattered collection of scraps her mother had left her, and a surge of resentment burned away the last of her weakness.

When the priest came in, she met his eyes calmly. Why not? She no longer had anything to hide. The handsome boy, Jeriah, came in with him and sat at the desk, pulling out writing supplies, obviously prepared to take notes on the conversation.

"So." Master Lazur walked around her, like a farmer looking at a pig he was thinking of buying. She refused to twist her neck to look at him, even when he spoke behind her. "You weren't affected by my truth spell before. Let's see if you can do it again."

He laid his hand on the back of her neck, beneath her hair. The power of the spell churned through her and clenched around her gut. There'd be no evasion this time.

He made sure the spell was established before he moved around to lean against his desk, watching her with hard, cold eyes. "How did you resist my truth spell before? In particular, how did you do it without my sensing it?"

The answer swirled up in her—she couldn't defeat it, so she didn't try. Let this cold, tricky, bastard know how careless he'd been. "I didn't resist it, you just didn't ask the right questions."

"What do you mean?" He was frowning now. Good.

"You asked if I knew the sorceress or some such thing, and there is no sorceress, so it was easy enough to say no."

He blinked in surprise. "But you are the sorceress. We saw you leading the goblins yesterday. I saw you in my scrying crystal, making plans. There's no doubt—"

"Oh, I'm your enemy, all right. The one you've fought so long, sent so many men to kill. But I'm just a simple hedgewitch, not a sorceress at all."

"You're joking." But he knew she wasn't. His face filled with astonishment. "How could you . . ." His expression changed, a dozen perceptions rearranging themselves behind his eyes as he fitted things he thought he knew into new patterns. But his first words startled her. "What a pity."

"What?"

"If you're not a sorceress, then you must be a very fine tactician, and we'll have great need of tacticians in the next few years. What a waste! I don't suppose . . ." She could see things rearranging themselves again in his mind.

"Sir." It was Jeriah, disapproval plain in his voice. "You can't do that! She's a murderess, how many times over? She—"

"Five times," Makenna told him. "No, six. I killed five men and one unborn babe." She had no idea what the priest was thinking, but Jeriah seemed to, and she gazed at both of them curiously. There was no compulsion on her to answer Jeriah, but she added. "I'd kill all but the babe again, if I had the chance. They'd blood on their hands, every one of them."

"Goblin blood?" the priest asked.

"It's as red as yours," she told him. "And the tears their kin shed just as bitter. Aye, I'd kill them again, and a few more if I could get my hands on them."

"Then there's no chance you'd consider working for me?" He gazed at her expectantly. Jeriah shook his head.

"That's mad! How could I work for you?" Makenna asked.

"Because I can give you a cause worth abandoning whatever drove you to take up with those vermin."

He leaned forward, a fanatical gleam in his eyes.

He told her that the desert barbarians were going to invade all the Hierarch's realm. It sounded insane. She glanced at Jeriah for confirmation, and he nodded reluctantly. As the priest spoke on, of drought, famine, and defensible borders, it slowly began to make sense. Was this why the knight had deceived them? Aye, likely. He struck her as the sort to sacrifice all for a noble cause, and if you cared for humankind, this might seem like one.

"So you see, girl, we'll need leaders of your intelligence and ability in the coming years. You could live! Have no doubt, you've earned death for the men you've slain, even if your demon-drawn power hadn't condemned you. But you can live and serve a great cause, if you'll only work with us, instead of against us."

His voice was butter smooth, like a pitchman at a fair. It was a wonderful pitch, too, Makenna thought, with reluctant admiration. Flattery, honor, and fear, all used against her. But a pitchman was only a pitchman, and peasants learned early to be wary of them. On the other hand, there was one thing she wanted, and if he could give her that . . .

"What about my goblins?"

"What about them?"

"Will the church still be killing goblinkind? You've gone and put them into the same position you say the barbarians have put you in—driven out of their homes, with no place to go. Can you put a stop to that?"

"My girl, goblins are lesser minions of the Dark One. As servants of the Seven Lords of Light, we must destroy them." So gentle, so rational. He probably even believed it himself, though with this man, you'd likely never be sure.

"My power's supposed to come from him, too, but you're willing to overlook that." It wasn't a question. He was a man willing to do anything to further his cause.

"Naturally, you'd have to forsake that power if you joined us." The priest frowned, his voice losing a little of its smoothness. "You must understand—to revoke the Decree of Bright Magic would be to admit that the Hierarch made a mistake. Now, when we're asking the entire realm to abandon their homes and move, on the strength of the Hierarch's word, we can't afford the appearance of weakness. But if you gave up your allegiance to the Dark One and entered the service of light, you could be spared."

"Aye, I understand. And magic is something I might willingly give up. But I'll not serve you, priest. For I think you're a man who does great evil in the name of good, and if I served you, I'd likely end up doing far worse than killing five killers and one babe."

A flash of insight seized her, tightening her throat. This priest had become what he was because he let nothing stand in the way of saving his people, just as she had let nothing stand in the way of saving her goblins . . . and avenging her mother. Had she betrayed her mother's teaching when she sought vengeance for her death?

If magic and life were part of each other, was dealing death—even to humans—a betrayal of magic?

The priest shrugged. "Well, it was worth a try. Jeriah?"

The boy jumped. He'd been staring at his master, almost in a trance. Had she shown him something he hadn't seen before?

"Record that the prisoner confessed to six murders and showed no repentance."

Only for the babe. But she didn't say it. Why bother?

"She also confessed to serving the Dark One and refused to surrender that allegiance. She is therefore condemned to death, by my authority. There. I'll sign it now. As soon as we're certain the goblins aren't going to try to free her, we can carry out the sentence and get out of here. This has already taken far too much time."

"Wait a minute. You're keeping me alive because you're expecting my people to attack? You're using me as bait?" The answer was plain on both their faces, and something else as well. She cursed her loose tongue, but it was too late.

"Why? Don't you think they'll try for you?" the priest asked.

For the first time, Makenna fought the spell, but the fist around her gut squeezed and the words rose in her throat and burst out. "Of course they'll try. They'll likely not give up till I'm dead or they are." She gritted her teeth and choked the rest of it down, but the damage was done.

He asked her where the goblins were now and what plans they might make, but since she truly didn't know, they learned nothing more. Demon's teeth, they'd learned enough!

They broke camp shortly after that and set out for the settlement. Makenna kept her face impassive as they tied her to the saddle and tied the horse she rode between two others, but her mind seethed. How could she have been so foolish? If she'd just kept her mouth shut they might have killed her before the goblins had time to try anything. She had little hope that her forces would succeed—all of them together wouldn't be able to defeat the men who guarded her now, and she'd been the one they relied on for the subtle, sneaky plans that had been so successful.

Now she knew why the settlers and explorers had kept coming, despite all her efforts. No wonder the knight said she couldn't raise the stakes high enough to send them elsewhere. There was no elsewhere!

Sooner or later the humans would fill this forest, and the goblins would be hunted and destroyed. All but the toughest and cleverest would die, as inevitably as the snow killed the grass. Even if she lived, there was nothing she could do to stop it.

The sun was going down. Makenna huddled against the log to which they'd chained her wrist, her head resting on her arms. She didn't look up as footsteps drew near. There had been plenty to come and gawk, once they reached the settlement. She had spent a full day and most of a night on horseback, and after they arrived at the settlement, no one bothered to give her more water. After a time she stopped replying to taunts, but the sound of human voices, haunting and alien, filled an emptiness within her, and she listened, though she didn't look up.

"So that's the sorceress." *Goodwife Garron's voice?* "I suppose she looks a little like our hired girl, but to say that she's the same one is ridiculous!"

"Aye. She did come to spy on us, but we spotted her and drove her off at once," the guard explained.

"Well, I'm glad we have men like you to protect us!"

Laughter swelled in Makenna's throat and she bit her lip, glad her arms concealed her face.

"Might I go closer?" Goodwife Garron continued. "I'd like to see if she really looks like the girl who worked for us. Not if it's dangerous, of course, though I'm sure you'd protect me."

"Ah, she's no danger now." A rough hand grabbed Makenna's hair, jerking her head back, and she stared up at Goodwife Garron. The small woman narrowed her eyes as if she was nearsighted, leaning very close, her body concealing a cloth-wrapped bundle that slipped from her hand and lit by Makenna's feet. The goodwife twitched her skirt over it. "My, she certainly is a messy creature. I see no close resemblance between her and the girl we hired, and so I shall tell folk." She took the guard's arm and pulled him away. "You wouldn't believe the malicious things people are saying." And she distracted him with a few of them while Makenna stretched out her feet and pulled the bundle closer. There was almost six feet of chain between her wrist and the log, and she could move easily enough. She would open it later, when it was dark.

They lit torches in a circle around her, after the sun set, but the six guards faced outward. Makenna investigated the bundle and found a jug of water, bread, and meat. She managed to drink and eat without them seeing her. As she ate, tears ran down her face for the first time since her capture. She had seen so much of human brutality—she'd all but forgotten that some of them practiced kindness.

Her mother would have liked Goodwife Garron. Would she have liked the woman her daughter had become? Makenna feared the answer.

She hid the remains of her meal under the log as best she could and settled back. The night wore on. Makenna was dozing when she heard the next voice. "I must speak to the prisoner—alone."

She looked up, her eyes widening, for in all the time she'd known him, through all the threats and fights, she'd never heard that haughty, authoritative tone in the lordling's voice.

He even looked different, with his armor glittering in the torchlight. He was clean, that was part of it, and shaved, but mostly it was his expression. She'd never seen him look arrogant before, and it sat oddly on his plain face.

The guards evidently didn't think so. They said, "Yes, Sir Tobin," nicely as trained dogs.

Of course. He was a hero now.

"So, wench." He sneered down at her. "We meet again. But this time it is I who have the upper hand!"

He'd gone mad. It was the only explanation she could think of. He leaned forward, the sneer still on his face, and hissed, "Demon's teeth, stop gaping at me and say something nasty! In about half a minute you have to attack me to cause a diversion so Cogswhallop can get under the log!" He straightened again and said loudly, "Not so sharp when you're the one in chains, are you?" And he kicked her ankle—hard.

Her mind sprang into motion, all at once. "Oh, aye. No doubt kicking a person in chains is your definition of a witty argument." Her heart raced. A torchlit ring in the very center of the settlement, and six guards. Were they all mad? But if they'd gotten this far, she'd no choice but to play along.

He drew back, and she prayed his exaggerated scowl wouldn't make the guards suspicious. She peered at them from the corners of her eyes. They'd drawn closer, listening avidly, approval on many of their faces. An army of goblins could have gathered in the darkness behind them.

"You . . . you . . ." He looked to be running short on insults, so she decided to help him out.

"Me, me," she mocked. "Aye, you've got the whip hand now—and you know a deal about whips, don't you?" Several of the guards gasped. Whatever he'd been flogged for was public knowledge, poor boy. "But you had to get an army to take me! When it was just you against me, I had you running in circles with your britches down! And once—"

"You had an army, too!" A flush rose in his cheeks and the defensiveness in his voice was real—much more convincing. "When it was just you against me, I captured you. If it hadn't been for the goblins . . ." He remembered his role, and the unnatural smirk came over his face again. He was almost within her reach. "Soon there'll be no more goblins. If they try to save you now"—his eyes narrowed on the word—"we'll capture them as—"

She sprang. The chain around her wrist barely let her reach him, but she did, clawing ineffectively at his face. Her instinct was to shout, but she didn't want to attract the attention of anyone but her guards, so she fought in silence.

He tried, equally ineffectively, to grab her hands, and he cursed—but not loudly. She thought they must look like squabbling children and was about to attack him in earnest when the guards grabbed her arms and kicked her feet from under her.

The knight stepped forward, lifting his hand, and then hesitated. No doubt he thought it dishonorable to strike both a woman and someone who couldn't hit back.

Fool of a lordling, don't balk at it now! "You spineless muckworm, you couldn't—"

He slapped her face twice, just hard enough to make it look real. It wouldn't have stopped her, had there been anything she really wanted to say, but she was certain the goblins had been given enough time. She also feared he was nearing the limit of his acting ability. When the guards released her, she subsided meekly against the log, protecting her face with her arms. Behind their shelter, she could see him glaring at the guards.

"What are you doing here?" he snapped. "This is a private conversation. Get back to the perimeter and keep watch. And I want to see you looking out, like guards, not peeking at me like gossiping grandmothers! Go!"

There was a pause while she continued to huddle, hiding her grin, and the guards withdrew. "They're watching," he murmured. "But they're out of earshot if we keep it down. Are you all right?"

"I'm fine. Unlike some, who seem to have gone mad! Lazur's not a fool. You'll never pull this off."

"Aye," said Cogswhallop's voice behind her. "But it's a lovely plan, gen'ral. Bring your wrist back where I can reach it and stop squirming!"

The knight scowled down at her. "Stop looking like that. Grovel or look angry or something. You look too happy."

"And you look far too nervous."

She felt Cogswhallop's hands pluck at the chains and

heard him murmur, "Now, don't jangle, sweet ones."

"What are you doing, lordling? First you get me taken and now you're setting me free? Make sense!"

"It doesn't make sense to me anymore," he admitted. "When I planted the stone, I didn't know, didn't realize . . . . When I understood about the goblins, I got it back, but then I got sick, and then it was too late. So now"—he took a deep breath—"I'm doing what I can to set it right."

Gazing at him as he spoke, she noticed that most of the buttons on his fine, clean shirt were gone. That, more than anything, made the truth plain to her. "So now you're betraying your own folk for the sake of mine. Poor honorable knight."

"Stop looking at me like that! I don't know about honor anymore. I just know I have to do this." But he looked confused and miserable. She thought of Goodwife Garron's kindness and understood exactly how he felt. How long had it been since she sympathized with a human . . . with another human?

"No use," Cogswhallop grunted softly. "Can't pick it. I've got the twists in, but I'm not strong enough to break the chain. It's up to you, soldier."

The knight straightened abruptly and glared at the guards again—several of them guiltily turned their eyes away. He threw back his cloak with a sweeping gesture. "How long will it take the Sleepers to affect them?" he asked nervously.

"You've got Sleepers out there?"

"Depends on the man," Cogswhallop answered. "How tired he is, how much natural resistance he has to that kind of spell, how much he wants to stay awake."

"What if some of them have spell-resistance charms?" Makenna hissed, feeling ignored. She'd always been in charge of rescues before. To be on the receiving end was unnerving.

"They don't," the knight told her. "That's one of the reasons we didn't do this sooner. We had to arrange for six unprotected men to be on guard at the same time."

His eyes widened and Makenna, looking where he looked, saw one of the guards sit down and lean against a tree, yawning.

"How in this world did you manage that?"

"Jeriah's in charge of setting up the guard." Was that pain in his eyes? "I just made a few suggestions. He's my brother."

Another guard lay down.

"Your brother! But—"

"I know. He takes after my mother."

"I wasn't going to say that." She smiled, amused by the small flash of vanity. "Won't he be in trouble?"

Definitely pain. "I don't know."

Several more guards had gone down, and the last swayed on his feet. Even as they watched, he lay down on the ground.

"Now, soldier. And keep it quiet. If you clank things about and wake one of them, it's all over."

"Right." He dropped to his knees beside her.

Cogswhallop popped out from below the log. He was covered with mud. "You'll have to get under it. The weakest link is where they attached the chain to the bolt, and they rolled the log so it's on the bottom."

The knight wiggled beneath the log.

"What happens if someone looks this way and sees no guards, and him crawling around the chains?" she asked her lieutenant.

"Then we're cooked. That's why we wanted to do it late."

There was a loud clank and they both winced, but the sleeping guards didn't stir. The knight swore.

"Here's your hiding charm, gen'ral. The soldier took a bit of a risk and stole it back." He fastened it around her neck. "We've all got one. Once we're away they'll not find us."

"Why do you keep calling him soldier?"

"He thinks like one," Cogswhallop told her. "When he's put to it. And he doesn't make excuses, even when—"

A snap sounded and the knight slithered out. "Wrap the chains around you, and try to keep them quiet," he advised. Cogswhallop reached under the log and pulled out a drab servant's cloak, and the knight dropped it over Makenna's shoulders and arranged the hood to hide her face. "It'll do."

Makenna staggered stiffly to her feet, grateful for the helping hand that caught her elbow. "You'd best use your cloak as well," she said.

He looked down at his filthy armor, as he pulled his cloak around him. "You said I should get some mud on my armor. Are you satisfied now?'

"It's a start," she told him as they crept toward the line of sleeping guards.

The inevitable soft clanking kept her heart racing as they passed the guards, but none of them stirred. Once they were out of the torchlit ring, she breathed easier. "What next? Anyone looking this way will see I'm gone, and the alarm goes up."

"That's why we're getting out of here fast." The knight picked up his pace, striding rapidly through the darkness. "And that means horses." They were already saddled and waiting. He helped her mount and set Cogswhallop up behind her, tucking the goblin beneath her cloak. "You're just a servant, so keep quiet," he told her as they rode toward the camp's perimeter.

Makenna, who knew more about this kind of escapade than he ever would, nodded meekly, amusement warring with indignation. Both emotions died at the guard's challenge. "Halt. Who passes?"

There were two of them—they looked bored and sleepy.

"Sir Tobin," the knight replied. "Leaving for the city."

"In the middle of the night?" said the guard incredulously.

"Master Lazur's been interrogating the sorceress and

267

he discovered something the Hierarch must learn imme-diately. Or so he says. I think it could have waited till morning." He smiled. He did niceness much better than arrogance, she noted.

"Aye, well." There was cheerful sympathy in the guard's face. "We're all under orders. You're—"

"She's escaped!" The cry was distant, but perfectly clear. "Call out the guard! Close the perimeter!"

"By the saints!" The guards reached for their swords, but they looked at the darkness around them, not at the knight or her. "Sorry, Sir Tobin, but—"

He got no further, for the knight's fist lashed out, knocking him down. The second guard spun, opening his mouth to shout, but Makenna kicked him in the face, and then kicked her horse till it galloped wildly down the road.

She concentrated on staying in the saddle, for she wasn't a skilled rider. When the knight spun his mount and abruptly left the track, her horse followed his and she almost fell. Only Cogswhallop's firm grip kept her aboard.

They rode in near silence for some time. She'd asked Cogswhallop about the number of casualties and the answer, though not as bad as she'd feared, left her with no desire to chat.

It was morning when they finally rode into a clearing filled with goblins, and the knight pulled his horse to a stop. They pressed around her, cheering, laughing, touching her, and it was several minutes before she was free to look about.

The shelters of brush and woven grass were all but invisible, unless you knew what to look for. But Makenna knew, and the sight of the desperate, shabby little camp, the bandages, the few treasures they'd managed to save, filled her with helpless fury. She had seen into the future, and it was full of sights like this one. "What can I do?" she whispered. "Ah, Bright Ones, what am I to do?"

"I—we've got an idea about that." The knight looked dirty and weary, much more like himself.

"What do you mean?"

He didn't answer immediately but led her to a hollow at the far side of the clearing. She flinched when she saw the blood-stained bandages around Erebus' head, but he beamed at her with all his usual cheeriness, and the tightness in her gut eased.

"We've been talking a lot, the past day or two," the knight told her.

"And mad meetings they were, with him having to run off to deal with those priests every five minutes," Cogswhallop grumbled. A Maker brought him a hacksaw and some rags, and he tucked them between her wrist and the shackle and started to cut.

"Anyway, Jeriah said that you've been told about the barbarians . . ." the knight went on. "So you know humankind is going to settle beyond the wall." There was a long pause, broken only by the saw's rasp.

"We can't stop it, mistress. Not forever," Erebus told her gently.

"Aye." Bitter, bitter to admit it. "But what else is there? You've said the barbarians killed off all the goblins in their lands. If we can't dwell there, and we can't dwell here . . . We can't survive in the frozen wasteland of the far north, either. What's left for us but to go down fighting?"

"Well." The knight looked oddly embarrassed. "There is—at least I'm told there is—the Otherworld."

"The Otherworld? That's madness!"

"But people have gone there. St. Agna. Some priests . . . and others. It is an actual place."

"Aye, they go there, but they never come back! No one knows what becomes of them. Even if we could go, it's likely suicide!"

"It's suicide to stay here," Cogswhallop put in calmly. The shackle fell from her wrist with a clank. "It's just a long, slow suicide, instead of a short, fast one."

"You're not in favor of this!" She had always relied on Cogswhallop's pragmatism. If he approved of a plan this mad . . .

He shrugged. "I don't know, gen'ral. I haven't got a better idea. He"—he nodded at Erebus—"loves the idea. 'A whole new world to discover!'"

Erebus flushed. "It's easy to pull another's plans apart, but you haven't got—"

"I don't think you have any choice." The knight

interrupted quietly. "Not in the long run. And the sooner you go, the more lives you'll save."

"Oh, that's fine. There's just one flaw in this wonderful plan. We can't get into the Otherworld without the help of a lot of powerful priests, and somehow I don't think we're going to get it."

"But you can cast magic," said the knight.

"Don't you listen to anything I say? I'm naught but a common hedgewitch. I can cure the harvest sneezing or chase off mice. What you ask is as far beyond my power as the moon is beyond the treetops!"

"But Erebus says you can use the power of the wall to strengthen your spells." They all looked at her expectantly. "He says you've done it often."

"Aye, for a look-away spell. Something I know back to front. I haven't the faintest idea how to open a portal to the Otherworld. It didn't happen to get into my mother's books. And they're gone anyway." She felt a stab of loss at the memory.

"We thought about that," said the knight. "The spell is in Master Lazur's books. He told me so himself."

"And my great-great-grandfather's aunt recorded that two hundred and seventeen priests put their magic into the wall," Erebus added helpfully. "Surely that's power enough?"

"Oh, that's enough power to level the wood! And I'm flattered you think I could control it. But how, pray, are you planning to get Master Lazur's books? Stroll in and ask him nicely?" She faced the knight. "They'll know you helped me escape. You're not a hero anymore."

"I know." Pain again, in his eyes, but it didn't reach his voice. "I think we could steal them. For us to go back is the last thing they're expecting. It's probably the safest place we could be."

She smiled in spite of herself, but then sobered. "To open a portal is beyond my skill. Even my mother couldn't have done it. I'm sorry, but I can't."

Something stirred in his face. "I didn't take you for a quitter."

Anger flared. "I'd fight to the death for these people!"

"Yes, but you're not afraid to die. It's easy to do something you aren't afraid of. I'm going to get those books, and when I do, see if you can face your people if you don't try to use them. I'm betting you can't." He rose to his feet. "I'm going now." And he walked away.

She stayed where she was. If she gave him no help, he'd have to turn back. He couldn't do it alone. He knew he couldn't do it alone. He mounted and rode away. The silence lengthened.

"He'll come back," said Makenna.

Cogswhallop snorted. "I warned you this day would come. But no, you had to go and build obstacles."

"He has to come back," Makenna said. "He can't do it alone."

"No one can do it alone," said Cogswhallop. "Maybe it's time you learned that, girl."

"He'll come . . . ah, dung!" She had never been able to lie to Cogswhallop. "He isn't coming back," she said.

Then she began to plan.

CHAPTER 18

The Knight

TOBIN'S PALMS WERE SWEATING despite the cool mist drifting around him. It was one thing to risk your life when you believed you were serving the Bright Gods and your people, pleasing your father, and if you died it would bring you honor. It was another to take that risk when you knew that dying would get you nothing but dead and disgraced.

He wiped his hands on his thighs and gazed through the branches at the settlement's dinnertime business, waiting for Jeriah to come out. Jeriah always checked to be sure his charger was settled for the night—almost always. With a pang of loss, Tobin hoped the person who had bought Fiddle would recognize his worth and treat him well.

There were only a handful of soldiers left in the camp; the rest were out hunting for the escaped sorceress. And for Tobin, probably. That was what he'd been hoping for. What he hadn't expected was that the peasant boys would take their places as perimeter guards. They looked more alert than the soldiers. Tobin sighed, and a small hand patted his arm comfortingly.

He looked down at Regg and smiled, despite the surge of guilt. Guilt, because if something happened to the child because of his need for a Charmer he'd never forgive himself, and because of what he planned to do. He fought the emotion. After his all-too-public escape last night, he couldn't accomplish this without a Charmer, and the children were the only ones who'd followed him from the camp.

Tobin had seen for himself that Makenna feared working difficult magic. He'd been certain that if he just kept walking she'd give up her stubborn refusal to face her fears, but she'd outstubborned him. He sighed again. Then Regg's comforting hand tightened on his arm. Following the boy's gaze, Tobin saw Jeriah toss a laughing comment to the perimeter guard and leave the camp, going toward the horse pasture.

"Into the bag," he hissed at Regg, pulling up the flap of the pouch attached to his belt. "Start the spell as soon as he gets near enough, and if anything goes wrong, kick me in the ribs and then save yourself. Understand?"

Already half in, the little goblin nodded briskly and burrowed into the bag. Tobin saw the flap stir and knew that Regg was watching Jeriah's careless approach. He walked slowly, shoulders hunched, a troubled expression on his face. *Oh, Jeri, I'm sorry!* As he neared the grove where Tobin was concealed, Jeriah hesitated a moment and shook his head, as if to shake away an odd thought. When he walked on, his scowl had relaxed. Regg's spell at work? There was only one way to test it. "Jeri," Tobin whispered. "Don't shout! Over here. I have to talk to you."

Jeriah jumped and looked around. "Tobin? Where are you?"

"Here." He signaled, and his brother came to him. Would he have done so, even without Regg's enchantments? He'd never know, and his throat ached with the grief of it. He'd have gambled his own life on his brother's love—he had no right to risk the goblins' lives on it. He hoped desperately that someday he'd have a chance to explain, that Jeriah would understand. But for now he'd rely on Regg's insistence that Jeriah trust his brother, regard all his suggestions as reasonable, and do what he said.

"Tobin, what have you done?" Jeriah's voice was anguished. "You had it all fixed, and then— Why?"

"I have reasons, Jeri, good ones. I'll explain it to you when . . . if I can, but I don't have time now."

Jeriah looked puzzled. "But you can't ever come back. You're wanted."

"Yes, I know." It was the sight of the spell working on his brother, not the knowledge that he'd gone from hero to outlaw, that tightened his throat.

"Jeri, I need to get into Master Lazur's tent and

borrow his spell books." Jeriah shook his head sharply, and Tobin spoke quickly, soothingly. "You know I was working for him? Well, in a way I still am. I'm trying to get rid of the goblins and the sorceress, but I have to borrow his books to do it. You don't think he'd mind lending them to me, if it would accomplish his goal, do you?"

"No." Jeriah blinked in confusion. "No, of course he wouldn't. I've been talking to him, and I don't think there's anything he'd object to, if it helped the relocation. He's been the moving force behind the relocation from the beginning, and he's only a fifth-circle priest. Talk about determination! If he'd been in charge of the rebellion, we might have had a chance."

"He wasn't part of your rebellion, was he?" asked Tobin, surprised.

"No. In fact, he's succeeded in convincing me that reform of the laws will have to wait until after the realm is safely resettled behind the wall. It won't do much good to reform the government if the barbarians kill us all, will it?"

"I suppose not," said Tobin. Part of the reason Master Lazur was so persuasive was that in some ways he was right. It was only in the muddled middle ground that he was so very wrong. "But for now, I need to borrow his spell books. To help get rid of the goblins, remember?"

Jeriah frowned. It was clear something troubled him, despite Regg's spell. "But how do you mean to get into camp? The guards will stop you."

"I'll walk with you," Tobin told him. "And pull my cloak over my face. If we're talking, I don't think they'll stop me."

"You're probably right." Jeriah's frown cleared. "Why not let me get the books for you?"

It didn't take the nudge in his ribs to tell Tobin that the spell wouldn't last once Jeriah was away from Regg.

"That wouldn't work as well," he said, thinking fast. "Besides, I have a favor to ask you. Fiddle has been sold to someone in Brackenlee. Would you . . ."

They strolled though the perimeter without a check, chatting about horses. It got them through the camp as well. Why not? Master Lazur's aide escorting some knight to his tent was no doubt a common sight. As they neared the tent, Tobin took a deep breath. "Jeri, if we see Master Lazur, I'm going to capture him. I'm afraid he might not understand that my taking his books is for his own good. It's simpler this way, you see?"

He waited, sick at heart, for his brother to struggle against the spell, but Jeriah said cheerfully, "You won't have to fight him. He's not in there."

Thank the Bright Ones! "Where is he?" Tobin asked, lifting the tent flap. He walked in and Jeriah followed. Several hard blows struck his side. Regg! But what—

Jeriah gasped and stiffened, staring at him with wide, horrified eyes. The spell was broken! Tobin leapt forward, punched his brother's jaw, and caught him as he fell.

He jerked the tent flap closed, dragged Jeriah inside, and dropped him, reaching for his knife to cut a strip off his shirt for a gag. "Regg, what happened?"

"I don't know." The goblin scrambled out of the bag. His small face was beaded with sweat. "As soon as we came into the tent my spell just went away."

"Never mind. You did fine. Wonderful. Can you get out on your own?"

"Of course," said the child. "But how will you—"

"That's my problem." He hoped he could come up with a solution when the time came. He stuffed the strip of cloth into Jeriah's mouth and cut another to tie over it. "But it'll be harder for me if I have to worry about you. You understand, Regg? You won't stay around and try to help me?"

The boy shook his head. "I'm not as silly as Onny. I understand. I'll see you outside." And he vanished.

Jeriah stirred, moaning behind the gag. Tobin grabbed his brother's arms and lashed his wrists with the cord he'd brought for this purpose, though he'd prayed it wouldn't be necessary. But now he was glad it had happened. He'd rather fight Jeriah honestly than fog his mind with spells. He tied his brother's ankles, rolled him over, and flinched at the pain and betrayal in his eyes.

"I'm sorry, Jeri, I'm so sorry." He touched his brother's face, and Jeriah cringed as if he'd burned him. "Oh, Bright Ones, don't. I'm not crazy, Jeri, I'm doing this because . . . because . . ." The impossibility of explaining washed over him. If he had time and freedom and Jeriah's trust, he could have made his brother understand, but he had none of those things. "I'm sorry, Jeri. I know what it looks like, dishonor, betrayal, and maybe it is, but sometimes . . ." A wry smile twisted his lips. "Sometimes honor doesn't get it done. Forgive me."

"He may," said Master Lazur's quiet voice behind him. "But I doubt if I will."

Tobin rose and turned, slowly. The priest's gaze was as cold and steady as the crossbow pointed at Tobin's heart.

Tobin had to swallow before he could speak. "I wasn't—"

"Spare me the protests, boy. I'll learn all I need with a truth spell. It will be interesting to discover the source of this girl's fascination. I know you're too sensible to throw your life away for a pretty face."

The face that appeared in the doorway behind the priest's back didn't look pretty, even though she'd washed away the dried blood—it was grim and wary as an assassin's. Tobin had never been so glad to see anyone in his life.

CHAPTER 19

The Hedgewitch

THE KNIGHT'S EYES WIDENED. She glared at him fiercely and he looked hastily back at the priest, who hadn't turned around, Bright Ones be praised.

"It isn't her at all," said the knight, his quiet, intense voice designed to hold attention. Good lad. Keep it up.

Jeriah stared at her, wide eyed above the gag, but he didn't make a sound, and she thanked him with a nod as she crept forward.

The crossbow was the problem. If she hit the priest on the head as she'd planned, and his finger tightened on the trigger, he could hardly miss hitting the knight. But if she used her first blow to knock the crossbow up, the priest would have time to shout, and one yelp was all it would take to bring the guards to kill them all.

The knight asked Lazur why Regg's spell failed when they entered the tent, and Makenna marked his warning—though with this cursed net clinging to her arm, it hardly mattered. The knight braced himself as she drew near—nothing obvious, just a small shift in posture, but she knew she'd best move before that sharp-eyed priest noticed it, too. Now!

She stepped forward and kicked the bow up. Even as the bolt whizzed harmlessly overhead, the knight sprang, his hands closing around the priest's throat before he could do more than gasp.

The momentum of the knight's leap carried them both down, with the knight on top. She grabbed the priest's hands, pinning them so he couldn't break the knight's grip or gouge at his eyes. He was already turning purple, his face contorting. She felt a moment's fear that her champion would weaken, but one glance at his grim face assured her. A moment later the priest's straining muscles went limp.

"You gag, I'll tie." His shaking voice contrasted oddly with the brisk commands. "And don't forget to put that net around him. How did you get it?"

"Erebus. That's how he was hurt, going back for it."

He worked rapidly and efficiently and she followed his example, tearing strips from her shirt for the priest's gag, just as he had. "How long will this one stay unconscious?"

"Not very long. And you can make a lot of noise through a gag. We'd better get out of here fast," he said.

She yanked the final knot tight. "Then maybe you'd better finish what you started?"

There were some humans, perhaps even most, who

should be spared—but Makenna wasn't sure this man was one of them. The net seemed eager to leave her arm, curling around the priest's limp body like a cat. At least he wouldn't be freeing himself with spells when he woke.

"Don't push it, hedgewitch." The knight glared at her with the eyes of a man who was rapidly reaching his limit, and she was too experienced a commander not to recognize it.

"As you will," she said soothingly. Then a thought struck her. "How did you know I'd go for the bow instead of hitting him over the head?"

"I didn't. Grab those cursed books, will you?" He pulled a large bag from the pouch on his belt and tossed it to her.

Her fingers lingered on the spines, stroking them despite the need for haste. Here was true magic, complex, codified, complete. This was what her mother had wanted for her.

"Hurry, will you!"

She stuffed the last of the books into the bag. But instead of coming to help her, he went to Jeriah, who sat in silence, watching. She saw him search for words.

"I love you," he said finally, and pulled his brother into his arms, kissing his head. "Tell Mother I love her. Tell Father . . . tell Father it was the right thing to do." He let Jeriah go and stepped out of the tent ahead of her, pulling his cloak around him.

She glanced back and met Jeriah's tear-bright eyes.

"I'll watch out for him," she promised. "And you'd better keep an eye on that one." She jerked her head at the motionless priest. "It's a trap, you know, thinking all the right's on your side, and none on the other. A trap of the mind, more vicious than steel spikes. Heavier than chains. And he's in so deep, he'll never even see it. Bright One's grace, I swear, I pity him. Win or lose." Was there a flicker of understanding in the boy's eyes? Makenna couldn't be sure. She pulled up her hood and followed her ally into the night.

He was waiting for her, trying to look confident as he scanned the quiet camp. "Do you have a plan for getting us out of here?" He took her arm, leading her in the direction of the horse lines. How long had it been since a human had touched her, in friendship?

"I was hoping you'd have one," she said.

"This is no time to develop a sense of humor. What about the goblins?"

"I told Cogswhallop to get the lot of them to the gap in the wall, and wait for us. I'll try to cast the spell when we get there, though I still don't think—"

He came to a stop and stared at her. "You sent them on ahead? You said you thought I couldn't do it!"

"I still don't." She took his arm and pulled him along. "But if by some miracle we bring this off, having the goblins scattered from one end of the wood to the other would be like having a cow with a full udder and no pail. Shh! Don't laugh like that. Someone'll recognize you and we haven't the time."

"Then you'll all be leaving as soon as you cast the spell." He sounded thoughtful. Wistful? "I wish—"

Muffled shouting came from the tent behind them, and several late-awake guards started cautiously in that direction.

The knight grabbed her hand and ran for the line where the horses were tethered. Makenna flung herself at the nearest beast, but when she put her foot in the stirrup and started to step up, the saddle rolled off the horse's back and fell on top of her. She sat on the ground and looked up at the knight, who was gazing blankly at the limp bridle that had fallen off the horse's head when he grabbed it. Then she understood and began to laugh, full, free, and joyous, and no thought of danger could stop the sound. Goblins! How she loved them.

The knight cursed, dragged her to her feet, and tossed her up to the horse's back.

"The books," she gasped. He thrust them into her arms, yanked the reins from the useless bridle, wrapped one around her mount's neck, and handed her the ends.

He took the other rein for himself, pulled off the other horse's saddle with one quick jerk, and leapt to the beast's broad back, compact and easy as a house cat leaping to a window sill. He kicked his horse to a gallop, and Makenna followed.

She wasn't trained to ride bareback as the knight was. She dropped the rein and wrapped both hands in the horse's mane, the awkward bag of books clutched in front of her. She was glad her beast followed his, for as they rode through the seething settlement she had no thought to spare for its guidance.

Freed livestock darted, bawling, hither and thither, with the owners in pursuit. Half a dozen flapping chickens, followed by a man with no boots on, made her mount shy, and she wobbled dangerously on its slippery back.

The alarm bell started ringing, and the confusion intensified as some ran for the church and others looked for weapons that were unaccountably missing. She passed a tent that bulged and bellowed furiously and laughed again when she saw that its flaps had been sewn shut.

Other horses appeared, running unbridled through the chaos with goblins clinging to their broad backs, two or three or four to an animal. For a moment Miggy rode beside her with Regg hanging on to his belt, his face alight with pride and terror. "I did it," he cried. "I was in command! I'm the one that did it!"

When they reached the perimeter the guards leapt for them and fell flat. Someone had tied their bootlaces together. Makenna was still laughing when they reached the road and set off toward the wall, galloping into the darkness after the knight.

CHAPTER 20

The Knight

〜❦〜

TOBIN STOOD ON THE WALL, looking back down the road into the woods. They'd come all the way by road, hoping Master Lazur would assume they'd leave it and waste lots of time searching for tracks—after he'd reduced the chaos to order, caught some horses, and stitched the tack back together! A reminiscent grin lit Tobin's face, in spite of his tension, for it had been gloriously funny. How she had laughed at it all.

He looked down at the girl as she scrambled over the rocks around the gap in the wall to set yet another careful rune. Some of the runes glowed faintly in the gray predawn and some were dark. He'd asked her why some glowed and some didn't, and she'd snarled that she hadn't any idea and then demanded the Otherworld stone as an "essential object," whatever that was. Since she seemed to need it, he was glad he'd forgotten to give it back to Master Lazur—and even more glad the hiding charms would keep the priest from scrying it.

He wrapped his arms around himself to fight the chilly air, his eyes wandering over the sea of small dark forms crowded around the gap. There were thousands of goblins, of every sort he'd ever seen and a few he thought he hadn't, but he couldn't be sure, for they milled about in the dimness, searching for friends and loved ones.

Cogswhallop had dashed up when they first arrived and reported that all who were willing to go were here, which was the best he could do in a day and a night. Tobin was about to ask about the unwilling, but Makenna simply nodded, and the goblin dashed off again before he'd had a chance.

Tobin looked down the road again and prayed with all his heart that those who were here would be able to escape. Makenna spoke softly a word he'd never heard. She was standing in the center of the gap, reading aloud from one of the books piled at her feet. He fought down a surge of impatience. It was a new spell and she was working at a level, and with powers, she'd never used before—and any mistake would kill all who followed her. She had every reason to have taken almost two hours about it, and maybe she should have taken longer.

A small part of Tobin's mind had been following Master Lazur's imagined progress. It would take time to restore order and get men organized and mounted. But he'd never underestimated the priest, and now he watched the road with increasing tension, for he knew they'd be here soon. He hoped that the goblins and the girl would be gone when they came.

He wished with all his heart that he could go with them.

It had first crossed his mind when they rode away with the books, and he realized with astonishment that they'd succeeded. Until then he'd thought only of making the escape possible. Once it was possible, he had suddenly realized that they'd all be leaving. Without him.

It was ridiculous, he thought angrily, that people he'd only known a few weeks (and for most of that time as enemies!) should have a stronger grip on his heart than his own family and friends.

But as they warred, quarreled, and finally strove together, he'd caught glimpses of a girl who was neither hedgewitch nor commander, but simply herself. They weren't even friends, not really, but he'd seen enough of this girl to know she was someone he wanted to befriend. And the goblins he simply loved. He couldn't imagine the world without them.

He looked down again. She'd shut her eyes and was chanting now. The book had fallen to her feet. He hoped she was getting it right.

He had duties in this world, he reminded himself. The humans, his people, were about to engage in a desperate fight for their very survival. And he now understood Jeriah's desire to change the government, for his own eyes had been opened to the need for reform. But that was the work of a lifetime, and he wasn't sure he had the strength to endure a lifetime of fighting to change a people whom he had seen perhaps too clearly.

He closed his eyes for a weary instant, blocking out the vision of a future of duty and service, of trying to reshape something he no longer cared about.

But he loved his family. He'd promised Jeriah he'd come back. Even if he couldn't return openly, that oath still bound him.

He opened his eyes and saw mounted men with torches charging down the road. They'd be here in minutes! Wild visions of blocking the road with his body and commanding them to halt filled his mind. But they were more likely to ride right over him than to stop at his command, and his dead body would make a poor roadblock. Could he draw them away, as Makenna had when they attacked the village? He needed a horse!

He spun about and stopped, staring in frozen wonder. The ragged gap in the wall's gray stones held a shimmering sheet of radiance. The light came, not from her, but from the air around her, and her face was joyous and serene as he had never seen it. He'd forgotten she was beautiful.

Goblins streamed toward her, a moving river of bodies, and when they entered the wall of light they vanished. They moved so much faster than humans—the crowd of thousands was more than half gone. Tobin climbed down.

From the ground, he could see into the light—there

were trees beyond it, and a meadow. But they were young trees, not the dense, ancient forest of the Goblin Wood, and a mountain rose in the distance where no mountain stood in his world.

Standing there, with her people flooding past and the light shimmering around her, she looked every inch a sorceress, and also a stranger, and the thought of her as a stranger left something cut and bleeding inside him.

I can't go with you.

Then she opened her eyes, and the mockery in them made her familiar again. "Coming, are they?"

"Uh, yes, but they won't be here for a few minutes. You did it. And in time, too."

"Didn't think I could, did you?"

"You were the one who thought that." The stream of bodies was lessening, and she reached down and began to gather up the books, stuffing them back into the scrip bag.

"What are you going to do with those books?"

"Take 'em with me, of course."

"Of course."

The mockery in her eyes deepened, but there was a gentleness in them, which was new to her. "He's taken enough from me. I don't mind robbing him. Are you coming, lordling?"

"My duty is here. My family. My people. Though I'm an outlaw now."

She snorted. "Don't let that worry you. Just tell them some tale about how you slew the fearsome sorceress and all her goblins. Say you made me fumble a spell or some such thing, and we all disappeared in a blast of light."

"They'd never believe that."

"Why not? We'll all be gone. They'll have to accept it, sooner or later. Master Lazur's a practical sort, he'll forgive you once he's sure we're really gone. You'll be a hero again. If you were a priest, they'd likely make you a saint!"

I can't go with you. My parents. Jeriah.

The last small bodies darted past her. He could see them in the meadow, laughing, cheering. The sun was rising there, too. He heard hoofbeats pounding nearer.

Makenna heard them, too; she looked at him and smiled. "Lordling . . . Tobin, thank you."

In her smile he saw the loneliness of all her life to come—a life where, for all the friendship around her, she would hear no human voices, and her own humanity would slip away and be lost. She turned and walked into the Otherworld, and the shimmering portal began to fade.

I am supposed to be the good son. . . .

"Ah, dung," said Tobin. He followed her.

The Goblin

〰️

OGSWHALLOP CROUCHED BENEATH THE WALL, watching the stamping hooves outside his hideout. The
hole was too small for humans to enter, so the foolish great ones ignored it.

Natter crouched at the back of the cave, weeping
silently, Nuffet asleep in her arms. Daroo knelt beside
him, staring out and listening to the sweet steel jingle of
the bits.

He'd had a ghastly time getting everyone to the wall.
Even though he knew he was best fitted to organize the
journey, it had galled him to leave that fool Miggy in
charge of rescuing the gen'ral. At least she'd arrived
unhurt and in time. He had thankfully handed over command and dashed off to where he'd left his own small
family, but Daroo had gone hunting for his friend Regg,
and Natter had taken the little one and gone in search of
him, and by the time he'd finally gotten them together
again the shimmering gate had disappeared and the

humans were almost upon them.

So she was gone, his gen'ral, leaving him with a debt of impossible proportion—how do you repay someone for the saving of all your kind? At least he'd been able to send her off heart-healed, and in good company. But that didn't begin to repay the burden she'd stuck him with this time! Tears stung his eyes, and he blinked them back. It was good she'd gone. If she'd stayed much longer, he'd never have been able to clear what he owed her. Now, in her absence, maybe he had a chance.

That thought pleased him. He knew she'd hated to abandon the war, though she was a good enough commander to know when retreat was forced on her. There were enough of them left to continue the fight. Subtly, of course. It wouldn't do to let the humans realize they were still here.

Perhaps if they waited a generation or two. He smiled down at his son. If his gift with iron and steel continued to breed true . . . no one would ever suspect goblins of sabotaging metalwork. Yes. An eternity of metal foxers, sworn to continue the war, would be a fitting payment for the saving of his kindred. The humans were doing more with steel all the time.

She might even come back someday, to check on his progress. Just because no one else had returned, that didn't mean his gen'ral wouldn't.

Humans and goblins had shared the world since the beginning. It seemed a shame to let things change *too* much.